The Verdict:
Who Killed Sonia Verma?

The Verdict:
Who Killed Sonia Verma?

By Dr. Sujay Kantawala

Represented By: Nidhi Kaushik

NU VOICE
PRESS

Praise for the Author

As cinematic as Delhi Crime, as morally haunting as The Firm.

– Justice VC Daga, Former Judge, Bombay High Court, Senior Advocate, Supreme Court of India

Raw, intense, and morally charged – the kind of story you feel in your gut.

– Saurabh Kirpal, Author, Senior Advocate, Supreme Court of India

Sujay has done a wonderful job. The story from the start grips the reader. The Verdict – A must-read!!

– Justice J P Deodhar, Former Judge, Bombay High Court

India's John Grisham at his fearless best – Explosive, razor-sharp, and disturbingly real.

– Justice Deepak Verma, Former Judge, Supreme Court of India

Taut, visual, and unsettling – a legal thriller that demands to be seen on screen.

– Mukul Rohatgi, Senior Advocate, Supreme Court Of India, Former Attorney General For India

First published by NU VOICE PRESS 2025
An imprint of Hubhawks Pvt. Ltd
www.nuvoicepress.com

This is a work of fiction. Space and time have been rearranged to suit the convenience of the book.Any resemblance to persons living or dead or the real events are purely coincidental. The opinions expressed in the book are those of the characters, and should not be confused with that of the Author.

ISBN: 9788199353121
Typeset by Pooja Sharma
Published by Nu Voice Press

This book is dedicated to my beloved parents, Late Anjani Nitin Kantawala and Late Dr. Nitin R. Kantawala, to whom I remain completely indebted forever with folded hands....

Author's Note

Law without justice, is a wound without cure

While on a family trip to the lovely state of Sikkim, I deliberately stayed at Offbeat Homestays and would wander off for hours, just ambling away on forest trails, listening to the sounds of the mystical forests. Distant chimes and temple bells sounded so beautiful, and the millions of colourful flags fluttering in the gentle breeze intoxicated me. Every time I took a break, it was near a tea stall and almost always, I saw smiling faces. I used to pay more, and that enabled the start of a conversation. Everyone spoke in Hindi, and I gathered a lot of knowledge and heard loads of folklore. Tales about the forest, about spirits that abound, what talisman brings good luck, as to what brings bad luck and how one should avoid the evil eye made me wonder about the variety of beliefs that have percolated down generations till date. India is truly a fascinating country. Every region is unique, and to experience the ground-level reality, the best way is to traverse on foot. At some juncture, at one tea stall, I saw a facial sketch of a young girl who was missing for a long time and the group of villagers sitting there were muttering various theories and glancing around the vast expanse of the thick wooden forest. Suddenly, I experienced an explosive Eureka moment, and a thrill of excitement ran through my body. This compelling story, though fictional in nature, is inspired by that incident. All the poetry, written by me, is splashed at various bends. It has also been curated and woven to be seamlessly weaved into the fabric of the storyline.

The Verdict: *Who Killed Sonia Verma* Playlist

SCAN THIS

Scan the code above and tune into the atmospheric mood of *The Verdict* to go on a thrilling journey along with Karan in the misty hills of Pelling.

Prologue

The past is a place of learning, not a place of living.

The mist pressed against the windows like an impatient visitor, swallowing the town of Pelling in its silent embrace. Somewhere in the distance, the temple bells tolled, their chimes lost in the wind that slithered through the valleys.

She ran. Jagged stones sliced into her bare feet, leaving a trail of red across the slippery jungle path. The slick mud pulled at her heels, each stride a battle to stay upright. Rain hammered her face, blurring her vision. Breathing in sharp bursts, her lungs strained, making her ribs ache as her heart slammed against her chest, each beat a warning drum. The torn *kurta* clung to her skin as she tried to clutch it close, with blood-slick fingers, stumbling, catching herself, pushing forward. Pain burned through her legs, but stopping wasn't an option. Behind her, the night felt alive - watching, waiting.

The night was supposed to be her ally, shielding her from prying eyes. But in a town ruled by fear, there was no such thing as safety. She stumbled near the old banyan tree, her knees hitting the wet ground. A sob escaped her lips as she tried to rise, her body trembling, broken.

Then she heard a footstep behind her. Deliberate and measured.

She turned, gasping, her vision blurred by tears and the rain that dripped from her lashes.

A shadow loomed in the fog.

"You should've kept your mouth shut," a voice murmured, calm. Almost amused.

Her heart pounded against her ribs. "Please..."

The laughter that followed was soft, almost gentle. It sent a shiver down her spine.

"Too late for that now."

The first kick drove into her stomach, folding her in half and ripping the air from her lungs in a strangled gasp. The second slammed into her shoulder, spinning her to the ground. She landed hard, mud splattering her face. She tried to get up – hands slipping, nails digging into the earth, but fingers clamped around her hair, wrenching her backwards.

A rope slid around her throat, coarse and cold. It tightened, cutting deep into her skin. She clawed at the hands behind her, heels scraping furrows in the wet ground, choking on rain and panic. Her chest convulsed, lungs burning for air. The world tilted, narrowing to the sound of her heartbeat pounding in her ears, then faltering, slowing, fading into darkness.

She never saw the blade.

When it was done, the drizzle thickened into steady rain, washing away footprints but not sins. Her body was dragged across the forest floor, leaving a dark trail in the mud. Gasoline splashed over her bruised skin, its acrid scent mingling with rain and blood.

A match flared.

Flame met flesh.

By the time the fire died, half her body was reduced to charred remains, just enough to blur the truth, just enough to make sure no one ever asked the right questions. Only one thing remained untouched by the flames: the deep, clean slashes of a *khukri*, carved deliberately into her skin like a signature.

By morning, the mist had already begun to erase her

The official story would be simple:

A tragic accident. A leopard attack.

A case closed before it truly ever began.

And just like that, Sonia Verma ceased to exist.

Contents

Chapter 1
A Holiday Interrupted

Knowing others is wisdom.

Knowing yourself is enlightenment.

– Lao Tzu

The narrow road to Pelling coiled through hills still wet from the night's rain. The morning mist hung thick over the jagged peaks of Pelling, clinging to the land like a ghostly veil. Karan Negi leaned against the jeep window, watching the world slip by in shades of grey and green as the prayer flags fluttered from roadside poles, their colours dimmed by dew.

His car creaked and swayed as it wound its way along the narrow, treacherous road. He tightened his grip on the steering wheel, squinting through the fog, the headlights doing little to pierce the opaque whiteness. Beside him, the rental car's radio softly hummed with Patti Page's *Tennessee Waltz*, a song he hadn't heard in years, but one that somehow felt appropriate for the melancholic mood that weighed on him.

Pelling was supposed to be an escape, a place where the sprawling silence and untouched beauty could offer him something he hadn't felt in years: peace.

The small hill town nestled in the lap of Sikkim had seemed like the perfect destination. Its ancient monasteries, whispering forests, and a commanding view of Mount Khangchendzonga spoke of timeless serenity, untainted by the chaos of the modern world. He parked outside his modest bungalow, trying to shake the unease simmering beneath his skin.

His housekeeper, Amar Singh and his wife, Pushpa Devi, were waiting for him in front of his well-maintained house. The wooden floor creaked as he entered and observed the blend of rustic charm and subtle decay. Pinewood beams supported the low ceilings, and the air carried a faint scent of dampness and old books. A faint smile broke on his lips as he glanced at the dozens of photo frames that hung on all the walls around the house, speaking about his fifty-year journey. Finally, no more homestays or Airbnb; the house would be out of bounds for anyone but him.

A fireplace sat at the centre of the living room, its hearth cold and unlit. A stack of firewood leaned against the wall, waiting. Karan's gaze landed on a desk by the window, where a leather-bound journal sat, placed as if inviting him to open it. His jaw tightened. That journal held years of scribbled thoughts, half-finished stories, and memories he wished to forget. He had bought this house decades ago and always hoped to lead a peaceful and quiet life in the lap of the mountains. He had also created a lovely kitchen garden and had promised himself that every morning, after a walk, whatever had grown would be plucked and put in a mixer grinder, which would be his daily breakfast of fibre. If nothing would grow, the penalty was a fast till lunch.

Finally, he was here to write and enjoy his retirement. He poured himself a glass of whiskey from the decanter on the side table and stood by the window watching the fog swallow the forest quietly. The distant temple bell tolled again, its sound resonating deep within him. For the first time in decades, he tasted a freedom not written into verdicts or judgments.

He watched Amar Singh light the fire as he switched on the radio, and *Missing You* by John Waite filled the room – a song he hadn't been able to bear for years. The melody ached, bleeding into the silence that clung to the walls. As the liquor burned its way down, he thought of Nalini – her eyes the night she left, and of Kiara, their daughter, whose laughter still echoed in the corners of his mind. Then his thoughts drifted to his childhood. He thought of his father's belt, of the courtroom he had left behind, of every choice that had carved him hollow. The past pressed in like mist – cold, relentless, impossible to escape.

But he wasn't that man anymore. Not the judge. Not the husband. Not the son. For the first time in decades, he was tasting freedom, not the kind granted by verdicts or courts, but the kind that comes with surrender.

He was savouring his freedom at last, and was now looking forward to roaming the hills. Life is supposed to be light and simple, but our aspirations and ambitions make it so heavy. He was now going to spend the remaining years on his terms. A faint smile appeared on his lips.

This was supposed to be his final respite. But standing there, staring into the mist, Karan couldn't shake the feeling that the mountains were watching, waiting, and that peace would not come easily here. He could not understand why his gut was trying to convey some intuitive message, but he gave up trying to decipher it.

The crackling fire in the bungalow's hearth did little to warm the former judge as he sat in his armchair, his whiskey now abandoned on the side table. The mist outside pressed against the windows like an impatient visitor, its tendrils curling into every crevice of the view. The stillness was suffocating, yet it was what he had sought, wasn't it? Would he be able to now sing his song like a solitary bird in the wilderness?

His hand hovered over the leather-bound journal, then withdrew immediately. Some memories were better left locked away. He leaned back, sinking into the leather chair, and shut his eyes. Thoughts churned behind them – relentless, rising like a storm he could no longer hold back.

He opened his eyes and flexed his hands, the old reflex kicking in. Years of practising Krav Maga had taught him how to fight back and how to breathe through the chaos. It had started as defence, a way to survive the blows of his father's belt. Later, it became the one thing that steadied him when his mind turned against itself.

Just then, Amar and Pushpa's son, perhaps fifteen years old, appeared at the door, bowing slightly.

"*Namaste*, Judge *sahib*," the boy greeted, his voice soft but laden with respect.

"*Namaste*," Karan replied.

The boy led him to his room, a modest affair with a single bed, a desk, a cupboard, and a window that framed a partial view of the misty mountains. Karan nodded in approval and unpacked his bags with slow deliberation, methodically removing the few items he'd brought: a book on Buddhist philosophy, a notebook, his clothes, medicines, whiskey bottles, and a photograph of his seventeen-year-old daughter, now estranged for ten years.

A particular photo drew his gaze, and for a fleeting moment, his stoic expression softened. It was the last picture taken, of Karan and Kiara with a birthday cake smeared on his face, by her. He still remembered her as a seventeen-year-old. He felt tears welling up.

She must be around twenty-seven now, he thought.

"Someday," he muttered to himself. Someday, he would repair the fractured bond between them.

That night, Karan sat by the window, sipping whiskey, today exceeding his usual quota, watching the veil of mist outside that had swirled in strange, almost hypnotic patterns, obscuring the world beyond. He tried to focus on the outline of his book, which would determine the flow of the story, but the unease persisted, the silence too thick, too oppressive.

A faint rustling sound made him glance up sharply. It was distant, somewhere in the woods beyond the former homestay. Perhaps an animal or the wind, teasing the trees. He shook his head and turned back to his scribbling pad to once again start writing the outline of his book, but the distraction lingered.

He knew what the real problem was. It wasn't the silence or the mist - it was his past.

The radio softly hummed in the background as a soft flute picked up, a haunting song by Jagjit Singh – *Apni Aankhon Ke Samundar Mein*. The melancholy in Karan's chest deepened with the *ghazal's* lingering ache.

The memories of a broken marriage, his father's cruel hand, and the isolation of a life dedicated to justice. The scars ran deep, and even here, in this secluded paradise, they found him. The politics he faced due to the ganging up of the system. He had always accepted the fact that he had very poor PR skills and remained a Sessions Court Judge, and for some reason or the other, he was never elevated to the High Court.

All in the past now.

As the clock struck midnight, his phone buzzed, breaking the heavy silence. Startled by the sudden sound, he stared at the glowing screen, hesitant. His eyes were already droopy, and his speech had started slurring.

The caller ID read: Chief Justice Raghavendra Rao.

Karan's jaw tightened. He already knew this wouldn't be good news. Reluctantly, he picked up.

"Karan," Rao's voice came through, urgent yet apologetic. "I wouldn't disturb you if it weren't important."

"I take it this call isn't just to exchange pleasantries," Karan said, his voice measured.

Rao chuckled, but there was no humour in it. "There's a case. High profile. Delicate. And frankly, there's no one else I trust to handle it," he said, his tone heavy.

Karan's fingers tightened around the ceramic mug. "I'm retired."

"Yes, I know, my old friend," Rao almost pleaded, his tone softening, "One last time, I need you for a very important assignment. You know we go a long way, and I am fully aware of your potential. This one is completely different."

Different? That word hung in the air like a faint echo. Karan had heard it before, often enough to know it was never good news. He glanced at the mist-shrouded hills, their beauty now tinged with foreboding. This was the Chief Justice calling, also an old friend. Memories of both of them as young lawyers who started their careers together flashed in his mind. One retired as a Sessions Court Judge, and the other is occupying the highest position of the Chief Justice of the High Court of the State. Most probably, he'll be elevated to the Supreme Court of India. The flood of thoughts abruptly ended.

"Tell me," he said, the resignation in his voice unmistakable.

"A murder in Pelling," Rao began, his words slow, deliberate. "The victim: a young woman, seventeen, the eldest daughter of a local farmer, working at a hotel owned by MLA Thakur. The main suspect is Rohan Thakur, his son."

Karan exhaled sharply. "Rohan Thakur." The name carries weight, a reputation marred by whispers of entitlement, arrogance, and unchecked privilege.

"There are... complications," Rao continued hesitantly, "The investigation is sloppy. Evidence has gone missing. The local police are compromised. I suspect the autopsy report is also carefully manicured. And the town - well, the town is on edge. The case is volatile, with no arrests."

Karan placed the mug on the table, suddenly increasingly aware of its weight. "And you want me to do what?"

"Not want, Karan. Need," Rao said, his voice now a low plea. "This inquiry and investigation requires someone with your... resolve. Your reputation for being unyielding, for cutting through noise. The kind of inquiry report only you can deliver. The Chief Minister, on an SOS basis, has requested me to convince you to accept the assignment. Under the Commission of Inquiry Act, the notification will be issued tonight."

Karan's gaze drifted to the mist again. It seemed denser now, more oppressive. Pelling had called him here for peace, for a respite from the chaos of his life. Instead, it was drawing him into something darker, something he wasn't sure he wanted to face.

"I'll need a detailed Appointment Letter with the Terms of Reference setting out all the parameters, my powers, my remuneration, the assistance and security at my disposal and specifically, what my suggestions pursuant to the findings in the report would be required," Karan said curtly. "You know the usual drill," he added, his voice weary but resolute.

"The notification is being issued tonight as we speak and will be delivered to you with protocol at 8 a.m. at your residence. The terms of reference will be personally drafted by me; please be assured. Thank you, Karan," Rao said, relief flooding his tone.

As the line went dead, Karan leaned back into the rickety chair on the veranda. Karan stared at the phone a moment longer, listening to the faint hum of rain on the roof. The wind carried the faraway clang of monastery bells - a sound that somehow made the order feel heavier.

Duty had a way of finding you, even in exile.

From the living room, the radio crackled and shifted tracks. Manna Dey's voice floated through the air, *Kasme Vaade Pyar Wafa*. The irony wasn't lost on him. A song about promises, loyalty, and betrayal - it struck too close.

He poured himself a drink and reached for his journal. The mist rolled across the mountains like secrets too heavy to settle. He scribbled a few lines, then paused, staring into the distance. In all his years navigating power and prestige, why did peace feel like a stranger?

The more money you have, the more depressed you become.

It wasn't his original thought, but it had stayed with him. The Easterlin Paradox - a theory he once came across that explained why happiness plateaus beyond a certain income. Money bought comfort, even dignity. But after a point, it only bought distractions.

No matter how many things you gather in life, there is no container service in the end. From accumulation to true enhancement is the key.

He'd seen it firsthand. The desperation of the poor in his courtroom, their rights traded for survival. Money mattered. But beyond shelter, food, and safety, what truly nourishes happiness? Meaning. Purpose. Intimacy. The kind of connections that couldn't be bought or manipulated.

Perhaps this assignment wasn't a punishment, but a quiet offering. A chance to step outside the system, not to prove something but to redeem something. Not for accolades. Not for legacy. But simply because someone had to speak for the silenced.

The mist thickened, curling inward like a silent listener to his thoughts. A familiar tightness stirred in his chest, the old tension that came before a trial, before the truth began to show its face.

Pelling hadn't called him to rest. It had summoned him for reckoning.

And he couldn't turn away.

Too many daughters had vanished into the silence of bureaucracy and shame. Girls raped, murdered, forgotten. He thought of his own daughter. The sharp edge of fatherhood never dulled. He needed to do this, not for closure, but for justice.

This was his moment to put his experience to work. To wield truth like a scalpel. To excavate what the world had tried to bury.

Tomorrow, when he opened his eyes in this strange, mist-shrouded town, something would shift. Something would begin.

With that thought, he closed his journal. The glass emptied. The chair creaked as he got up and went to bed.

The night deepened. Somewhere, a dog barked and then went silent. He finally let sleep take him – deep, unresisting, and still.

Chapter 2

The Commission Of Inquiry

The law may be blind, but those who interpret it are not.

Justice depends on how long they can bear to keep their eyes open.

- Anonymous Judicial Saying

The next morning, Karan awoke to the faint hum of life outside his window. The mist had lifted slightly, revealing the jagged, imposing silhouette of the mountain, which seemed both majestic and foreboding, a reminder of the challenges that lay ahead.

Amar Singh and Pushpa Devi were preparing his favourite breakfast. A few carrots were also plucked from the kitchen garden and served with a steaming hot cup of coffee. The shower area overlooked the mountains, and he loved to shower with the window open as the cold air mixed with hot water was refreshing. He quickly shaved and dressed, his movements deliberate, as though each button fastened and cuff adjusted was a small step toward shedding the fragile peace he had come to Pelling to find. Just as he was heading out, Amar Singh came and handed him a letter which had been delivered in the morning. Karan opened it and read:

Government of Sikkim

Office of the Chief Secretary

Gangtok – 737101

Date: 18/6/2023

Ref. No.: CS/SK/INQ/2022-03

APPOINTMENT LETTER

To:

Shri Karan Negi (Retd.)

Former Sessions Judge

Government Guesthouse

Pelling, West Sikkim

Subject: Appointment as Commissioner of Inquiry under the Commission of Inquiry Act, 1952

Sir,

In view of the grave and disturbing circumstances surrounding the recent death of Ms. Sonia Verma, an employee of the Royal Pelling Hotel, the Government of Sikkim, in the interest of transparency and justice, hereby appoints you as the Commissioner of Inquiry under Section 3 of the Commission of Inquiry Act, 1952.

This appointment shall be governed by the following Terms of Reference:

Terms of Reference:

- To inquire into the circumstances leading to the death of Ms. Sonia Verma on the night of 13.6.2023, including, but not limited to, the sequence of events preceding and following her death.
- To examine the conduct of the concerned officials, including officers of the local police

station, forensic department, and any public servant who may have been involved in the handling, reporting, or investigation of the matter.

- To determine the veracity of the claim that the cause of death was an animal attack, and whether the same was an attempt to mislead or suppress facts.
- To assess whether there was any attempt at tampering of evidence, coercion of witnesses, or institutional failure in providing justice.
- To recommend actions, based on the findings of the inquiry, including administrative, legal, and institutional reforms or disciplinary proceedings where necessary.

Powers Granted:

- The Commission shall have the powers of a Civil and Criminal Court.
- You are empowered to summon witnesses, requisition documents, and direct production of records from any department or private individual.
- You may, at your discretion, engage experts, consultants, or advisors with prior approval of the undersigned.
- You may conduct hearings in-camera as deemed fit, keeping in mind the sensitivity of the case.

Remuneration and Support:

- A consolidated honorarium of ₹2,00,000 per month shall be provided, in addition to boarding and lodging at the Pelling Guesthouse for the duration of the inquiry.

- A dedicated team of administrative staff, research assistants, stenographers, and round-the-clock armed security from the Sikkim Police (4 personnel) shall be assigned to you immediately upon commencement of duty.

Timeline and Reporting:

- The Commission is to submit its Interim Report within 30 days and the Final Report within 90 days from the date of receipt of this letter.
- Your findings and recommendations shall be considered binding for administrative action unless otherwise directed by the Hon'ble Chief Minister's Office.

We are confident that your integrity, experience, and understanding of the judicial system will be of immense value in unveiling the truth and restoring public faith.

We thank you for accepting this responsibility.

With regards,

Yours sincerely,

[Signed]

A.K. Bhutia

Chief Secretary, Government of Sikkim

akbhutia@gov.sk.in

(Seal & Stamp)

The morning mist in Pelling was thicker than usual, clinging to the slopes like a reluctant farewell. The peaks were obscured, hidden behind a veil of grey. Karan stood on the small veranda of his bungalow, his briefcase by his side, watching the hazy outlines of prayer flags fluttering in the breeze. Both his bags were already packed, as till the Commission of Inquiry proceedings would end, he would have to shift into his official quarters and thereafter, return to this house.

It had been a brief escape, too brief to dull the edges of his restlessness. Now, the weight of duty pressed upon him again, as it always did. He took one last sip of the lukewarm black coffee from the clay cup in his hand and set it down on the railing.

The rhythmic rumble of approaching vehicles broke the quiet. Two new Mahindra jeeps emerged from the mist, their headlights slicing through the dense fog. The driver, a wiry man in his forties, with weathered hands and a wary disposition, stepped out and tipped his cap. Four constables also stepped out, along with a State Government official in a dark suit, who promptly handed over the notification and the terms of reference.

Pleasantries exchanged, the driver asked, "Ready to leave, *sahib*?" his voice, tinged with curiosity. Karan suspected the man was used to ferrying tourists who lingered for weeks. His abrupt departure must have seemed strange.

"Let's go," Karan said, his tone clipped.

The driver loaded Karan's suitcase into the back of the jeep as he turned for one last look at the bungalow. The slate roof glistened with rain, and the wooden beams groaned softly in the damp air. Mist gathered around the porch, curling through the garden like breath. For a moment, he felt it - the stillness, the solitude, the fragile peace he'd almost managed to make with himself. The thought of staying flickered through him, brief and dangerous. But the decision was made. Amar Singh and Pushpa Devi stood by the steps, their hands folded, eyes glistening with unspoken words as he said goodbye.

As the jeep trundled down the narrow mountain roads, the landscape unfurled before him. Dense forests of Rhododendron and Oak framed the path, their branches entwined like ancient sentinels. In the distance, a monastery bell tolled – low, resonant, a sound that seemed to fold the valley back into silence. The local driver muttered, "*Aba*, fog won't lift till noon, *la*," his voice thick with the easy rhythm of the hills. Karan gave a small nod, half-smile; he had grown used to conversations that ended before they began.

Karan leaned back against the back seat, his thoughts as tangled as the roots of the trees outside. The official sitting in front next to the driver started explaining, "Sir, there is a file on the seat next to you. This contains various documents, newspaper clippings, etc., for your kind perusal. Next to the court building, there is a bungalow, and on the ground floor will be your office. Your assistants, stenographer and personal secretary will be at your aid and disposal. Two constables will be on duty around the clock with 12-hour shifts, so that, if you need anything or any assistance, they will be available. These two armed constables will be staying on the same floor. There will also be a cook, and his wife will be the maid for cleaning and washing purposes. If anything is lacking, please don't hesitate to contact me even at midnight." Karan had a satisfactory smile on his lips, as even when he was a Sitting Judge, he did not enjoy these protocols.

Karan flipped it open. The pages detailed the victim's background and the circumstances of death. Rohan Thakur's face had been plastered across newspapers and television screens for weeks, a privileged scion now accused of cold-blooded murder. He went through the Chemical Analysis Reports, photographs of the crime scene, and the autopsy conducted were all in the file.

Karan's mind churned with questions. *How airtight was the evidence? How far would the Thakur family go to shield their son? And what of the victim?* She was more than just a name in a file. Someone's daughter, someone's friend – now reduced to a tragic headline. She needed closure. And he was damn well going to ensure that she got it.

The jeep came to a sharp turn, jolting Karan from his thoughts. He was still scanning the contents. So many photographs of the crime scene, already fading forensic reports, and witness statements to the police. It was all there, stark and clinical, the investigation done so far. The manner in which the file was prepared clearly meant that a team had worked on it at bullet-train speed for him to start reading.

Karan's grip on the file tightened. The weight of responsibility settled heavily on his shoulders. This wasn't just another case. It was actually him on a trial. A trial that would test the limits of justice in a country where power often held sway over truth.

The jeep emerged from the mist into a bustling market square. Locals moved about, their chatter punctuated by the occasional honk of a car horn. The scent of steaming momos and freshly brewed tea wafted through the air.

"Five minutes' stop here, *sahib*," the driver announced, pulling the jeep to a halt near a small teashop.

Karan stepped out, stretching his legs. His eyes caught sight of a vendor selling prayer wheels and intricately carved wooden masks. He wandered over, his fingers brushing against the smooth surface of a mask resembling Dzonga, the mountain deity.

"For protection," the vendor said in halting English, his weathered face breaking into a smile.

Karan hesitated, then bought the mask, slipping it into his bag. *Protection* – perhaps he would need it in the days to come.

When the jeep resumed its journey, the mist seemed less oppressive, the mountains receding into the distance. He was leaving the quiet of the hills behind, heading toward the action in the Enquiry Room. The fog thickened with every mile, muffling the crunch of gravel under the tyres.

The driver, unable to control himself, broke the silence. "You're heading into a storm, sir. This case... The Thakurs have roots here, deep ones. They'll protect their own." His eyes darted to the rearview mirror, meeting Karan's gaze for the briefest moment.

Karan said nothing. The man's words confirmed what he already knew: this was no ordinary case. The air in Pelling felt charged, as though the mountains themselves were holding their breath.

The makeshift office to conduct the Commission's proceedings sat atop a crumbling hill, an old colonial bungalow repurposed for the town's justice. Instead of the towering, polished structures of Metropolitan

Courts, this was a crumbling relic of colonial times. Perched precariously on a weather-beaten hill, it seemed to lean into the mist, as though seeking refuge from the relentless elements.

Karan stepped out of the battered jeep, his leather case in hand. A chill wind whispered through the courtyard, carrying the faint aroma of damp earth and wildflowers. The courthouse loomed before him, its faded white walls streaked with moss and its windows dark with neglect.

He adjusted his coat and climbed the uneven stone steps, each one creaking underfoot. At the entrance, a wooden plaque swung lazily in the breeze, its letters barely legible: Pelling District Court. Its faded white walls bore scars of weather and time, much like the cases it now witnessed. Just for the kicks of it, he decided to take a tour of the Courthouse, this time, as a 'civilian'.

The chaos of the courthouse mirrored the chaos of the town's justice system. Inside, it was even more decrepit. The walls bore the stains of countless monsoons, and the air smelled of mildew and old paper. A creaky ceiling fan whirred ineffectively, failing to dispel the oppressive humidity. Karan's shoes echoed hollowly on the wooden floorboards as he walked toward his chambers. The room was modest, with a desk cluttered with dusty, ageing files, a single chair with fraying upholstery, and a window that overlooked the misty hills. The glass was smudged, but through it, Karan could make out the outline of Mount Khangchendzonga, its jagged peaks piercing the clouds.

As he walked out from the rear side door towards his official bungalow adjacent to the courthouse, he was greeted by the cook and his wife. They welcomed him with a *namaste* and showed him the lounge, a small workspace and the huge dining area. A prayer flag fluttered at the doorway, and Karan, out of habit, removed his shoes before stepping across the threshold – an old Sikkimese courtesy he'd picked up years ago. Near the staircase, he noticed the extra guest room where both the constables would be staying around the clock in shifts.

The couple escorted him to his room on the first floor, where each window flooded the entire room with abundant sunlight, and the view of the mountains was mesmerising. He opened the windows and took a deep breath, soaking in the fresh air.

After they set his luggage down, he lingered for a moment in front of the large mirror. The journey, the altitude, and the weight of recent years seemed to show faintly in his eyes. With a small, practised motion, he straightened his tie, smoothed the creases of his visibly weary suit, and drew in a long breath as though gathering himself back into form.

The courthouse wasn't far, but each step through the narrow lanes felt like crossing between two worlds – the serenity of the mountains behind him, and the solemn gravity of justice awaiting ahead. By the time he entered his office, the sun had shifted, casting slanted beams across the old wooden desk and a worn-out leather chair. He hung his blazer carefully on the peg, sat down, with a sigh.

The room carried the faint scent of paper and dust – a familiar companion through the years. He adjusted a few files, letting the silence settle, when the door creaked open.

"Welcome to the Pelling judiciary, sir. It's not glamorous, and it doesn't get any more interesting," said a man with a thin moustache and a hint of dry humour in his voice. "I'm Kumar – your clerk."

Karan nodded, taking in the man's faint smile and sharp eyes, the kind that missed nothing. "It'll do," he replied, his expression unreadable.

Kumar smirked. "It'll have to. Pelling has a charm, though. You'll see it eventually. Probably after the first monsoon flood washes away half the files."

Before Karan could respond, a bright-eyed young woman with a notebook clutched to her chest entered.

"Good morning, sir," she said, her voice clear and confident. "I'm Leela. Your intern. It's a privilege to learn and help you bring justice!" Her dark eyes scanned the room with curiosity, barely containing her excitement. Though Karan couldn't help but notice, her idealism seemed out of place in Pelling's murky landscape.

"Leela," he said, nodding in acknowledgement. "Are you from Pelling?"

She shook her head. "No, sir. I'm from Gangtok. But I've been here for a while, studying law."

Kumar chuckled, stepping past her. "She's the idealist of the lot. Still believes justice is more than a word to put on a plaque."

Karan looked at Leela with a faint smile and said, "Let's hope you still believe that by the end of this inquiry. After all our efforts, ultimately, when I prepare my report, it is up to the government to consider and act on the report and the suggestions incorporated after the collection of all the evidence, coupled with my findings," said Karan, as he broke into a chuckle.

Leela's eyes brightened.

Kumar groaned. "The whole town's already buzzing about it. You've been here less than an hour, and the gossip's beating you already." They all laughed. The atmosphere was now more relaxing.

Karan glanced at the files neatly placed on his desk.. He hadn't even opened them yet, but already the weight of the case pressed down on him like the mountains outside.

"Let's get to work," he said softly.

As Karan began unpacking the details of the case, Kumar brought him the police case file, which read like a checklist of political interference. He flipped through the photographs clipped to the inside cover. The victim, a young girl whose identity was still under speculation, was found dead near the forest's edge with bite marks on body parts that they could salvage from her charred body, and under mysterious circumstances. The girl stared back at him – mud streaked across her cheek, eyes half-open, caught between fear and something that looked almost like defiance. She was identified as Sonia Verma, a seventeen-year-old daughter of a local farmer who had filed an FIR with the police accusing Rohan Thakur.

For a moment, he couldn't move. The curve of her face, the faint dimple in her chin, even the way her hair framed her features – it all struck too close to home. For a heartbeat, he saw Kiara instead, her laughter echoing somewhere at the edge of memory. His throat tightened.

He blinked hard and shut the file. The paper rustled like a whisper he didn't want to hear. When he looked up again, his expression was all business.

He immediately collected his thoughts, as whenever he conducted trials as a Judge in cases of unnatural death and mysterious circumstances surrounding such a death, the postmortem report was of utmost significance. Anti-mortem and Post-mortem injuries or marks actually convey a message to alert the investigator, as a dead body never lies. But the criminals who disfigure a dead body to misguide the investigator create a danger of a misleading event, which can completely derail the investigation.

The deceased girl's body was partially burnt. In a case where a person is burnt while alive, the airways and lungs would have soot particles, as the victim was breathing, but if the victim is burnt after murder, to misguide the investigator, there would be no such particles in the airway. Through years of conducting trials and asking millions of questions, he had developed a keen and alert sense of what exactly was happening in a particular case. Fortunately, he had a strong intuitive power, which almost every time proved to be correct.

After an hour of quiet reading, he closed the file and let the silence stretch, pondering the next steps. The Thakur family was a name that carried weight in Pelling, and not in a good way. Rohan Thakur's reputation as a brute, a man with a penchant for violence and intimidation, was well-known.

Kumar abruptly entered the room without knocking and self-appointed himself as part investigator. He stood in front of Karan and announced enthusiastically, "First up is Rohan Thakur. You've heard of him, haven't you? Local bigwig. Known for his 'charming' ways with the women in town, if you know what I mean. And let's not even start on his *family*." Karan knew he had to deal with this over-smart character, as Kumar knew details about all the characters involved.

Karan didn't miss the emphasis on the word 'family'. He had already gathered that the Thakurs were well-entrenched in the political and social fabric of Pelling, with their influence stretching far beyond the courtrooms. That, he knew, was going to be the first real obstacle in this case.

"Judge Karan," Leela entered the room, her voice high-pitched with excitement. "I've been going through the files, and it seems like there's more to this case than we thought. Thakur's got a pretty shady past. But what's even more concerning is the way the police handled the investigation. It's... well, compromised."

Karan raised an eyebrow. "Compromised how?"

"Political interference," she explained, her face scrunching up. "The investigation was supposed to be straightforward, but there are signs that the police were directed to keep it quiet. Thakur's father, the MLA, had his hands in it. There are rumours, too. Some locals think the whole thing's a setup."

Karan's mind raced. The more he learned, the clearer it became that this was not going to be a simple inquiry proceeding. "So the case isn't just about the murder. It's about power."

Leela nodded. "Exactly. And as much as I want to be optimistic, I'm afraid justice might not be as easy to find here as we'd hoped."

Karan glanced at Leela. "Who's the lead investigator on this case?"

Leela hesitated before answering. "Inspector Vikram Singh. But… he's more interested in keeping things quiet than finding the truth."

Karan knew the name. Vikram Singh had been on his radar from the moment he'd arrived in Pelling. The man had a reputation for being a political puppet, someone who did the dirty work and kept his hands clean. Karan had no illusions about the man's integrity.

"I'll need to speak with him," Karan said, his voice cold.

Kumar leaned back in his chair, the smirk never leaving his face. "You think he'll talk to you? With the Thakur family pulling the strings?"

Karan didn't answer immediately. Instead, he stared out of the small window, where the view of the mist-covered hills beyond Pelling's borders seemed to mock him. There was something about this place, something old and ominous, that seeped into the very air. It was as if the land itself had absorbed the secrets of generations, and now, they were waiting to be unearthed.

Karan's resolve tightened. This was why he was here. To navigate this murky world, where truth was obscured by the weight of local politics and personal vendettas. He couldn't let Thakur's influence overshadow the law. Not on his watch. He shot off orders to issue summons to all of them, which were to be hand delivered by evening for the day after tomorrow, the Commission would commence its preliminary inquiry hearing.

"We'll start by looking into Thakur's history," Karan said, his voice firm. "But we need to proceed carefully. No one here seems too eager to bring him down."

Leela and Kumar exchanged a look, both of them sensing the depth of Karan's determination. Beyond the window, a prayer wheel creaked in the breeze, its rhythm steady, unhurried. Karan's gaze followed the spin – a circle without end, like the truth he was about to chase.

Chapter 3
The Hills Have Secrets

In the Court of Justice, both parties know the truth – it is the Judge who is on trial.

The Outer Inquiry Room was packed, the air electric with tension. Farmers, who had to work on their fields and orchards in the afternoon, with weathered faces, sat shoulder to shoulder with shopkeepers of the town who would later in the day go to sit in their shops, wearing their crisp *kurtas*, their whispered speculations ricocheting off the wooden walls. This wasn't just an inquiry; it was a spectacle, the kind that only murder and scandal could summon in a town like Pelling.

Most had come out of curiosity, while a few out of a sense of duty, but all had one common firm belief in their minds and were just waiting for the inevitable – waiting to see how long Karan could withstand the powerful inferno of Pelling's politics. A gladiatorial perverse pleasure was flowing through their veins.

The hum of conversation died the moment Karan deliberately strode in his nicely tailored suit and stood tall and commanding in front of the audience gathered in the outer room to witness the proceedings. As he walked into the inner room where the proceedings were to be held in camera, the air around him crackled with authority as his sharp eyes scanned and noted every twitch, every subtle glance exchanged among the gathered townsfolk, inhaling the quick soft murmurs and thoroughly enjoying the attention.

"SILENCE," Kumar let out a huge shout, and the chatter instantly died, replaced by an oppressive silence.

Karan walked to the inner room and took his seat at the table set up as the inner room was converted into a makeshift court. The cameras were placed in the centre, facing him, and on one side, the victim's parents and the State Appointed Prosecutor and on the other side, the accused, Rohan Thakur, sat, his face a mask of arrogance with his lawyer. Rohan's sharp suit and well-coiffed hair clashed with the rustic surroundings, a symbol of privilege in a room full of struggle.

Only the person summoned and his lawyer, along with the constables and State-appointed Prosecutor to assist the Commission of Inquiry, were allowed in the inner inquiry room by Karan's orders. Right now, his role was to ask questions and gather evidence. The state-appointed Prosecutor and the Defence Lawyer were also given the freedom to have their say at any stage of the proceedings. Karan had, at the outset, explained the procedure which he had devised in order for full participation, which was understood by all. He wanted everyone to experience the seriousness of a courtroom so that the inquiry could be conducted in a disciplined manner.

On the other side, the victim's family sat huddled together, their eyes red and faces drawn. The girl's father, a gaunt-looking man with calloused hands, clenched his prayer beads tightly, his lips moving soundlessly.

"Let the process begin," Karan said, his voice cutting through the tension like a blade.

The prosecutor, Harsh Bhatia, in an attempt to be the first one, arose from his seat, a thin, nervous man with a perpetual frown. "Your Honour, the evidence will show..."

"Spare me the preamble, Bhatia," Karan interrupted. "Proceed with the facts."

Bhatia faltered but nodded, shuffling through his papers. "The victim, Sonia Verma, worked at the Thakur family's hotel. She was last seen alive on the night of September 15th. Her mutilated body was discovered in the forest the following morning."

Karan leaned forward slightly, his expression giving nothing away. "And Mr. Thakur?"

"Mr Thakur was seen arguing with the victim earlier that evening. Witnesses place him near the scene of the crime shortly after midnight."

Rohan's lawyer, Sunil Tiwari, a rotund man with a booming voice, rose to his feet. "Your Honour, this is circumstantial at best. My client is being accused based on hearsay and conjecture. There is no physical evidence tying him to the crime."

Karan turned to the Defence Attorney, his gaze unyielding. "And yet, here we are. Let's see where the evidence leads us before making sweeping statements. I propose to conduct this inquiry as per the procedure devised by me, which is very informal in nature, which you must have already noticed, sir."

The lawyer sank back into his chair, his expression sour. As the day wore on, the Commission heard from witnesses, each one adding another layer to the tangled web of the case.

The first to testify was a young hotel worker, trembling as he stepped up to the witness stand. His thin frame and sunken eyes made him look older than his years. The prosecutor approached him with a sympathetic tone.

"Please state your name for the record," Bhatia, the prosecutor, began.

"Jatin... Jatin Rai," the young man stammered, his voice barely audible. He avoided eye contact, his hands fidgeting with the edge of his shirt. Each one in the room watched him intently, a sea of eyes weighing every move he made.

"And your occupation?"

"I work as a bellboy at the Thakur family's hotel."

Karan leaned forward slightly, observing the witness closely.

"Jatin," Bhatia continued, "did you know the victim, Sonia?"

"Yes, sir. She was... she was the receptionist. A good person." His voice broke on the last words.

Bhatia nodded. "You were working the night of September 15th. Did you see anything unusual?"

Jatin hesitated, glancing nervously at Rohan Thakur, who sat impassively at his table, his fingers drumming softly on the polished wood.

"It's okay, Jatin," Karan said, his voice calm but firm. "Just tell the truth. I will record your deposition as told by you. You don't need to fear anyone."

Jatin took a deep breath. "I... I saw Rohan *saab* near the service entrance," he said hesitantly. "Around nine, maybe a little later. He was arguing with someone outside the staff quarters."

"Arguing with whom?" Karan pressed.

Jatin hesitated, his fingers twisting the hem of his shirt. "I... I saw him arguing with Sonia near the staff quarters. He was shouting at her, saying things like, 'You'll regret this,' and 'You don't know who you're messing with.' I didn't see clearly. It was dark, and I didn't want to get involved."

A murmur rippled through the room.

"But you're sure it was Mr. Rohan Thakur?"

"Yes," Jatin said quickly, almost too quickly. "His voice... it was loud. I couldn't mistake it."

Jatin glanced nervously toward Rohan, who was seated at the back of the room. Rohan leaned back in his chair, a smirk playing on his lips. His nonchalance stood in stark contrast to Jatin's trembling form.

Karan's gaze hardened. "What else did you see?"

Tiwari shot to his feet. "Objection, Your Honour! This is hearsay and purely speculative!"

Karan raised a hand, silencing him. "Sir, let the witness finish."

Jatin looked down at his hands. "Later that night, I saw him leave the hotel around midnight. He was driving fast, heading toward the forest road."

Tiwari smirked, rising again. "Rai, are you implying that my client's late-night drive is somehow incriminating? Isn't it true that Mr. Thakur often takes midnight drives to clear his head?"

"I... I don't know," Jatin admitted, his voice barely above a whisper.

"Exactly," said Tiwari, turning to Karan with a flourish. "This testimony proves nothing."

Karan tapped his pen against the bench. "This is not a court proceeding. My job is to elicit all the facts from each and every individual directly or indirectly connected to the case. So, let's stick to the facts, gentlemen. Jatin, did you see Mr. Thakur return?"

"No, sir. I went to bed after that."

Karan's eyes narrowed. "Thank you, Jatin," he said, dismissing him. But his gaze lingered on the young man as he shuffled back to his seat, his fear almost palpable.

The next witness was an elderly woman who ran a tea stall near the forest entrance. She was a stout woman in her fifties, her silver hair pulled back tightly. She walked, looking straight at Karan with her sharp eyes despite her wrinkled face. She carried herself with a quiet dignity, and her silver bangles jingled softly as she folded her arms across her chest and stood facing Karan.

Bhatia approached her with respect. "Please state your name for the record."

"Kamla Devi," she said, her voice steady.

"Mrs. Kamla, were you at your stall on the night of September 15th?"

"I was, sir," she replied, "I always stay open late. Travellers often stop for tea before heading into the forest."

"And did you see anything unusual that night?"

"I saw him," she began, her voice cutting through the room like a whip. She jabbed a finger in Rohan's direction. "That boy. Driving like a madman down the main road at 1 a.m. Almost ran into my cart!"

Rohan chuckled, leaning back further in his chair. "And you're sure it was me?" he asked, his tone dripping with mockery.

Then, regaining composure, Kamla hesitated, shifting her gaze towards Rohan Thakur. She added, "Later, I saw his black SUV parked near the forest entrance around 2 a.m. He got out and walked into the trees. He was wearing a dark jacket."

"Could you identify this man?" Bhatia asked.

She squinted at Rohan. "It was dark, but he looked like that man over there." She pointed a trembling finger at the accused.

The room erupted into whispers.

Rohan smirked, leaning back in his chair. "And you're sure it was me?" he drawled, his voice oozing condescension.

Instantly, the Defence Attorney rose again, his tone mocking. "Mrs. Kamla Devi, how can you be so sure? It was dark, and you're not exactly young anymore. Isn't it possible you made a mistake?"

Kamla's eyes flashed with defiance. "I may be old, but my eyes are sharp. I know what I saw." Kamla stared angrily. "Don't act smart with me, Rohan Thakur. You think your father's name can save you from everything?"

Karan thumped his fist on the table sharply. "Let's keep this civil and stick to the facts." Keeping his tone steady but authoritative, he turned to Kamla, "Thank you, Mrs. Kamla Devi. You can leave the room."

With her gaze still locked on Rohan, Kamla said, "Don't tell me I'm mistaken. I'd recognise that fancy car of his anywhere," Kamla replied, crossing her arms. "And there was someone with him. I couldn't see their face, as they slouched down, trying to stay hidden."

Rohan leaned over to Tiwari, whispering something that made the lawyer's face tighten. Karan noticed but said nothing, filing the moment away for later.

The next deposition was of Ajay, a Forest Ranger, a grizzled man with a no-nonsense demeanour. His testimony was straightforward but chilling.

"I found the body around 6 a.m.," he said, his voice rough from years of barking orders in the wilderness. "It was clear she'd been dragged there. There were tyre track marks leading to the spot."

Bhatia nodded, "Did these tyre tread marks match any vehicle?"

Ajay pulled out a small notebook. "The treads matched the SUV owned by Mr. Thakur."

Tiwari groaned audibly. "Circumstantial again!"

Karan fixed him with a sharp look. "We'll determine what's circumstantial and what's not. Let's get the facts first. Continue, Mr. Ajay."

Ajay nodded. "The body was found near a clearing used for illicit activities. We've caught poachers there before, but this time… this was something else."

The Commission resumed after a short recess, and the prosecutor called the final witness for the day, "Inspector Vikram Singh."

The doors opened, and a tall man in a neatly pressed police uniform strode to the stand with an air of authority. His sharp features and piercing gaze gave him the aura of a man who'd seen it all. He sat down, his back ramrod straight.

Karan leaned forward slightly, his pen poised to jot down notes.

"Inspector Singh," the Prosecutor, Bhatia began, "you were the first officer on the scene when Sonia's body was discovered. Please describe what you found."

Singh adjusted his collar before speaking. "I received a call early in the morning about a body in the forest. When I arrived, I found the deceased lying in a clearing, partially covered in leaves. The victim had multiple injuries, including deep lacerations on her neck and torso."

"Were these injuries consistent with foul play?"

Singh hesitated. "Initially, they appeared suspicious. But upon further inspection and consultation with wildlife experts, it became evident that the injuries were caused by a leopard. This area is known for frequent leopard sightings and attacks."

Tiwari seized the moment, standing with a triumphant expression. "So, Inspector Singh, in your professional opinion, this was nothing more than a tragic accident caused by a wild animal?"

"That is correct," Singh replied firmly.

A murmur rippled through the room. The townsfolk had been whispering about the panther prowling the outskirts, its presence both a menace and a mystery.

Bhatia frowned but continued. "Inspector, are you aware of the Forensic Report that found tyre tracks leading to the clearing?"

"Yes," Singh admitted, "but tyre tracks alone don't prove foul play. This is a popular area for locals and tourists. The tracks could belong to anyone."

Bhatia stepped closer, his tone sharpening. "And what about the witness testimony that places the accused, Rohan Thakur, near the forest that night?"

Singh shrugged, his expression impassive. "Circumstantial. Without concrete evidence tying him to the crime, we cannot disregard the likelihood of a leopard attack."

Karan's fist struck sharply against the desk. "Inspector Singh, you can safely assume that you are under oath. Have you ruled out the possibility of human involvement entirely? And you think a leopard killed Sonia?" Karan asked, his tone laced with scepticism.

Singh hesitated, clearly irritated by the question. "We've considered all possibilities, sir. But without definitive proof, we cannot classify this as a homicide."

Karan's gaze bore into the inspector. "Inspector, was there anything at the scene that could definitively link the leopard attack theory to this particular incident?"

Singh shifted uncomfortably. "There were animal tracks near the body, and the injuries were consistent with claw marks. Beyond that, no."

Karan leaned back, his face unreadable. "Thank you, Inspector. You may leave the room. We will look into the charring of the body in due course, after I carefully examine once again the post-mortem report and the accompanying photographs." Karan very tactfully let out his intention to gauge the response. He saw beads of sweat for the first time on the forehead of Rohan Thakur.

Inspector Singh also wiped his sweat beads and started walking slowly out of the room, as Karan's gaze followed him, sharp and probing. There was something about the Inspector's testimony that gnawed at him. The leopard attack theory was too clean, too convenient, a puzzle piece forced into place without truly fitting. The charring comment was deliberately thrown in by Karan, and he had thought of a clever ace up his sleeve to be revealed at a later date.

The whispers in the room grew louder as people present began debating the plausibility of Singh's testimony. Word was also spreading in the outer room, and rumours were flying fast and furious.

"Leopard, my foot," someone muttered in the back. "This whole thing stinks."

The tension in the room was palpable. Karan scanned the room, his mind racing. Bhatia looked frustrated, while Tiwari seemed smug.

Karan made a note in his pad: *Investigate Singh's handling of the case. Speak to forensic experts directly. Dig deeper into Thakur's connections.*

The session adjourned for the day, and as the room emptied, Karan flipped through his notes while his mind replayed the testimonies.

Was Singh's leopard theory an attempt to cover up something bigger? How could he have completely ignored the charred body? The postmortem report did not give a clear picture at all and was prepared in a hasty and haphazard fashion. Apart from being the Commission of Inquiry, he would also have to put on his detective hat.

Each piece of testimony seemed to connect, but there were gaps, important ones. Karan's thoughts were interrupted by a subtle shift in the air, a faint rustling from the open window behind him. He tapped his pen against the edge of his notebook, deep in thought. Sonia's life and death held secrets he hadn't uncovered yet.

"Long day, huh?" a voice interrupted his thoughts.

Karan looked up to see Bhatia's Assistant Prosecutor, Priya Kapoor, leaning against the desk, a steaming cup of coffee in her hand. Her sharp features softened as she smiled at him.

"Long and frustrating," Karan admitted, sitting back in his chair. "There's something we're not seeing."

Priya raised an eyebrow. "You're thinking this was just a personal grudge?"

"I'm certain of it. But connecting the dots is proving harder than I thought." He gestured at his notebook. "Rohan's argument with Sonia, his midnight drive, the forest tracks – it all seems deliberate, yet too convenient."

Priya sipped her coffee. "Maybe we're looking in the wrong places. Have you been to the crime scene? And what do we know about Sonia's personal life? Any enemies, debts, relationships?"

Karan nodded. "Exactly what I was thinking. I'm going to visit the crime scene and dig into her background. There has to be a lead somewhere."

"Need help?" Priya asked and winked. Karan had to admit that she was one hell of a smart woman whose help would be essential at all stages. No wonder the State Government had also appointed her as an expert to assist the Commission.

Karan hesitated, then nodded. "Let's meet outside after an hour. The sooner we start, the better."

He looked at the mountains outside, looming in the distance, their peaks shrouded in perpetual mist. With a sigh, he rose and left the room. Karan knew that the case was far from straightforward, and the web of corruption surrounding Rohan Thakur was already spinning faster than he could untangle it. Yet, in his gut, Karan knew one thing for sure: he wasn't going to back down. Not now, not ever.

As he stood to leave, Kumar leaned over and whispered, "Good luck, Judge *saab*. You'll need it."

Karan smiled. "I've been through worse," he said as they walked to his chamber.

He felt the weight of the room pressing in on him. The makeshift Commission's Headquarters in Pelling was far from the polished institutions he was used to, and every creak of the wooden floorboards seemed to echo the fragility of the justice system in this corner of the world. The walls, barely more than thin sheets of corrugated metal, offered no protection from the cacophony of the town's daily life. But he had to admit that all the tools for research, laptops, the internet and assistants were a big help.

Yet, as the evening sun filtered through the gaps, illuminating the dust motes dancing in the air, Karan couldn't help but feel that this was where he was meant to be, at least for now.

He observed his team. Kumar, the clerk, sat opposite him, scribbling notes in a ledger with an air of detached indifference. His eyes, sharp and calculating, occasionally darted toward Karan, his lips curling into a slight, almost imperceptible smirk as if aware of something Karan was yet to fully grasp.

Beside him, Leela shuffled through a stack of papers, her expression a mixture of determination and youthful enthusiasm. She was the kind of intern who believed that a single courtroom victory could change the world, and in many ways, Karan admired her optimism. And there was Priya.

"Sir, I've collected, organised and reviewed the files for the Thakur case," Leela said, her voice bright but laced with an undercurrent of uncertainty. "It's... It's complicated. The police reports are riddled with gaps, and there's talk of political influence over the investigation. It's hard to know where to start."

Karan looked up from his own papers, his gaze steady. "We start where the truth is buried, Leela. And then we dig."

Kumar let out a dry laugh, his pen tapping rhythmically against the desk. "Digging sounds like the right approach, Judge *saab*, but in this town, you might just end up digging your own grave." Kumar had an uncanny manner of conveying, in the frankest manner possible, the most dreadful and honest message.

Karan's eyes narrowed, the comment hitting closer to home than Kumar realised. There were too many people here who wanted to keep their skeletons hidden, too many who thrived on the corruption that poisoned every facet of Pelling's existence. Karan had seen it before, small towns where power and influence were wielded like weapons, where the innocent paid the price for the sins of the guilty. Mercy was always a luxury for the powerful. The less fortunate were always found guilty.

"Let's assume the worst, for a moment," Karan said, turning back to his staff. "Let's assume that Rohan Thakur is involved in this murder. What then?"

Leela's eyes widened, but she didn't flinch. "We build a case. We find the evidence and make an ironclad report for the State Government to act upon."

"And if the evidence is fabricated?" Karan pressed. "What if the entire investigation has been tainted from the start?"

Kumar shrugged. "Then we start digging into the right places. But be prepared, when you dig in Pelling, you're likely to stir up more than just dirt. People don't like their secrets exposed. Ask Priya," he chuckled.

Karan ignored him, took a deep breath and stood up. "Leela, let's check out the crime scene first. There's no point in waiting for the investigation to come to us. If we want the truth, we'll have to find it ourselves."

Leela stood with him, her eyes bright with determination. Kumar, however, remained seated, his gaze fixed on Karan with a calculating look. "Good luck, Judge *saab*," Kumar said, his tone dry, "You'll need it."

As they left the bungalow, Leela and Karan met Priya and went to investigate the crime scene first. The two constables were in the jeep behind.

The bustling noise of the morning had faded, leaving only the hum of the distant hills and the occasional call of a bird soaring high above. The narrow streets, lined with worn-down buildings and faded signs, seemed frozen in time, stuck somewhere between history and a future that seemed uncertain at best.

Priya and Leela followed closely behind Karan, their eyes scanning their surroundings with the same sharp attention he had grown accustomed to. Leela was eager, yes, but also cautious. It was a delicate balance that Karan had learned to strike over years of dealing with places like Pelling, where danger wasn't always obvious, but it was always present.

They reached the edge of the town, where the road split, winding up the hillside toward the dense forest. It was here, in the shadows of the trees, that the body had been found. The locals had claimed it was an accident – just another case of an innocent life lost to the leopard.

The scene was cordoned off by a few hastily erected wooden posts, the yellow tape fluttering weakly in the breeze. No officers were around. The investigation, it seemed, had been abandoned, or at least deliberately overlooked. Karan stepped past the tape without hesitation, Priya and Leela following closely behind him.

"Here," Karan said quietly, pointing to a patch of disturbed earth just beyond the clearing. "This is where they found her body."

Leela crouched down, examining the ground. The soil had been dug up in a few places, but there was no sign of blood. No obvious signs of a struggle. She frowned. “It doesn’t make sense. There’s no sign of her having been murdered here. No signs of anything unusual.” Nature has virtually wiped out everything. The preservation of evidence is the most critical aspect of the investigation. Whatever is lost and what is remaining is always less. It’s not as easy as plucking low-hanging fruit.

Karan’s eyes narrowed as he surveyed the area. “It’s not what’s here that’s important, Leela. It’s what isn’t.”

She looked up at him, confused.

“Why bring the body out here?” Karan asked, his voice low, almost to himself. “Why leave it in a place like this, so far from everything? Have you both heard of the Innocence Project? Dedicated people must ultimately work towards finding clues, and the truth must ultimately be told, or the victim will never find closure”. Both women were listening intently.

A little while later, Priya blinked and asked, “You think someone moved it?”

Karan stood up, scanning the trees surrounding them. He could feel the weight of the silence pressing in on him as if the entire forest was watching. “This wasn’t a random place to dump a body. Whoever did this knew it would be overlooked. There’s no one around for miles. It’s the perfect place to hide a crime.”

Leela followed his gaze, her brow furrowed. “But why? Why would anyone go through the trouble of bringing her here?”

Karan’s voice was steady but filled with the sharpness of realisation. “To make it look like a leopard attack? They wanted the investigation to fail before it even began. That's why there's no sign of a struggle. It's too clean. Too easy."

A shiver ran down Leela's spine as she looked around again. "But the Thakur family... Rohan... do you think they...?"

Karan held up a hand to stop her. "We don't have enough to make any accusations yet. But we can't ignore what's right in front of us. There's something wrong here, and I'm going to find out what it is. As an impartial Inquiry Commission, I have to be completely neutral, and none of my personal prejudices can affect the sacred process of the inquiry proceedings."

Leela nodded, though her expression was one of concern. "So what now?"

Karan took a long breath, the chill of the mountain air filling his lungs. His eyes were focused, sharp, and resolute as he turned toward the trees.

"We start looking for answers. And we don't stop until we have them."

They moved further into the woods, each step feeling heavier as if the trees themselves were silently warning them to turn back. The forest was dense, its overgrown underbrush making every movement feel slow and deliberate. As they ventured deeper, the silence grew thicker, more oppressive.

Leela's voice broke the stillness. "Sir, do you think the police were involved in hiding something bigger? Or is it just the Thakurs pulling strings to protect Rohan?"

Karan didn't answer immediately.

"It's not just the Thakurs, Leela," Karan said, his tone firm. "There are too many layers here. There are people in this town who have a lot to lose if the truth comes out. Come, let's go back and search for more details and potential witnesses. We need concrete pieces of evidence and uncorrupted witnesses. Let's go back and get some rest and continue the investigation tomorrow."

Chapter 4
Delving Deeper

The worst prison in the world is to have the talent and intelligence

to achieve something great, but lacking the courage to go out and do it.

The inquiry had ended for the day, but its echoes followed Karan as he walked back to his quarters. He wanted to be left alone and instructed his guards to go ahead and wait for him at the quarters. Under the moonlight, as Karan was ambling on the winding path back through the edge of the forest, the chirping of cicadas grew louder as night fell, and the air felt heavy with the scent of damp earth and moss.

He paused midway, struck by a sudden silence. The forest had gone still as if holding its breath. The back of his neck tingled, and he scanned the treeline, his heart beating faster. Was that a shadow moving, or just the play of moonlight through the branches? He could almost feel eyes on him, intense, unblinking.

The snap of a twig broke the spell. Karan spun around, his fists clenched, "Who's there?" he called, his voice steady despite the chill spreading through his chest, but the path was empty. His breath was shaky as he quickened his pace, telling himself it was just the stress of the case getting to him. He finally reached the quarters and straightaway went to his room and switched on the radio.

On the table beside it sat an unopened bottle of single malt and a glass. He poured himself a generous serving, the warm liquid catching the dim light of the lamp as the distant echo of *Aisa Lagta Hai* by Chitra Singh seeped into the room.

He sank into the armchair, the glass cool in his hand, and stared out at the ghostly outline of the mountains beyond the mist, savouring his drink.

The first sip burned slightly, but warmed him as it went down. He savoured the familiar bitterness, letting it anchor him as his thoughts spiralled and replayed that day's events. Jatin's fear, Kamla's fiery defiance, and Singh's stubborn insistence on the leopard theory all swirled in his mind. But the image that lingered was Sonia's.

He let his thoughts drift, as they always did at this hour, to the weight he carried, the memories, the losses, and the unyielding drive that had brought him to this moment.

Justice. The word felt heavy, pressing against his chest. For him, justice wasn't just a profession; it was a necessity. Memories of his failures haunted him, none more painful than the case of the young girls groomed, abused and sold. The families were silenced by money and power, their lives destroyed by powerful men, leading to the guilty walking free despite his best efforts. He had failed them, and that failure had carved a permanent wound into his soul. Questions raced through his mind – *why does a court not order that for the death penalty when a monster sniffs out the life of an innocent girl? Did she deserve to suffer, get raped and then get killed? Does this not fall within the rarest of rare cases, warranting the death penalty? What more does a victim need to suffer to enter the category of rarest of rare cases? Is it the subjective satisfaction of a particular judge who decides to grant the convicted criminal a sentence of life imprisonment? Does the taxpayer have to suffer the misery and pay all the expenses till the rascal dies? Instance after instance has now instilled some kind of courage in criminals that they will not hang and continue to live, while the victim's families go through untold misery and pain due to the untimely loss of their loved ones. Is this real justice?* He tipped the glass to his lips again.

"Not this time," he whispered, his voice resolute. The haunting melody of *Udan Khatola* and Mohd. Rafi, at his best, made his eyes moist.

Sonia's face flickered into his thoughts, her warm smile from the photograph he'd studied earlier that evening. Her smile in the photograph seemed almost alive, full of promise. She wasn't just another victim - she was a reminder of why he fought. She had dreams, a future. Now, she was gone, her life extinguished under mysterious circumstances. Karan's grip on the glass tightened.

Setting the glass down, he went to his bed. As he lay down, the day played over again in his mind: the faces of the witnesses, the misty streets, and the faint, unsettling sense that someone was always watching. The warmth of the whiskey dulled the edges, pulling him into an uneasy sleep.

Karan woke before sunrise, his body attuned to the demands of his profession. The faint light of dawn barely pierced the thick mist outside his window. The night's dreams lingered like shadows at the edges of his mind, disjointed flashes of Sonia's face, the leopard's low growl, and Rohan's smirk.

The guesthouse was cloaked in silence, the kind that amplified every creak of the floorboards and the rustling of the trees outside. He swung his legs over the side of the bed, the cool air biting at his skin, and rubbed the lingering fog of sleep from his eyes.

Pulling back the curtains, he was met with the sight of Pelling in its morning stillness. The monastery bell chimed softly in the distance, its haunting cadence floating through the air like a hymn to the unknown.

He turned away from the window and reached for his coat, shrugging it on over his pressed shirt. His movements were methodical as he collected the file from his desk, flipping through it while he ate a heavy breakfast and rushed to the courthouse early.

As he stepped into his office, Karan paused by the glass pane beside his desk, looking at his faint reflection in the morning light. His tall, lean frame, now wiry with age at almost sixty-three, stared back at him but still carried the strength of a younger man. His muscles, though marked by the passage of time, remained firm, bearing the quiet memory of discipline, of practising Krav Maga and not vanity. Silver hair, meticulously combed, framed an angular face etched with lines of experience and countless sleepless nights. Yet, it was his eyes, piercing and unyielding, that commanded attention, their intensity undiminished, capable of unsettling even the most seasoned lawyers in the courtroom.

He was determined to review the evidence with fresh eyes. The images in the forensic report were stark and cold: Sonia's body positioned unnaturally in the clearing, the smudged tyre tracks too close to the scene, and animal prints that seemed placed rather than incidental.

Karan stood at the window, the cold glass fogging slightly as his breath met the morning chill. Then, he turned away from the window and straightened his coat with the file in his hand. "Animal tracks," he muttered to himself, flipping to the photographs. "Conveniently near the body, but not leading away. And tyre marks at the scene, what leopard needs a ride?"

He walked back and sat down in his chair, rubbing his temples. Singh's confident dismissal of foul play didn't sit right. If it were a simple animal attack, why were there no clear patterns of drag marks from the body? And why had Singh seemed so eager to close the case?

Karan had seen this pattern before: a hastily constructed narrative, convenient enough to be believable, yet fragile under scrutiny. He moved to the armchair near the window and sank into it, the worn leather creaking under his weight. He decided to meet the local forensic expert, Dr. Meena Iyer, who was also an old acquaintance.

Dr. Iyer's cramped office was a sanctuary of order amid the chaos. In her early fifties, she was known for her precision, her sharp intellect matched by her calm demeanour, exuding an air of quiet authority. Her hair was pulled back into a sleek ponytail, shimmering under the fluorescent light, accentuating the sharp angles of her face. Though her frame was petite, the intensity in her eyes and the precise, almost surgical way she moved made it clear that she was not one to be trifled with.

She adjusted the collar of her pristine white coat as Karan entered the room. The faint scent of antiseptic hung in the air, sharp and acrid, mingling with the soft hum of fluorescent lights above. Karan looked around for a place to sit. The office was a contradiction: cramped yet immaculately organised. Folders were stacked in perfect alignment, a microscope sat gleaming on the counter, and the faint scent of antiseptic lingered in the air.

As Karan sat down, his gaze flicked to the stacks of papers on her desk, each marked with colour-coded tabs. Whatever she had called him in for, it wasn't trivial.

"Karan," she said, gesturing to the lone chair across from her desk. A faint but knowing smile played on her lips. "I've been expecting you."

"You're always ahead of the curve, Meena," Karan said, leaning back slightly in the chair. He forced a smile, but his tone carried an edge of unease. "Your reputation for being prepared is starting to make the rest of us look bad."

Dr. Iyer met his gaze without a flicker of amusement. "Flattery, Karan?" She raised an eyebrow, her voice clipped but tinged with dry humour. "Save it for later. We have more pressing matters."

Sliding the folder across to him, she locked eyes with him. "This is the forensic report," she said, her voice dropping to a sombre note. "And I'm not going to sugarcoat it. What's in there..." She inhaled sharply, and pursed her lips. "It's troubling, to say the least."

Karan opened the folder, his eyes scanning the neatly typed report and the accompanying photographs with practised efficiency. The images were stark and unsettling: close-ups of Sonia's injuries, the peculiar angle of her limbs, and detailed shots of what looked like bite marks. But it was the accompanying analysis that made his pulse quicken.

His lips parted as though to speak, but he hesitated, the words stuck in his throat.

"These markings…" Karan began, his brow furrowing. "You're saying they're not consistent with a leopard attack?"

"The blunt-force trauma suggests a cylindrical object was used; there are also ligature marks," she explained, "and the claw marks… too symmetrical. Likely made by a weapon designed to mimic an animal's attack."

"I thought as much," his voice barely above a whisper. "This doesn't make sense," Karan muttered, glancing up at Dr. Iyer and continued, "The post-mortem doesn't align with the evidence at the scene. At the time of death, there's a gap." Then leaning in, he whispered, "This wasn't a straightforward case, was it?"

Dr. Iyer just nodded.

"Okay, what about the time of death and the ligature marks?" Karan asked.

Dr. Iyer glanced at another report, "Between 11 p.m. and midnight, based on body temperature and lividity. That lines up with the timeline Singh presented, but it doesn't line up with the location of death. She was killed elsewhere, Karan. They brought her to the clearing hours later.

"The injuries suggest there was a struggle, but here's where it gets interesting," she continued, leaning forward slightly, "They're faint but clear. There are signs of restraint, faint ligature marks on her wrists. Whoever did this wanted to control her first. She was restrained before the attack.

"Also, the tox screen found sedatives in her system, not enough to kill her, but enough to impair her judgment.

"The claw marks on Sonia's body don't match the spacing of a leopard's paw," Dr. Iyer explained, gesturing to an enlarged image on her laptop. "And these puncture wounds are too precise. They could've been made by a weapon."

Karan's stomach twisted. "So you're saying this wasn't a random animal attack?"

Dr. Iyer nodded, her expression grave. "There's more. The soil samples near the body contain traces of motor oil, consistent with the tyre marks found at the scene. This wasn't just about making it look like a leopard attack. The body was transported there."

She hesitated. "All I'm officially saying is that the evidence doesn't fully support that theory. It's possible someone staged it to look like one."

Karan closed the file, his mind racing. "Any DNA?"

Dr. Iyer's expression darkened. "Trace amounts, but inconclusive. The samples were compromised, probably by the conditions at the scene."

Karan felt a rush of anger mixed with grim vindication. "So, we're dealing with a cover-up." He clenched his jaw, his mind racing. "And Singh? He was too quick to shut down the investigation."

Dr. Iyer's eyes narrowed. "I've known Singh for years. He's ambitious, but he's not usually sloppy. If he's involved, it's because someone's holding the strings."

Karan closed the folder and set it on the desk, his expression hard. "This confirms what I suspected. Sonia's death wasn't an accident; it was premeditated. And someone went to great lengths to hide the truth."

Dr. Iyer tilted her head, her gaze searching. "What's your next move?"

Karan stood, the file clutched in his hand. "I'll start where every trail begins, with the people closest to her. Rohan, the Thakurs, and anyone else who had something to lose. And if Singh's involved, I'll expose him too."

Dr. Iyer's voice softened, a rare note of concern breaking through her professional demeanour. "Be careful, Karan. Whoever did this has resources, influence, and the kind of power that doesn't take kindly to being exposed. If you push too hard..."

He gave her a faint smile, though it didn't reach his eyes. "I've dealt with their kind before, and careful isn't exactly my style, Meena. But thanks for the warning."

As he stepped out of the office, the weight of the case pressed down on him. The stakes were higher than ever, and the lines between ally and enemy were blurring. But one thing was clear: he couldn't stop now. Sonia's face flashed in his mind again, her life cut short and her story silenced.

Karan's stride quickened as he headed back toward the Inquiry Room. He was ready to shake the foundations of this small, quiet town to uncover the truth. And no matter what or who stood in his way, he wouldn't stop until Sonia got the justice she deserved.

At the Outer Room, the lobby buzzed with murmured conversations and the shuffle of paperwork. Karan found

Singh speaking to a junior officer, irritation flickering across his face as Karan approached.

"Inspector, a word?"

Singh turned, crossing his arms. "Judge, what now?" He had a funny smirk on his face, which also reflected defiance.

"The forensic evidence doesn't fully support the leopard attack theory," Karan said bluntly, but was also throwing in the dice. "Dr. Iyer's findings raise serious doubts about the injuries."

Singh's jaw tightened. He knew that Karan was playing a shrewd chess game. He had to give some sort of reply. "Dr. Iyer is just speculating. I've been in this region for years. I know what a leopard attack looks like," Singh blurted.

Karan stepped closer, lowering his voice. "Do you? Or are you too eager to wrap this up and move on?" The eagle eyes were at their piercing best.

Singh bristled. "I suggest you stick to your role, Judge. Let the police handle the investigation." Singh's face darkened as he brushed past Karan and left. The battle lines were drawn.

In the office, the hum of computers and the sporadic chatter of officers created a charged atmosphere. Leela, Karan, and Priya sat at their desks, combing through Sonia's files. Employment records, phone logs, and social media activity sprawled before them as they searched for anything that could lead them to the truth.

They began piecing together all the information they had gathered. They laid out photographs, reports, and witness statements on his desk, trying to see the bigger picture. The evidence pointed to a carefully orchestrated conspiracy, one that involved not just the Thakur family but also local authorities and perhaps even higher-ups.

"Look at this," Priya said, sliding a printed document toward Karan. "Sonia's phone records show multiple calls to a number registered to a 'Vinod Kumar'. He's not on the witness list, and there's no mention of him in her personnel file."

Karan frowned, his gaze narrowing on the document. "Who is he? A friend? Family?"

Priya shook her head. "I ran a quick background check. Vinod Kumar owns a small logistics company. There's no immediate connection to Rohan or Sonia's workplace, but it's suspicious."

Karan tapped the paper thoughtfully. "She called him five times on the day she disappeared. We need to figure out what they were talking about."

Priya paused, her pen clicking absently against the desk. "True, but we also need to consider her personal life. Sonia could've been involved in something unrelated to her job."

Karan nodded. "Right. Tomorrow we start with Vinod. Let's see where that takes us. But we also need to revisit the crime scene and speak to her neighbours. Maybe there's something we missed."

Karan leaned back in his chair, the file open before him filled with reports that painted a picture more chaotic than he had anticipated. On one side were rumours – whispers of a man-eating leopard prowling the forested slopes beyond town, its presence stirring unease in every household. And on the other, the kind of predators Karan knew too well – the ones who wore uniforms, carried official seals, and killed without claws.

He had seen case files altered overnight, evidence manipulated, narratives changed. Justice, he thought, rarely bled in Pelling; it simply faded, quietly, like sound swallowed by mist.

As he worked late into the night, a knock at the door startled him.

"Come in," he called, his voice firm.

Leela stepped inside, her face pale but determined. "Sir, you need to see this," she said, handing him a small envelope.

Karan opened it carefully, his heart sinking as he pulled out a single photograph. It was a blurry image of him walking through the forest earlier that day, his expression tense and focused.

"Someone's watching us," Leela said quietly.

Karan's eyes hardened as he stared at the photograph. "Good," he said after a moment. "That means we're on the right track. Let's rest and meet again tomorrow."

Karan trudged back to his room in the sprawling, now-empty bungalow, the silence of the night pressing against him like a suffocating weight. The shadows outside his window felt alive, creeping into the corners of his mind. He didn't bother drawing the curtains. He was too tired and numb to bother.

He reached for the bottle of whiskey – his constant companion. With trembling hands, he unscrewed the cap. The sharp scent of this amber liquid was a temporary escape from the memories that clawed at him. He poured a heavy drink and downed it in one go. The burn gave him a brief respite from the chaos in his mind as he leaned against the table, staring at the darkened landscape outside. The steady ticking of a clock on the wall seemed to echo in the silence of the room.

Flashes from his memories rose from the depths like ghosts in the night. He saw himself as a young boy, running through the narrow streets of his childhood village, the bustling market alive with the sounds of barter and negotiation. His father, a shopkeeper, was a man of authority in that small town. Karan had watched, horrified, as the old man cheated customers, tipping the scales just enough to make a quick profit. But when Karan, still a boy, called him out on it, his father's fury knew no bounds. The belt had cracked across his back, each strike burning with the injustice he'd tried to expose.

He remembered the sting of the belt on his back, a constant reminder of the price he paid for speaking out honestly and warning the customers to be careful. His father's angry voice still echoed in his ears, accusing him of embarrassing the family in front of customers, of being too honest for his own good. But it wasn't the pain of the belt that haunted him; it was the injustice. He had learned two truths: Honesty is painful, and silence is comfortable for everyone except the one who refuses to bend.

He couldn't stand to see the dishonesty, the manipulation, and the exploitation of others, especially the poor, who had no voice. That sense of injustice had burned inside him, making him vow that one day he would fight for the truth, no matter the cost. That desire had led him to law school, to the courtroom, and eventually to the badge he wore now.

But life, as it often did, had a way of complicating things. His mind shifted to his wife, Nalini, a diplomat who had always been graceful, poised, and elegant. At first, she had admired his integrity, his drive for justice. Their marriage had been filled with promise, the kind of intellectual conversations and shared goals that two ambitious people in the world of politics and law could appreciate. But over time, his rigid honesty, his refusal to turn a blind eye to the wrongs around him, had become a burden for her.

She wanted a life of comfort, a life of diplomacy and compromise, not a life tied to the truth that Karan insisted on seeking. Her tolerance for his unyielding sense of justice wore thin, and soon, she started to look at him with disdain, which felt like a dagger to the heart.

Karan's daughter, Kiara, had been drawn into their conflicts and nasty fights. Nalini managed to turn her against him, making her believe that his honesty was nothing more than arrogance, that his pursuit of justice was an obsession that kept him from being the father she needed. She followed her mother's path, her eyes hardening towards him, abandoning the man who'd once been her hero. "*You care more about dead strangers than your living family*," Kiara had accused.

The more Karan tried to prove his love and dedication to them, the more they drifted away, until, one day, he found himself completely alone in the fight for justice he had always believed in. No family. No allies. Just a hollow sense of duty to fight for justice that no longer mattered to the people he loved most.

He took another swig of whiskey, the burn in his throat a welcome distraction from the emotions swirling inside him. His life had been a battle on two fronts, one to uphold the truth and the other to protect his family from the consequences of that truth.

The knock at the door broke his train of thought. He opened the door. The husband and wife, caretakers, stood at the door with a trolley of food.

"Dinner, sir," the man said quietly, his voice soft.

Karan nodded, taking the plate from the lady, and set it on the table. "Thank you," he muttered, his thoughts still elsewhere while the couple served him.

As they left, Karan watched the couple disappear into the drizzle – their shoulders brushing, their laughter low but easy. There was a rhythm to their silence, a kind of understanding that needed no words. Even in their poverty, they shared something rare – comfort in each other's company.

Karan ate mechanically, his mind spinning with the memories of his past, the echoes of his childhood, and the cold betrayal of the system and most of all, his wife and daughter. The food barely registered in his senses.

Later that night, as he lay in bed, the shadows of his memories merged with the darkness around him. His dreams were vivid and fragmented; he saw flashes of his younger self, running through the streets, his father's belt striking his back, his daughter's face twisted in anger, morphing into the faces of the victims who had once come to him for help. Tears started streaming and entered the cracks of the ageing skin on his face.

His father's angry face morphed into a man that he had prosecuted, his mother's disappointed expression merged with his daughter's cold stare, his wife's icy silence, fused with the faces of the countless victims who had sought his help and he couldn't save. Their eyes, wide with fear, merged with Nalini's cold expression, with his father's cruel, unrepentant glare.

Suddenly, he was standing in front of a dark forest, protecting his daughter from something, or someone. The dream swirled into chaos as his wife's and daughter's faces blended with Sonia's and Pooja's faces, and Karan woke with a jolt. His heart raced in his chest as he wiped the sweat from his forehead. He lay there, breathing heavily, the echo of the growl from his dream still lingering in his ears.

Karan woke with a start. Sweat clung to his forehead, and his chest heaved as if he'd been running. His dreams had been relentless, a tangled web of faces, accusations, and the stinging belt that seemed to echo in his ears even now. He sat up in the darkness of his room, the faint glow of dawn filtering through the window.

Rubbing his temples, he reached for the glass of water on his bedside table. His reflection in the window caught his eye – dishevelled hair, face etched with exhaustion and regret. The man staring back at him seemed a stranger.

Today, he told himself. *Today will be different*.

Chapter 5
Cracks In The Case

The Rashomon effect is the phenomenon of the unreliability of eyewitnesses.

- Akira Kurosawa (inspired by the film Rashomon)

Leela, Karan and Priya sat in the dimly lit office, the hum of computers and the occasional chatter of officers creating a tense backdrop. Karan reviewed the evidence with a sharp focus, the files spread across the desk in meticulous order. Leela sat nearby, scrolling through photographs on her tablet, while Priya reviewed the autopsy report and combed through employment records, phone logs, and social media activity.

"The ligature marks on Sonia's wrists indicate she was restrained for a significant period," Priya began, her tone measured. "The abrasions are faint, but they suggest she was tied with something like a synthetic rope or plastic zip tie; tight enough to hold but not deep enough to cut into the skin."

Karan tapped his pen against the desk, his expression thoughtful. "What about the sedatives?"

"She had traces of midazolam in her system," Priya replied, flipping to another page. "It's a benzodiazepine, commonly used for sedation. The dose wasn't lethal, but it would have rendered her drowsy and disoriented."

Leela looked up from her tablet. "And the claw marks? The ones Singh insists were from a leopard?"

Priya sighed, pushing her glasses higher up her nose. "They're irregular. The spacing is inconsistent with a leopard's paw anatomy. A leopard's claws typically leave four evenly spaced punctures – these have five, and the depth varies. The forensic pathologist noted that the injuries appear to have been made with a blunt, claw-like instrument. It's staged, plain and simple."

Leela looked up from her tablet. "Rohan Thakur was seen arguing with Sonia at the hotel the night she disappeared. Multiple witnesses confirmed it."

"And yet," Karan said, his voice dry, "Inspector Singh conveniently omitted this from his initial report."

"Why wouldn't he?" Priya asked, leaning forward. "Rohan's father essentially bankrolls half the town. The Thakur family funds infrastructure projects, sponsors local events, and has ties to the police department. Singh has every reason to cover for him."

Karan frowned. "If Rohan is involved, he's not working alone. A crime of this complexity requires meticulous coordination, someone who knows how to manipulate both the scene and the narrative."

Just then, Kumar entered, carrying a sealed envelope. "Dr. Iyer sent this over," he said, handing it to Karan.

Karan opened the envelope and scanned the attached forensic report. His jaw tightened. "The fabric fragment we recovered at the crime scene contains traces of motor oil and human DNA. It's a perfect match for a hotel employee."

Leela grabbed her notebook. "The hotel staff?"

Karan said, his voice hard. "A hotel worker with a spotless record, until now."

"Take a look at this," Priya said, sliding a freshly printed document across the table toward Karan. "These are Sonia's phone records. She made multiple calls to one number the day she disappeared."

Karan leaned forward, scanning the highlighted entries. "Whose number is it?"

"Registered to a Vinod Kumar," Priya replied. "He's not on any of the employee rosters or listed in her personnel file. No formal link to the hotel or to Rohan."

Karan's brow furrowed. "Friend? Relative?"

She shook her head. "Unlikely. I did a preliminary check; he owns a small logistics business on the outskirts of town. No known connection to her professionally or personally. But she called him five times on the same day she went missing."

"Five times? That's not casual. Either she was panicked… or trying to warn him about something."

"Exactly," Priya said. "It could be nothing, or it could be the missing piece. We need to find out who he really is and why she kept calling him."

Karan nodded slowly, tapping his finger against the page. "Start digging. Cross-reference his company records, look into any prior police complaints, financials, or if he has any link to Thakur."

Priya hesitated, then added, "We also shouldn't rule out the possibility that this has nothing to do with the hotel or her work. There could be something in her personal life we haven't uncovered yet."

Karan looked up, thoughtful. "True. But five calls to a man no one's mentioned, just hours before her death;

that's not a coincidence. It's a lead. We need to find out what they talked about."

He thoughtfully looked at the file open before him, filled with reports that painted a picture more chaotic than he had anticipated. He thumbed through the pages, pausing at a grainy photograph of another young woman. Her name was Pooja Yadav. Found at the edge of the forest three months ago, her death had been attributed to a 'leopard attack,' though the coroner's report raised more questions than answers.

The rumours about Rohan, a name that kept surfacing in conversations, added fuel to the fire. Rohan, the son of a wealthy businessman with deep political connections, was allegedly the last person seen with this girl, too, on the night she died. But the town's collective silence about his involvement was deafening.

Karan took a deep breath and shut the file. "First, let's get to know Sonia, her life and all the people she interacted with. She lived in a rented apartment near the market. We might get to know who Vinod is, and I think we need to revisit the crime scene. We also need to look beyond the story and the rumours floating around."

"Yes, neighbours notice the small details, especially unusual behaviour or visitors. Sonia's colleagues, her friends and anyone she interacted with regularly. These are the people who knew her rhythms," Priya said.

"Do we split up?" Kumar asked, glancing between the three of them.

"Yes," Karan said firmly. "Priya, you stay here and see if you discover anything else, especially Vinod. Leela, Kumar and I will go in a methodical but approachable manner. Priya and I will lead the questioning. Leela, you handle the documentation."

Leela, Karan and Kumar stepped out of the courthouse area towards the town square. The morning air was crisp, the scent of pine thick as they walked to the town square, which was alive with activity. Children ran through narrow lanes, which were lined with stalls selling everything from fresh produce to handcrafted trinkets. An occasional roar of an engine echoed around as jeeps ferried tourists to the nearby hills.

On their way to Sonia's house, they decided to stop at a corner shop run by a wiry man with sharp eyes that missed nothing. He was an unofficial chronicler of the town, his shop serving as a hub for information and gossip.

"Judge *sahab*, what brings you here so early?" the shopkeeper asked, his smile cautious.

"I hear you know this town better than anyone," Karan replied, his tone casual. "I'm trying to understand why this leopard attacks only girls. Can you help me?"

Taken aback, he glanced nervously around his shop, ensuring no one was within earshot. "It's best not to talk about it too much. People here don't like questions."

Karan leaned closer, his voice firm. "And what about answers? What if those questions could save someone else's life?"

His fingers twitched as he rearranged a stack of biscuit packets. "People say a leopard killed them. The police even found paw prints near their bodies. But..."

"But what?" Karan pressed.

"Not all marks on their bodies looked like they came from an animal," the shopkeeper whispered, looking scared. "Some looked… human."

"Do you know Sonia Verma?" Karan asked, his tone polite but probing.

The man nodded, his weathered hands busy arranging the biscuit packets. "Sonia *bitiya*? Of course. She was a sweet girl. Always bought groceries from me."

"Did you notice anything unusual about her recently?" Karan continued.

He sighed. "She seemed worried these past few weeks. She asked me once if I knew a good lawyer."

"A lawyer? Did she say why?"

"No," he replied. "She just said she needed advice about a 'problem.' I thought she meant something small, like landlord trouble, maybe."

"Did she mention anyone by name?" Leela asked.

The vendor shook his head. "No. But now that you mention it, there was a man who came looking for her one day. He asked if I'd seen her. He seemed… angry."

"What did he look like?" Karan pressed.

"Medium build, clean-shaven, wearing a grey jacket," the vendor recalled. "He left quickly when I told him I hadn't seen her that day."

A customer stepped into the shop, and the man's attention drifted. Leela took it as her cue to leave. She slipped a visiting card across the counter and said, "Let us know, in case you remember anything else."

Next, they reached Sonia's apartment complex, a modest three-story building with peeling paint and narrow corridors. Karan knocked on the first door. An elderly woman in a floral *sari* opened it, her eyes widening slightly at the sight of the group.

"Mrs. Mehta?" Karan asked, his voice calm but authoritative.

"Yes," she said, her tone cautious.

"We're investigating Sonia Verma's death. She lived here. May we ask you a few questions?"

"Oh, Inspector! Have you found anything new about poor Sonia?" she asked, clutching her shawl, stepping aside to let them into her small living room.

"We're still working on it," Karan replied. "But I wanted to ask if you noticed anything unusual about her recently. Any visitors, arguments, or changes in her routine?"

Mrs. Mehta frowned, thinking. "She was such a sweet girl, always polite. But now that you mention it, she seemed... different these past few weeks. Nervous, like she was always looking over her shoulder. I asked her once if everything was alright, and she just smiled and said, 'Everything will be fine soon.'"

Karan enquired, "Did she have visitors? Anyone who seemed out of place?"

Mrs. Mehta frowned, thinking. "There was a man. I saw him a few times, tall, with a thick moustache. He came late at night, usually around ten. They always talked in hushed tones."

"Do you know his name?" Karan asked.

"No," she said apologetically. "But Sonia seemed tense whenever he was here."

Leela jotted down the description as Priya asked, "Did you hear anything unusual the night Sonia disappeared?"

Mrs. Mehta's lips pressed into a thin line, her eyes darting toward the window. "I remember – there was shouting. I couldn't make out the words, but it sounded like an argument. Then there was a thud, and everything went quiet. I thought about calling the police, but… I didn't want to get involved."

Karan's jaw tightened. "Anything you remember could help, Mrs. Mehta. Even small details."

She hesitated before adding, "There was a car parked outside that night. A white sedan. I hadn't seen it before."

"Did she ever mention a Vinod Kumar?" Karan asked.

Mrs. Mehta shook her head. "No, but she did get a lot of phone calls lately. Sometimes, I'd hear her voice through the wall; she sounded angry, almost scared."

Karan's brow furrowed. "Thank you, Mrs. Mehta. This is helpful."

As they rose to leave, Mrs. Mehta's hand lingered on the edge of the doorframe. "If only I'd known, maybe I could have done something..."

"You did what you could," Karan said softly. "Now, it's up to us."

As they walked down the narrow lane, Priya Kumar broke the silence. "Sonia was distracted but avoided help; it all points to someone pressuring her. And if Mrs. Mehta is right about that late visitor..."

"We need to confirm who it was," Karan said, his tone steady. "Someone in this town knows more than they're letting on. Let's go to the next piece in the puzzle – the Royal Pelling Hotel, where Sonia worked as a receptionist."

The Royal Pelling Hotel loomed ahead, its grand façade softened by the swirling mist. Inside, the lobby was warm and dimly lit, the polished wood and gleaming brass fixtures lending it an air of subdued luxury. Karan adjusted his tie, his breath visible in the chilly mountain air, before stepping through the glass doors. The lobby was bustling with activity; guests checking out, bellboys carting luggage, and a concierge attending to queries with mechanical politeness.

The place was a labyrinth of corridors and dimly lit rooms, the air thick with the smell of old wood and dust. The hotel had been around for decades, its grand facade a shell hiding the shadows beneath. He'd heard rumours of illicit dealings and backroom politics tied to the hotel, and now, as he walked through its halls, he wondered what secrets it held. The lobby buzzed with muted activity, hotel staff moving like pieces on a chessboard. His eyes scanned the room until they landed on the reception desk, and he began walking towards it, where a young woman with short black hair, sharp features and a crisp uniform stood. At the reception desk, Karan flashed his credentials "I am Karan Negi, the judge appointed for Sonia Verma's case. She was a receptionist here."

The receptionist's eyes widened, and she hesitated before nodding. "Oh! How can I help you?"

"We need to speak to someone who was working the night Sonia Verma disappeared," Karan said, his voice calm but firm.

Regaining her practised composure, she said, "That would be Aditi. She's in charge of housekeeping. I'll call her for you."

A few minutes later, a petite woman in her late twenties arrived, her expression guarded. Aditi's uniform was neat, but her hands fidgeted nervously as she approached.

"Ms. Aditi," Karan began, "we're investigating Sonia Verma's death. We understand you were on duty that night. Can you tell us what you saw?"

Aditi hesitated, her eyes darting to the receptionist and then to the floor. "Rohan Thakur came to the hotel that evening. He was with Sonia," Aditi said, her voice trembling slightly before continuing, "but she left alone around midnight. I saw her arguing with him in the lobby before she walked out."

"What time did this happen?" Priya asked, her pen poised over her notepad.

"Just after 10 p.m.," Aditi replied. "Sonia left after work, alone, around midnight. She looked upset."

"And Rohan?" Karan asked.

"Rohan left early the next morning. Didn't seem worried at all. Just… annoyed."

Karan's gut tightened. Sonia had left alone, late at night, into the very forest now infamous for a so-called man-eating leopard.

"Thank you, Aditi," Karan said, his tone softening. "If you remember anything else, please let us know."

Back at the Commission's Office, Priya had tracked down Vinod Kumar, and one of the constables hand-delivered a summons to appear before the Commission of Inquiry. The constable brought him in for questioning. The Inquiry Room was quiet, the hum of the ceiling fan punctuated only by the shuffle of papers.

Priya took a seat across from Vinod, placing her notepad and pen neatly in front of her.

"Mr. Kumar," Priya began, her tone calm but firm. "Thank you for coming in. We're here to discuss your relationship with Sonia Verma and any information you might have regarding her death. I'd like to remind you that just like your statement under Section 161 of the old Code of Criminal Procedure, this is an official inquiry. I request you to speak the truth, as it will be recorded."

Vinod shifted in his seat, his eyes flicking nervously to Karan before returning to Priya. "I... I don't know how I can help. Sonia was a friend. That's all."

"Friends," Priya repeated, her tone neutral. "You were in frequent contact with her in the weeks leading up to her death. Phone records show multiple calls, sometimes late at night. Can you explain what those conversations were about?"

Vinod swallowed hard. "She... she needed advice. Personal matters. She was worried about someone."

"What kind of advice?" Priya pressed.

He hesitated. "Personal matters. She didn't go into details, but she was worried about someone. Said they were threatening her."

Karan stepped in, his voice cutting through the tension. "Who was threatening her, Vinod?"

Vinod hesitated, his fingers twitching on the table. "She didn't tell me his name. But she said he was someone powerful. Someone who wouldn't take no for an answer."

Priya leaned forward slightly, her pen poised. "Did she mention why this person was bothering her?"

"She didn't give me specifics," Vinod said quickly. "But I got the impression he was trying to... get close to her. Flirt with her. She wasn't interested, and it made things tense at work."

Karan's gaze darkened. "Tense how?"

Vinod said shakily. "She said he would find excuses to be around her. Make comments. At first, she thought she could handle it, but then..." He trailed off, his eyes darting to the mirror.

"Then what?" Karan pressed.

Vinod sighed, his shoulders slumping. "She found something. I don't know what, but it scared her. She said she needed to 'take care of it.' I told her to go to the police, but she said no one would believe her."

Priya, who had been silently taking notes, finally spoke. "Did she mention what she found?"

Vinod shook his head. "No, but she hinted it was related to her job. Something about shipments and strange payments. She told me it didn't add up."

Karan exchanged a glance with Priya, the pieces of the puzzle starting to align in his mind.

"You said this person was powerful," Priya said, her voice steady. "Was she referring to Rohan Thakur?"

Vinod's eyes widened slightly, and he leaned back in his chair. "I... I don't know. She never mentioned his name directly. But the way she talked about him, it sounded like someone who thought he could get away with anything." It was a smart ploy. The day you plant the seed is not the day you eat the fruit.

Karan's jaw tightened. "Did Sonia ever mention the forest? Or why she might have been there the night she disappeared?"

Vinod hesitated, his gaze darting between Karan and Priya. "She said she had a meeting. I don't know with whom, but she was nervous. She told me not to call her that night, that she'd handle it."

Priya jotted down notes rapidly, her pen scratching against the paper. "One last question, Mr. Kumar. Where were you the night Sonia disappeared?"

Vinod's face flushed. "I was at home. Alone. You can ask my neighbours, they saw me come back from work that evening."

Karan's piercing gaze lingered on Vinod for a long moment before he finally nodded. "You're free to go for now, but don't leave town. We may need to speak with you again."

Vinod stood quickly, his chair scraping against the floor. "Of course. I'll be available."

As Vinod left the room, the tension remained thick. Karan turned to Priya and Leela, his expression grim.

"Rohan isn't just a suspect," he said, his voice steady but filled with purpose. "He's the thread connecting everything: Sonia's fear, the missing payments, and her death. We need to dig deeper into his connections and what Sonia discovered about him."

"And the forest?" Priya asked.

Karan's gaze shifted to the window, where the mist curled around the trees like a living thing. "The forest is a stage," he said quietly. "A distraction. Whatever Sonia was trying to uncover, someone wanted it buried, along with her."

Later that evening, Karan sat across from Priya in his chamber to discuss the developments from various angles. Fixing her crisp, white, well-pleated *sari*, she sighed, removing her glasses and rubbing her temples. "There's more to this than meets the eye. The rumours about the leopard? They've been fanned by certain... interested parties. The local MLA owns the news channel, pushing the leopard angle. Convenient distraction, don't you think?"

Karan's mind raced. "The question is, who benefits? And why was Sonia such a threat to them?" he murmured, his elbows resting on the worn wooden table. "What was Sonia trying to sort out? If the leopard was a cover story, then who was behind it, and why? How and why is Rohan connected to all this?"

Priya hesitated, her brow furrowed. "From what Vinod said, Sonia was looking into something at the hotel shipments and payments that didn't add up. She wouldn't have connected it to Rohan without a reason."

"If she stumbled onto something incriminating, it's no wonder she was scared. And if Rohan was harassing her at the same time..." Karan said thoughtfully.

Priya interjected, her voice rising slightly. "She might have thought no one would believe her. A young receptionist accusing the son of a powerful businessman?" She shook her head. "The system is stacked against her from every angle."

"Possibly," he said, his voice heavy with contemplation. "But Sonia wasn't passive. She was trying to fight back; Vinod said she was planning to 'sort it out herself.' That means she had a plan, however desperate."

Priya leaned forward, her eyes narrowing. "What do you think she found?"

Karan took a slow breath. "Rohan's family owns multiple businesses, including logistics companies. If Sonia discovered something illegal – smuggling, poaching, or worse – it would explain why she was silenced. The payments she noticed could be bribes, cover-ups, or evidence of transactions tied to something far bigger."

Priya's pen hovered over her notepad. "And the forest?"

Karan's gaze shifted toward the window, where the mist outside pressed against the glass like an unspoken threat. "The forest is the perfect cover, remote, unmonitored, and easy to control. If the leopard narrative holds, it keeps people out and questions at bay. But it also means Sonia might have been lured there under false pretences."

Priya nodded slowly. "If the forest was a meeting place, it wasn't random. Someone knew she'd be there that night and planned for it."

Karan rose abruptly, his decision made. “I want to revisit the crime scene. If Sonia’s murder was staged to look like an animal attack, the evidence will betray them. Call Dr. Iyer and Ajay. We need a forensic eye on this.”

The forest at dusk was alive with muted sounds: the distant call of a Himalayan thrush, the rustle of leaves disturbed by the faint evening breeze, and the persistent hum of unseen insects. The towering trees created a canopy that let in only shards of fading sunlight, while the mist clung stubbornly to the forest floor, shrouding everything in a pale veil.

Karan, Priya, Dr. Iyer, Ajay and the two constables at a distance behind moved carefully through the uneven terrain, their boots crunching softly against the damp soil. Dr. Iyer crouched near the spot where Sonia’s body had been discovered, her gloved hands sweeping away the top layer of soil with precise, deliberate motions.

“This soil is unusually compact,” she noted, her tone professional. “It rained heavily the night Sonia was killed. The moisture would’ve made it easier to conceal something, but also harder to keep it hidden for long.”

Karan stood nearby, scanning the area with sharp eyes. “If the body wasn’t dragged far, then they weren’t trying to hide it. They wanted it found, but not easily. The stage was set to reinforce the leopard story.”

Ajay, standing a few feet away, adjusted his rifle strap as he spoke. “Pelling does have a leopard problem, but it’s not what most people think. Leopards here are opportunistic hunters, primarily preying on dogs, goats, and sometimes livestock. Human attacks are rare, and when they do occur, they’re quick and brutal. No unnecessary injuries.”

Dr. Iyer straightened, gesturing toward a nearby tree trunk. “Look at this. These scratch marks are inconsistent with leopard behaviour. Leopards typically use their claws for territorial marking or climbing. These are too uniform, almost like someone used a tool to mimic claw marks.”

“A leopard that turns man-eater is rare, but not impossible,” Dr. Iyer said, adjusting her wide-brimmed hat. “But this case? It doesn’t fit the pattern. Leopards don’t drag their prey out in the open.”

“So, you’re saying the leopard isn’t the killer?” Karan asked to confirm.

Ajay said, “I’d bet my career on it. But the fear of a leopard can be a powerful tool, keeps people away from the forest, keeps them from seeing things they shouldn’t.”

Priya, notebook in hand, asked, “And the tracks? The ones Singh was so keen to point out?”

Dr. Iyer moved to the area where the tracks were found. She knelt down, inspecting the impressions carefully. “Superficial,” she confirmed, brushing a gloved hand over the edges. “They lack depth, which means they weren’t made by a heavy animal. The spacing is also too perfect. A real leopard’s stride would show variability based on its movement.”

Ajay added, “And if it were a kill, there’d be clear signs of a struggle, drag marks, blood spatter, tufts of fur. None of that is here.”

As Karan listened, his eyes scanned the immediate area. Something caught his attention: a faint glint of metal partially buried in the soil. He crouched down, brushing away the dirt to reveal a small button embossed with the initials *RPH*.

"A hotel uniform button," Karan said, holding it up for the others to see.

Priya leaned closer to get a better look. "That narrows the list of suspects. Someone from the Royal Pelling Hotel was here that night."

Dr. Iyer's gloved hands continued to sift through the soil, uncovering more fragments: a small length of frayed rope, a wrench, and a charred oil can, its metal warped and blackened. She held the items up, her expression grim.

"This rope could've been used for restraint," she said. "And the oil can? Likely an attempt to burn the body. But with the rain that night, the fire wouldn't have lit for long. Instead, it left traces."

Priya noted the evidence in her pad. "The rope ties in with the ligature marks on Sonia's wrists. And if this oil can was used, then burning the body was premeditated. This wasn't a panicked crime; it was deliberate."

Karan's jaw tightened. "Whoever did this knew the rain would make it harder to burn the body, but they tried anyway. It was a sloppy move. They were confident no one would dig deeper. The police were clearly compromised."

Dr. Iyer stood, brushing her gloves clean. "There's more. Look here." She pointed to a faint impression in the soil. "This is consistent with a *kukhri* blade, a traditional Nepalese knife. The curve of the mark suggests it was used to cut something, maybe during the struggle."

Ajay's face darkened. "A *kukhri* isn't uncommon around here. Many locals carry them for utility. But it's also a weapon."

Karan examined the scene, piecing the fragments together. "A *kukhri* for restraint, oil for disposal, a staged leopard attack... This wasn't random. This was calculated. But it's messy; too many tools, too many loose ends."

Ajay shifted uncomfortably. "I've heard whispers about poaching here. Leopards, musk deer, red pandas; Pelling is close enough to international borders to make smuggling easy. Pelts, organs, bones; they fetch a high price."

The group started their return journey as the light faded entirely, leaving the forest bathed in shadows and faint moonlight. The air felt heavier now, every sound amplified, the distant hoot of an owl, the crackle of leaves underfoot.

Karan's steps slowed as the sensation of being watched crept over him again, prickling at the back of his neck. He stopped abruptly, his sharp eyes scanning the trees.

"Something wrong?" Priya asked, her voice low.

Karan didn't answer immediately. His gaze remained fixed on the dense foliage. "We're not alone," he said finally, his tone flat.

Ajay unslung his rifle, his movements measured. "Wildlife?"

"Maybe," Karan replied. "Or someone who doesn't want us to dig around."

A faint rustling echoed from the trees to their left. Ajay raised his flashlight, the beam slicing through the darkness. For a moment, they saw nothing. Then, just beyond the edge of the light, a pair of unblinking eyes glinted in the shadows; watching, waiting.

Chapter 6
The Jungle's Teeth

Just as the river flows to the sea, the question is – when will I, too, be free?

Suddenly, the stillness was shattered by a low, guttural growl. The sound came from somewhere to their left, reverberating through the trees like a primal warning. Everyone froze, their breaths caught in their throats. The constables were about 100 feet behind.

"Was that…" Priya began, her voice barely above a whisper.

"Yes," Ajay replied, his hand instinctively reaching for his rifle. "It's close."

The growl came again, louder this time, and closer. Karan's flashlight darted toward the sound, illuminating the underbrush. For a moment, there was nothing but leaves and shadows. Then, a pair of golden eyes appeared, glowing faintly in the light.

"Move slowly," Ajay instructed, his voice calm but firm. "Don't run. Running triggers their predatory instincts."

The leopard emerged from the underbrush with an almost spectral grace, its sleek body blending seamlessly with the dappled light and shadows. Its coat, dotted with rosettes, seemed to ripple as it moved, every muscle coiled with latent power. It was no ordinary leopard. It was larger than most, with an air of calculated menace.

Leela took an involuntary step back, her boot catching on a root. She stumbled, letting out a small cry as she hit the ground. The sudden noise drew the leopard's attention, its ears flattening as it crouched, preparing to pounce.

"Leela, don't move!" Karan barked, stepping between her and the leopard. Ajay raised his rifle, the barrel trained on the animal, but he hesitated, his finger hovering over the trigger.

"It's watching," Ajay muttered. "Waiting for the right moment."

The leopard's tail flicked, its eyes fixed on the group with an unnerving intensity. For a heartbeat, the world seemed to hold its breath. Then, with a sudden burst of motion, the leopard lunged.

Ajay fired a warning shot into the air, the sharp crack echoing through the jungle. The leopard halted mid-pounce, its claws raking the air before it retreated a few steps, growling in frustration. The constables ran towards them, shouting to scare off the leopard.

"Get up, Leela!" Priya shouted, rushing to pull her colleague to her feet. Leela's ankle twisted as she stood, and she winced, clutching Priya for support.

The leopard, undeterred, began to circle, its growls low and guttural. Ajay kept his rifle trained on it, his movements mirroring the animal's. "Go," he said through gritted teeth. "Keep moving. I'll cover you."

"Not without you," Karan said firmly, his eyes never leaving the leopard.

"I'm right behind you," Ajay replied. "But you need to move. Now."

Karan nodded, placing a steadying hand on Priya's shoulder. "Help Leela. Let's go."

The group began to retreat slowly, their movements measured and deliberate. The leopard followed, its golden eyes gleaming with a predatory gleam. Every step felt like a negotiation with death, the tension thick enough to choke on. The constables were now next to them and were waving their sticks as if to scare off the leopard. Obviously, it was having no effect. It seemed like the animal was used to humans. The image of the famous man-eating leopard of Rudraprayag and Jim Corbett flashed in front of Karan's eyes.

As they neared a clearing, Ajay fired another shot into the air. This time, the leopard hesitated, its growls fading into a low rumble. It watched them for a moment longer before slinking back into the shadows, its movements fluid and eerily silent.

The group burst into the clearing, their breaths coming in ragged gasps. Leela sank to the ground, clutching her ankle as Priya knelt beside her. Ajay joined them moments later, his rifle slung over his shoulder.

"It's gone," she said, his voice calm but strained. "For now."

The jungle grew eerily silent after the chaos as if holding its breath. The leopard's retreat left behind an oppressive tension, the echoes of its snarls still ringing in their ears. Karan's breathing was steady, but his mind raced as he scanned the dark forest around them. Ajay stood nearby, his rifle lowered but ready, sweat glistening on his furrowed brow.

Priya crouched beside Leela, with her hand on Leela's shoulder. "Are you alright?"

Leela winced as she adjusted her weight, testing the sprain in her ankle. Despite the pain, her voice was steady, but her face was pale. "I'll manage. Just a sprain, I think."

Priya examined the injury, her tone reassuring. "It's not too bad. We'll wrap it and ice it once we get back."

Ajay exhaled deeply, wiping sweat from his brow. "That was no ordinary leopard," he said. "It wasn't hunting. It was defending territory."

"Or someone wanted it to seem that way," Karan said darkly, his mind already turning over the implications. "This wasn't just about us stumbling into its path. This was staged."

Priya's eyes widened. "You think someone… set this up?"

Karan nodded grimly. "Too many coincidences. Too many threads leading back to the same people. Whoever's behind Sonia's murder isn't just hiding, they're actively trying to scare us off."

Ajay's expression hardened. "If that's true, then we're dealing with someone who knows this forest and its predators better than we do."

Leela, sitting on a fallen log with her arm clutched to her side, winced as she shifted position. "So, someone's watching us, tracking us, even using the wildlife against us?" She shook her head, her voice tinged with frustration. "This is insane."

"Not insane," Karan corrected, his tone sharp. "Calculated. The same way they tried to stage Sonia's murder as an animal attack. It's their way of controlling the narrative, keeping us guessing."

Dr. Iyer crouched beside Leela, checking the scratch on her arm where the leopard's claws had grazed her. "You're lucky," she said quietly. "It could have been worse. A leopard this close to humans? That's no coincidence. If they're willing to weaponise the jungle against us, they must be desperate. That means we're close to something."

"Desperate people make mistakes," Karan said, his tone resolute. "This was sloppy. An attack like this? It's too obvious. Too pointed." He rose, his gaze fixed on the dark line of trees beyond the clearing. The jungle, now silent, felt oppressive, its secrets coiling tighter around them. "Fear won't stop us," he said, his voice cutting through the tension. "We go back to the hotel tomorrow. Someone there knows the truth. It's time we get answers."

Ajay slung his rifle over his shoulder, his movements measured, but tense. "If they wanted to scare us off, it means we're getting close. This forest doesn't just belong to the wildlife. It belongs to them, too."

Karan's gaze swept over his team. "Let's get some rest tonight. We regroup tomorrow, stay sharp, and stick together. This isn't just about Sonia anymore. Whoever's behind this has more to hide than we thought." It was a relief that the constables were also with them.

On his way back to the guesthouse, Karan was still shaken by the attack. Trying to calm himself down, he passed the marketplace, now emptied of its daytime vibrancy. The stalls, covered with tarpaulin sheets, stood like hunched figures, their once-bright wares hidden in the gloom. Somewhere in the distance, the faint toll of a monastery bell broke the quiet, its sound melancholy and haunting as it faded into the mist.

The streets of Pelling were nearly deserted, the usual chatter of vendors and clatter of tea stalls replaced by an oppressive silence. The mist clung to the narrow lanes, wrapping around the dim glow of streetlights and turning them into faint, ghostly orbs.

He glanced toward the Royal Pelling Hotel, its grand façade emerging like an island of opulence in a sea of shadows. The golden lights spilling from its windows illuminated the intricately carved wooden balconies and the manicured gardens below. But beneath its polished exterior, Karan knew it was a fortress of secrets; a place where wealth insulated its inhabitants from consequences.

The hotel's grandeur was a stark contrast to the rest of Pelling's modest surroundings. It catered to tourists who came seeking the town's natural beauty, blissfully unaware of the power dynamics and corruption woven into its fabric. The same money that funded its crystal chandeliers and silk-draped hallways also shielded people like Rohan Thakur from scrutiny.

As he passed the hotel, his mind circled back to the button found at the crime scene. The initials *RPH* were a direct link, and someone within those gilded walls had answers.

Karan entered his dimly lit guesthouse room, the weight of the day's events pressing heavily on his shoulders.

He set his briefcase on the table, its contents brimming with files, and reached for the bottle of single malt whiskey perched on the sideboard. Then he took off his coat, draped it over the back of the chair, and poured himself a large dose of whiskey from the bottle. He took his usual seat in the corner by the window, the amber liquid reflecting in the glass, its warmth a stark contrast to the chill of the room.

He swirled it absentmindedly, his thoughts racing. He gulped down the contents of the glass, attempting to calm his nerves. The button from the hotel uniform, the *kukhri* marks, the rope, the leopard attack, Rohan and Vinod... each piece felt like a thread leading to the same tangled knot, but the picture wasn't clear yet. Karan poured some more and swirled the whiskey in his glass, his gaze distant.

This case stirred memories of another investigation, years ago. A young girl, a teenager, bright and hopeful, had disappeared under similar circumstances. The trail had led to powerful men who thought they were untouchable. Back then, Karan's pursuit of justice had been relentless, but the system had failed him. The perpetrators had walked free, shielded by influence and wealth. The girl's family had been left to mourn in silence, their cries drowned out by the machinery of corruption.

Setting the empty glass aside, Karan reached for his notebook, flipping through pages of scrawled notes and observations. The pieces of the puzzle were beginning to align, but gaps remained.

"The forest isn't the end," he muttered to himself, his pen tapping against the notebook. "It's the beginning."

Karan formulated his plan for the next day. He decided to take the fight to the epicentre of it all – the Royal Pelling Hotel and Rohan. To peel the layers, he decided to start questioning everyone who had crossed paths with Rohan.

He rose from his chair, the notebook in hand, and paced the room. The rhythmic sound of his steps helped him think. Returning to his desk, Karan jotted down the final points of his plan before setting the notebook aside.

Exhaustion finally began to pull at him. Karan placed the empty glass back on the side table and moved to the bed. As he lay down, the day's events played over in his mind like a slow-moving reel.

The last thing he remembered, before sleep claimed him, was the sound of the wind outside, whispering through the trees as though carrying secrets he had yet to uncover.

The next morning, while eating breakfast, Karan switched on the television and immediately heard a TV anchor on the local news channel with a mix of frustration and curiosity. A woman with sharp features and a practised tone of urgency delivered her report as though it were breaking news.

As news of the investigation leaked to the press, the poaching angle ignited a media storm. Local and national news outlets latched onto the story, sensationalising every detail. Sonia's murder was no longer just a criminal investigation; it had become a political and environmental scandal.

"Another leopard sighting near the Pelling Forest Reserve," she announced, the screen cutting to a shaky clip of villagers pointing at trampled bushes. "Residents are on edge as rumours swirl about a man-eating leopard stalking the area. Authorities have advised caution."

Karan took a sip of his cooling tea, his eyes narrowing. The segment was sensationalised, complete with ominous music and quick cuts to terrified locals recounting exaggerated encounters.

The report shifted to a panel discussion. On one side sat a smooth-talking representative of MLA Thakur's office, insisting that measures were being taken to ensure safety. Opposite him was a fiery opposition leader, who seized the moment to criticise the Thakur family.

"This leopard scare is nothing but a distraction," the leader declared, jabbing a finger at the camera. "The real danger isn't in the forest, it's the unchecked privilege of the Thakur family. Sonia's tragic death is being swept under the rug, and we will not stand for it!"

The Thakur representative sneered. "The investigation is ongoing, and baseless allegations will not help the people of Pelling. The opposition should stop exploiting tragedies for political gain."

Karan leaned forward, his instincts sharpening. The debate was clearly orchestrated, with the leopard serving as a convenient diversion from the growing scrutiny on Rohan. The discussion devolved into shouting, the anchor struggling to maintain control.

But what caught Karan's attention was the brief mention of a recent poaching incident, almost buried under the noise of the debate.

"One last thing before we end," the anchor said hastily, cutting over the bickering politicians. "Reports suggest that an illegal poaching ring operating near the forest may be linked to the heightened leopard activity. Could this be connected to the fears in the region? We'll have more on that in our next segment."

The screen switched to commercials, but on his way to the office, Karan's mind stayed on the tantalising fragment of information.

Karan sat in his office, sipping coffee and flipping through the morning newspaper headlines: *"Whistleblower to Victim? The Dark Secrets of Bandhavgarh Forest", "Poaching Mafia Exposed: Murder, Money, and Corruption", "Thakur Enterprises Linked to Wildlife Trafficking?"*

The articles painted Sonia as a whistleblower who had uncovered an illicit poaching operation tied to powerful figures. Speculation ran wild, and with each passing hour, the pressure on Karan and his team grew.

The faint hum of overhead lights mingled with the occasional click of a keyboard as Karan and Leela worked through Sonia's records. A whiteboard at the far end of the room displayed a growing web of names, dates, and connections, with Sonia's photo pinned squarely in the centre.

Karan tapped his pen rhythmically on the desk, his sharp eyes scanning a stack of printed call logs. "Leela, these repeated calls to Vinod Kumar, what's the timeline? Did they happen right before she died?"

Leela shuffled through her notes. "Not exactly. The calls started three months ago and were frequent, almost daily. Then, two weeks before her death, they stopped completely."

"Why the sudden silence?" Karan mused aloud.

Leela leaned back in her chair, a frown creasing her forehead. "Maybe she found something during those calls. Something she wasn't supposed to." She turned to her laptop, typing furiously. "Let me check if Vinod Kumar reported any unusual activity during that period."

Karan nodded, his thoughts churning. "Meanwhile, I'll cross-reference Sonia's work shifts with those call logs. If she were making these calls on company time, it might point to something directly tied to Thakur Enterprises."

For the next hour, the room fell silent except for the faint rustle of papers and the occasional clatter of keys. Then, Leela let out a low whistle, her eyes fixed on the screen.

"Got something," she said, swivelling her laptop toward Karan. "Two weeks before Sonia's death, Vinod Kumar filed a police complaint about a missing truck. Cargo was listed as 'industrial equipment,' but the truck was never found, and the case was closed in under 48 hours."

Karan's brow furrowed. "Industrial equipment? Or something else entirely?"

Leela smirked. "That's what I thought, so I dug deeper. Guess what other cases got dropped around the same time? Two illegal poaching investigations. Both involved leopard pelts and ivory."

Karan leaned forward, his voice low and serious. "And Thakur Enterprises was their largest client?"

Leela nodded. "It's too much to be a coincidence."

Karan rubbed his temples, the pieces beginning to fit together. "If Sonia found out about the missing truck and its connection to poaching, it could explain why she became a target. She must have confronted Vinod or someone higher up before they silenced her."

"But why dump her body in the forest?" Leela asked. "Why not make it look like a robbery or an accident in town?"

Karan scribbled notes on a yellow pad, his mind racing. "Maybe the location wasn't random. The clearing could be a significant drop-off point, a meeting spot, or even where the operation was coordinated. We need to revisit the site and dig deeper."

Leela stood, determination etched on her face. "We should also bring in Vinod for questioning. He might crack if he knows we're onto him."

Karan glanced at the whiteboard, his gaze lingering on Sonia's photo. "Whatever they were protecting, it was worth killing for. Let's make sure her death wasn't in vain."

The clock on the wall read 11:37 p.m. when Priya and Leela burst into Karan's temporary office at the station, a sheaf of papers in hand.

"Karan," Priya said breathlessly, "we cross-referenced the dates of Sonia's calls with Vinod Kumar and Thakur Enterprises' shipping manifests. There's a pattern. Every time Sonia contacted Vinod, there was a shipment marked 'Priority' leaving the warehouse the next day."

Karan's eyes sharpened. "What was in the shipments?"

"That's the thing," Priya said, dropping the papers on his desk. "The manifests list them as 'equipment' or 'raw materials,' but there's no detailed description. It's deliberately vague."

Karan picked up the top sheet, his gaze scanning the columns of data. "And the destinations?"

Priya pointed to a highlighted section. "Most of them went to ports in Kolkata and Chennai, but one shipment stood out. It was routed to a private airstrip in West Bengal. No client name, just a reference code."

Karan sat back, the weight of the discovery settling over him. "Private airstrips mean superficial customs inspections. It's the perfect setup for smuggling."

"And Sonia figured it out," Priya said quietly.

Karan nodded and called Kumar. "Kumar, let's go to Rohan's school to find out his background, then check that airstrip and try to tie it to the clearing where her body was found. If it's part of their operation, it might explain why they went to such lengths to cover it up."

Chapter 7
The Principal's Wife

Talk to yourself at least once in a day. Otherwise, you may miss meeting the most excellent person in this world.

- Swami Vivekanand

The mist hung low over Pelling as Karan and Kumar entered the school grounds. The laughter of children playing in the courtyard struck a jarring contrast to the grim purpose of their visit. Karan adjusted his coat against the morning chill as he and Kumar strode toward the principal's office. A few students paused to stare at the unfamiliar visitors accompanied by constables, their curiosity quickly forgotten in the midst of their games.

Inside the office, the atmosphere was markedly different. Principal Sharma sat rigidly behind his desk, his face clouded with unease. Karan eased into a chair, his sharp gaze fixed on the principal, while Kumar leaned casually against the wall nearby, notebook in hand, his pen already poised, ready to catch every slip, every pause.

Mr. Sharma greeted them at the door with a polite but anxious smile, his demeanour suggesting he was well aware of the weight their visit carried. He motioned for them to sit, his hands twitching as he poured them tea.

"We need to talk about Rohan Thakur's history in this school," Karan began, his tone calm but firm. "From what I understand, he spent a fair amount of time here."

Sharma's fingers fidgeted with a pen. "Rohan… attended a few school events. His father's contributions to the school made it... difficult to turn him away."

Karan raised an eyebrow. "Difficult? Did his presence cause any problems?"

The principal shifted uncomfortably, his gaze dropping to the desk. "Rohan had a reputation. He was charming, yes, but also brash. Some of the younger staff, particularly the women, felt uneasy around him."

"Uneasy how?" Karan pressed, his voice taking on a sharper edge.

"There was an incident," Sharma admitted reluctantly. "One of our teachers said he made inappropriate advances during a school event. She resigned shortly after."

Karan leaned forward. "And you didn't report it?"

Sharma's face flushed. "I couldn't. Rohan's father is an influential man. Filing a complaint would've jeopardised our funding, our reputation… everything."

Nisha Sharma entered carrying a tray, with a polite smile that didn't reach her eyes, and her eyes avoided eye contact with her husband's.

Karan looked up as Nisha stepped inside, "I thought you might need some refreshments," she said, her voice measured.

The silk of her deep emerald *sari* caught the light, a whisper of it against her smooth, golden skin. A single loose curl slipped from behind her ear, trailing down the curve of her neck, swaying ever so slightly as she moved. The scent of jasmine lingered in the air, subtle, elusive, just like the woman herself. She was the kind of woman whose presence shifted the air in a room.

There was a quiet confidence in the arch of her brow, a deliberate slowness to her movements, as if she knew she was being watched but pretended not to notice. Yet, Karan didn't miss the flicker of hesitation in her step, the way her fingers tightened around the tray's edge for just a fraction of a second before she set it down.

"Tea?" she offered, her voice smooth.

She turned slightly, just enough for him to catch the gentle curve of her lips, not quite a smile, more like a practised expression, something polished and rehearsed. But her eyes... her eyes betrayed her. Dark, almond-shaped, lined with kohl, they flickered with something beneath the surface. Something guarded.

"Thank you, Mrs. Sharma," Karan said, studying her carefully.

She poured tea into the delicate porcelain cups silently with steady hands; her wrists adorned with gold bangles barely made a sound, almost as if she had learned to move in silence.

Her husband cleared his throat, breaking the moment.

"Nisha, there's no need for all this," Mr. Sharma said, his tone clipped, dismissive.

Her lashes fluttered before she straightened her *sari* and stepped back, her demeanour shifting. It was subtle, but Karan caught it, how she folded her hands before her, how the sultry grace in her movements dimmed just a little under her husband's gaze.

Still, when she finally spoke again, her voice remained soft but composed. "It's just tea, darling. Nothing more."

She sat down with her hands clasped in her lap, her lips pressed tightly together, as though holding back a flood of words. Her eyes flicked toward her husband whenever he spoke, a mixture of hesitation and anxiety evident in her expression.

Mr. Sharma gave a tight smile but didn't respond.

Karan sipped his tea, studying her over the rim of his cup. "So, Mrs. Sharma," he said casually, setting the cup down, "I imagine you must have seen Rohan Thakur around quite a bit over the years?"

Her fingers skimmed over the chain around her neck, a delicate touch, almost subconscious. "Now and then," she admitted, her voice light but not careless. "He was one of my husband's brightest students."

"Was he?" Karan mused, tilting his head.

She nodded, but didn't elaborate. Her fingers twitched slightly, her lips parting as if she wanted to interject, but no words came. She looked at Karan, her gaze lingering just a moment too long.

Mr. Sharma cut in swiftly. "Rohan had a troubled past, but that's behind him. I don't think there's anything relevant there."

Suddenly, she got up to leave but hesitated by the door, glancing briefly at her husband before meeting Karan's gaze.

"What about you, Mrs. Sharma?" His voice was calm, but deliberate. "Did you ever notice anything... unusual?"

Mr. Sharma frowned, cutting in before she could respond. "No, no, Nisha wasn't involved in such matters."

For a brief moment, Nisha's mask of composure slipped. Her hand moved to her necklace, fiddling with the pendant nervously. "Some of the girls... they were afraid of him," she said softly, her voice barely audible.

Mr. Sharma turned to her, his expression a mix of surprise and irritation. "Nisha, there's no need to bring that up now."

Karan leaned forward slightly, his eyes fixed on her. "Afraid of him? Did they ever confide in you?"

Karan noticed how her fingers curled slightly, gripping the folds of her *sari*. Nisha hesitated, her gaze darting to her husband. "They... didn't say much," she replied, choosing her words with care. "But their fear was evident. Some avoided him altogether."

Pursing her lips, she nodded slowly. "It was hard not to. Rohan acted like he owned the place. He made people uncomfortable, especially the women."

Her husband let out a nervous laugh, clearly eager to downplay the situation. "That was years ago, Mr. Karan. Rohan was just a troubled boy then. Kids grow out of these things."

Karan didn't respond. Instead, he shifted his attention back to Nisha, whose fingers were still toying with her pendant. "Did you notice anything unusual about Rohan's visits here after he left the school?"

Nisha's eyes flickered with a fleeting intensity before her expression returned to its practised neutrality. "He came to meet some of the staff," she said cautiously. "And... he would sometimes loiter near the school gate."

"Nisha," her husband interjected again. "That's hardly unusual in a small town. People are often around the school area." his voice dangerously smooth, "let's not get carried away with rumours."

Karan leaned forward slightly, "Fear isn't a rumour, Mr. Sharma. It's a reaction. A real one."

Nisha's throat moved as she swallowed. Then, in the softest voice, she said, "He had a way of making people uncomfortable."

Mr. Sharma let out a short, forced laugh. "Teenage boys can be reckless. Doesn't mean anything."

Karan's patience was running thin. He decided to take a different approach. "Mrs. Sharma, if there's anything you think might help, no matter how small, it's important that I know. The victim's family deserves the truth."

Nisha glanced at her husband, her lips trembling slightly. "Rohan... had a way of getting what he wanted..." she said finally, her voice tight.

Before Karan could press further, Mr. Sharma stood abruptly. "I think that's enough for now, Mr. Karan. We've told you everything we know."

Karan let his gaze linger on Nisha. Her eyes darted to the side for the briefest moment before returning to his.

There it was. That unspoken message.

Not here. Not now.

And then, as if nothing had happened, she smiled politely and reached for the tray. "More tea, Mr. Karan?"

He smiled back, slow and knowing. "Not right now. But thank you, Mrs. Sharma. You've been very helpful."

Karan drained the last of his tea. Mr. Sharma cleared his throat and looked pointedly at his wife. "Nisha, dear, don't you have some preparations to make for the parents' meeting tomorrow?"

Nisha hesitated, her lips parting as if to protest, but she quickly closed them again. She nodded, rose from her chair, and excused herself with a polite smile. Her eyes met Karan's fleetingly before she disappeared into the adjoining room.

Karan leaned back slightly, sensing the shift in tone. The principal shifted in his seat, checking his watch and tapping his fingers against the armrest of his chair.

"Well, Mr. Karan," Mr. Sharma said with forced geniality, "I hope this discussion was helpful. But I'm afraid I must attend to some urgent school matters. You understand how demanding this job can be."

Mr. Sharma opened the door, making it clear there would be no further discussion. Karan offered a polite nod, masking his annoyance at the abrupt dismissal. "Of course, Principal Sharma. Thank you for your time. I'll be in touch if I need any more information."

The principal escorted him out of his office, his steps brisk, his demeanour hurried. "Anything to assist the investigation, Mr. Karan. We all want justice, after all."

As Karan stepped out of the principal's office and into the quiet corridors of the school, the scent of jasmine followed him, faint, lingering, like an unfinished thought.

He looked around the school – though modest in size, it was immaculately kept. The polished floors gleamed under the fading daylight streaming through tall, narrow windows, and faint murmurs of students lingering after hours echoed faintly. It was serene, but Karan couldn't shake the tension lingering in the air.

As he made his way toward the exit, he noticed Nisha standing near a bulletin board at the end of the hall, her back to him. She appeared to be rearranging notices pinned to the board, though her movements were mechanical, her fingers trembling slightly as she adjusted a sheet of paper that was already perfectly aligned.

"Mrs. Sharma," Karan called softly as he approached, careful not to startle her.

She turned abruptly, clutching a piece of paper as if caught off guard. Her eyes flitted to the doors of the principal's office, then back to Karan, before lowering to the floor.

"You can call me Nisha," she said, her voice polite, but laced with an undertone of unease.

Karan took a step closer, lowering his voice. "Nisha, is there something else you wanted to tell me? Earlier, you seemed…" He paused, choosing his words carefully. "You seemed like there was more on your mind."

Nisha glanced nervously at the office door, then around the corridor, which was now empty, save for the two of them. She hesitated, gripping the papers tightly as if they might anchor her. Finally, she leaned slightly toward him, her voice dropping to a whisper.

"Karan," she said softly, her voice barely carrying over the rustling papers. Her posture was tense, her gaze darting nervously to the door as though expecting her husband to reappear at any moment.

"I... I'm sorry if I wasn't much help earlier," she began, her tone halting. "Sometimes it's hard to... remember things clearly."

Karan stepped closer, lowering his voice. "If there's anything else you'd like to share, Nisha, now would be the time."

Her grip tightened on the sheets, and she took a cautious step forward. "Rohan had a way of getting what he wanted. But it's not safe to talk here," she whispered, her words laden with urgency. "There's something you need to know. Meet me... outside by the school garden. Please."

Karan nodded subtly, his gaze steady. "I'll be there."

She nodded quickly, her gaze darting toward the office again. Karan noticed the fear that lingered in her eyes. This was more than simple unease – this was someone genuinely afraid.

"I'll be there," he said, his voice steady.

The sudden sound of a chair scraping inside the principal's office made Nisha flinch. The door opened a moment later, and the principal emerged, his expression a mask of geniality that didn't quite reach his eyes.

"Ah, Mr. Karan," he said, his tone overly cheerful, "I see you're taking a moment to enjoy the school's atmosphere. I hope Nisha hasn't been burdening you with too much information." He cast a quick, pointed look at her, who had already turned back to the bulletin board, feigning interest in a stack of flyers.

Karan forced a smile. "Not at all. Your school has a very welcoming environment."

The principal's smile tightened as he gestured toward the exit. "Well, I mustn't keep you. I'm sure you have plenty on your plate, and we have a busy evening here as well."

Karan nodded, walking with him to the exit and throwing one last glance over his shoulder as they reached the door.

As Karan stepped out into the misty evening, her cryptic words replayed in his mind. *Rohan had a way of getting what he wanted.* What exactly had she meant? And why did she seem so afraid to speak openly?

Karan found Nisha in the school's garden, her hands deep in a bed of marigolds. The bright yellow blossoms stood in stark contrast to the heavy clouds rolling over the hills, a reflection of the dissonance in the peaceful school and the storm of his investigation. She looked up as his shadow fell over her, brushing dirt from her fingers onto a crisp apron.

"Nisha," Karan began, his voice softer than usual, "Can we talk?"

She hesitated, then nodded, picking up a watering can as a prop just in case her husband came.

"You mentioned earlier that Rohan used people. What did you mean by that?"

Nisha leaned forward, clasping her hands tightly. "Rohan was... he wasn't just entitled; he was dangerous. He believed he could do anything and walk away from it. And he usually did."

Her voice carried the weight of something personal, but Karan didn't press her yet. She continued, her words flowing like a confession.

"I've seen it happen so many times. A young teacher here, Miss Rakhi, was bright, full of promise. Rohan took a liking to her. At first, it was subtle: compliments, small gifts, then more intrusive behaviour. He cornered her during a school event, touched her arm, and whispered things that made her uncomfortable. She left the school soon after, but no one dared to say why. How could we, with his father's shadow looming over us?"

Karan listened intently, his jaw tightening. Stories like these weren't new to him, but they never failed to fuel his disdain for those who wielded power as a shield.

"Rohan… had a way of getting what he wanted," she said finally, "sometimes, at the expense of others. Also, he used people… especially Suresh…"

Before she could say anything else, they noticed Mr. Sharma speaking to someone at the door. Nisha quickly turned, pretending to water the flowers and whispered, "Meet me at the school grounds tonight."

"Mr. Karan, still here? I trust you can find your way back to town?" the principal called out, his voice barely laced with the pretence of hospitality as he walked towards them.

Karan gave him a faint smile. "Of course, I was just admiring your lovely garden. Thank you once again," he said as he walked towards Kumar near the school gate and headed back to the office. He couldn't shake the growing sense of unease. Whatever Nisha needed to tell him, it was important and dangerous. Quickening his pace, he made a mental note to return to the school grounds after sunset.

Karan was seated in his office, nursing a cup of terrible machine-brewed coffee. His desk was cluttered with legal briefs, case files, and a notepad filled with scribbled questions from the night before.

He had spent hours sifting through old court records, land disputes, and town gossip, looking for something, anything, that might explain why Rohan had been "protected."

And why Nisha had looked at him the way she did.

A sharp knock on the frosted glass of his office door interrupted his thoughts.

Leela entered, clutching a thick folder to her chest. "Sir, the background check on Nisha and Rohan you asked for," she said, placing it on his desk.

Karan straightened in his chair. "Yeah. What do you have?"

She hesitated, glancing at the file before meeting his gaze. "Something… odd."

Karan gestured for her to continue.

He flipped through the pages of the file. "Any past cases tied to Rohan or his family?"

Leela hesitated again.

Karan glanced up. "Spit it out."

"There was… one incident," she admitted, lowering her voice. "A sealed case. A dispute between Rohan and another party. Settled out of court."

Karan exhaled through his nose. Sealed cases meant someone wanted it buried.

Leela nodded and added. "There's more. Nisha isn't just some principal's wife."

He glanced up, intrigued. “Go on.”

“She’s ten years younger than Mr. Sharma. Comes from a small village near Guwahati. Her family was poor, sent her younger brother to school, but stopped her education after the twelfth grade.”

It was a familiar story. The son gets an education. The daughter gets married off.

“She ran away at eighteen and married Principal Sharma,” Leela said.

“Oh! Why him?”

Leela hesitated. “Money, probably. Stability, Security. He was established, respected, and a powerful man in his own way. She probably thought he’d give her a better life… but the marriage…” She said, lowering her voice.

Karan took a deep breath. He had seen it before – young women escaping one form of oppression only to walk straight into another.

Leela pulled out another set of papers and continued. “But neither her husband nor the marriage was what she expected. There are hospital records, sir. Several visits over the years. Bruises. Fractures. Classic signs of domestic abuse.”

Karan leaned back, rubbing his chin. He had suspected control, maybe coercion, but this?

“She never filed a complaint,” Leela added.

“Of course, she hadn’t. A woman from a small village, married to a respected school principal, who would have believed her? Who would have fought for her? She endured all of that and still stayed,” he muttered.

Leela nodded. “Until now.”

Karan’s gaze sharpened. “What changed?”

Leela flipped a few pages, stopping at one in particular. “There’s something else. Something that connects her to Rohan Thakur.”

Karan leaned in. “Tell me.”

Leela swallowed. “Not directly. But…” She opened the file, pointing to a document. “There was an old police report. Some of the girls from the school had accused Rohan of harassment a few years ago. The case never went anywhere. Witnesses changed their statements, and evidence disappeared.”

Karan’s jaw tightened. “And?”

Leela turned the file toward him, tapping her finger against a name in the report. “The person who filed the complaint on behalf of those girls?”

Nisha Sharma.

Karan stared at the name, something clicking into place.

“She stood up to Rohan Thakur,” he said slowly.

Leela nodded. “And paid the price for it.”

Karan shut the file with a firm snap. That explained her fear. She had challenged Rohan once before and had been crushed for it. If she was hesitating now, it was because she knew the cost of speaking out.

And yet, she had still tried to tell him something in the school garden.

His jaw tightened. *She knows the truth. And if she was willing to risk speaking up back then…*

"She might have the key to uncovering what Rohan has done this time," he finished.

Leela exhaled. "But will she talk?"

Karan pushed back his chair and stood up with a smile. "She will."

Leela hesitated. "How can you be sure?"

Karan's gaze was steady.

"Because this time, she won't be standing alone." Karan closed the file, exhaling slowly. "I need to meet her tonight."

Chapter 8
Meeting at the Banyan Tree

One day, you will realise that the same person is not found twice in life. Not everyone is replaceable.

The moon hung low, its silver glow spilling over the school grounds. Shadows danced as Karan adjusted his jacket, his breath misted in the chilly air, and he scanned the deserted courtyard. He walked towards the secluded jungle path, his footsteps echoed softly on the cobblestones, the quiet amplifying his growing anticipation.

The wind had died down, but the air was thick with tension, as though the jungle was holding its breath. Karan approached the ancient banyan tree, its twisted roots rising from the ground like skeletal fingers, gripping the earth. The tree, with its wide canopy and deep shadows, seemed almost alive, watching over the deserted school playground. The air was tinged with a faint floral fragrance, out of place in the earthy surroundings.

He had barely stepped off the main path when he saw a shadow move. A figure emerged from behind the tree, her movements fluid yet hesitant.

Nisha.

Her silhouette was almost ethereal. She was poised yet restrained, as if she had spent years perfecting the art of being unseen. Her deep red *sari* shimmered faintly in the moonlight, its fabric clinging to her frame. Shimmering in the moonlight, her hair cascaded over one shoulder, and she slowly tucked it behind her ear. As she stepped toward him, the clink of her bangles softly broke the silence.

Her kohl-lined eyes sparkled as they met Karan's, holding a mix of nervousness and quiet defiance. "Karan," she murmured, her voice low and smooth, with a touch of urgency. For a fleeting moment, Karan thought he saw a flicker of sadness, fear, or maybe regret.

She drew the *pallu* of her *sari* closer around her shoulders, as her eyes darted toward the empty windows of the school building.

"You made it," Karan replied, his tone steady but his gaze momentarily faltering at her unexpected appearance. "What's so urgent?"

Thank you for meeting me," she began softly. She glanced over her shoulder nervously before taking a step closer. The scent of jasmine followed her – intoxicating, yet grounding. "I didn't know who else to trust." She stepped closer, "I had to see you," she murmured, her voice almost a whisper. "I couldn't say everything earlier."

Karan nodded, his professional demeanour intact, though he couldn't ignore the undercurrent of intensity in her presence. "Go on," he encouraged.

She hesitated, her fingers playing with the edge of her *pallu*. "Rohan Thakur," she began, her tone soft but laced with disdain. "You've seen glimpses of it, but there's more, things no one dares to say out loud. He seems like a spoilt, charming man, but charm can hide the darkest of things. He's dangerous." Her eyes seemed to darken for a moment, and she looked away, swallowing hard.

Karan frowned, leaning in slightly. “Dangerous how?”

Nisha inhaled sharply, and she stepped even closer and tilted her head, her lips curving into a bittersweet smile. The night was still, except for the occasional rustle of leaves.

Karan nodded, pressing gently. “What do you know about him?”

Her gaze darted around the courtyard again, her anxiety palpable as she looked down at her feet, her voice trembling slightly as she continued, “He… he’s a predator.”

He listened silently.

“He’s used his father’s clout to cover up the things he’s done.”

Her voice broke slightly, but she steadied herself and looked around nervously again.

“Rohan… he’s used his father’s power to cover up so many things. There are girls, so many girls, who’ve suffered because of him. He treats them like playthings, discards them when he’s bored, and if they resist...” Her voice broke slightly, but she quickly composed herself.

Karan’s jaw clenched, “Go on,” his hands balling into fists. He had suspected Rohan of being protected, but this… this was worse.

Nisha’s eyes glistened, but she pressed on. “Pooja, the librarian’s daughter. She left town suddenly last year, with no explanation.”

Breathless, she continued, “Then Maya, a hotel staff member, vanished after… after a night Rohan spent there.

And Gracy…" Her voice faltered again, but she caught herself. "She was a teacher here. She spoke out against him, and the next day she was dismissed. Rohan's father made sure of it."

Karan felt a cold fury rising within him, but he kept his tone even. "And Sonia? Did she know Rohan?"

Nisha flinched and nodded, her hands now trembling. "She was different. She wasn't afraid of him. She confronted him once, right here in this courtyard. I saw them arguing. She accused him of… of things no one else dared to say aloud. She even threatened to expose him. And then…" Her words trailed off, but the meaning was clear.

Karan leaned closer, his voice low. "You think he killed her?"

Nisha hesitated, then nodded her head slowly.

"I don't know. But… I don't think he acted alone."

Karan's eyes narrowed. "Who else?"

Her fingers played absentmindedly with the edge of her *pallu*, almost as if she needed something to distract herself.

"I can't say too much here," she whispered, her gaze darting toward the school building. "But I need you to listen carefully."

Karan stepped closer, but kept a safe distance, sensing the fragile line between them. "I'm listening," he urged, in a cautious and controlled tone.

"But that's not what you need to focus on right now." She trailed off, eyes now glistening with something more than concern, fear, perhaps, or regret.

"Then what should I be focusing on?"

"There's something else you need to check. The CCTV footage."

Karan frowned. "From the hotel?"

Nisha nodded. "Rohan was there that night, but someone else was too. Someone no one is talking about."

Nisha's lips parted as though she wanted to speak, but then, as if realising the gravity of her words, she pressed her hand to her mouth, briefly hiding behind the delicate fabric of her *sari*.

She lowered her voice further, her tone heavy with the weight of an unspoken truth. "One of the waiters. He's been around both Rohan and the victim too many times. Watch him carefully. He may be the key to all of this."

Karan's eyes sharpened. "The waiter?"

She hesitated before finally saying his name. "Suresh," she said, "I saw him and Rohan at the school gate on the night Sonia was murdered, too."

Karan exhaled. "What's his connection to Rohan?"

Nisha's hands gripped the edge of her *sari* tightly. "He was always around Rohan, but not by choice."

Nisha's gaze drifted to the trees. "He's different. Quiet, obedient, but… afraid. Rohan treated him like a servant, barking orders and humiliating him in public. But there were moments when they seemed… closer. Too close."

She whispered, "I once overheard them arguing near the school gate. Rohan was furious, shouting about something Suresh hadn't done right. Suresh just stood there, looking like he wanted the ground to swallow him up."

Karan leaned forward, his curiosity piqued. "What were they arguing about?"

"I don't know," she admitted. "But it wasn't the only time. I saw them together around town, too, always in hushed conversations. It was like Rohan had some kind of hold over him."

Nisha's voice grew quieter, her next words carrying an edge of fear. "I've wondered if Suresh knows more than he's letting on. He was always around when Rohan stirred up trouble, though Suresh always seemed uneasy."

"Uneasy how?" Karan asked, intrigued. He was surprised. A new lead. A new thread to pull. "Do you think Suresh might know something about Rohan's activities?"

Nisha hesitated, then nodded. "Definitely. He was always around Rohan."

"Thank you for sharing this. It could be important."

"If it helps bring justice to that poor girl, I'll do whatever I can. That's the key…"

Karan's mind raced as he absorbed her words, but before he could respond, the sound of footsteps interrupted their conversation. Nisha's eyes widened slightly, her face softening with a forced smile, her demeanour shifting instantly. She took a step back, her fingers adjusting the pleats of her *sari* in a practised motion.

"I… I must go. My husband will be looking for me."

Karan nodded, but as she turned to leave, he caught something in her eyes. A silent plea.

"Wait," he called out quietly, his voice low. "Nisha, what do you mean by 'the key'? Are you suggesting…"

She turned back to him, her expression becoming unreadable for a moment. "I can't say more now," she whispered. "But… if you help me, I can help you."

Her gaze lingered on him a moment longer, her lips curling into a cryptic, almost sad smile.

"There are things you don't know, things about Rohan, things about this town. It's all tangled. But you must trust me, Karan. Go to the hotel," she emphasised.

There was a silent message in her gaze, a promise of more to come. She reached up, as if adjusting her hair, and subtly traced a circle in the air with her finger before disappearing into the shadows.

Before he could say another word, she turned away, melting into the shadows, leaving Karan feeling a strange mix of intrigue and unease.

He stood there for a moment longer, his thoughts swirling in the dark forest and her words echoing within.

If you help me, I can help you.

Karan stood rooted to the spot. There was something, an unspoken plea, a warning, maybe even a silent promise. The circle she had drawn, was it a clue? A meeting place? A warning? For a moment, it was as if she had never been there at all.

The jungle behind the school swallowed every trace of movement, the whisper of leaves and distant calls of nocturnal creatures returning to fill the void she left behind.

Karan exhaled slowly, his fingers flexing at his sides, trying to shake the unease creeping into his bones.

As the schoolyard grew still once more, Karan felt a knot tighten in his stomach.

What are you trying to tell me, Nisha?

The words echoed in his head as he turned and made his way back through the jungle path toward his car. The road leading to the guesthouse was deserted, save for the occasional flicker of movement in the undergrowth. A stray dog darted across the dirt path, its lean frame momentarily illuminated by his headlights before it disappeared into the night.

By the time Karan reached the guesthouse, fatigue had begun to settle deep in his bones. The day had been long, too long, and yet, sleep felt like the last thing his mind would allow him. The constables saluted him with a worried look.

The caretaker greeted him at the entrance with a polite nod. "Long day, sir?"

Karan managed a tired smile. "Something like that."

"Dinner's waiting in the dining hall. Thought you might be late, so I kept it warm."

Karan exhaled, grateful. "Thank you."

As Karan sat down and took his first bite, he barely registered the taste. The food, fragrant and warm, sat untouched. His appetite had disappeared the moment Nisha's voice replayed in his mind; soft, almost too quiet, but heavy with implication.

She was a riddle. Every answer she offered only led to more questions. There was a fragility to her, yes, but also something elusive, something she was withholding. Was it fear? Guilt? Or a calculated silence meant to protect herself… or someone else?

She unsettled him, not just as a possible witness or victim, but as a woman caught in a storm she wasn't ready to speak about. And that silence gnawed at him more than her words ever had.

After pushing the plate away, he poured himself a drink. The amber liquid shimmered in the glass as he sank into his chair, letting the soft vinyl scratch of *Knife… Cuts Like a Knife* by Rockwell, played in the background. But the warmth of the whiskey couldn't soothe the chill climbing his spine. His thoughts wandered, as they often did, to the ghosts the justice system had forgotten.

Another log cracked in the bonfire. The flames rose, shadows danced on the walls. Karan sat alone, the scent of whiskey thick on his breath and thoughts unspooling faster than he could control. He picked up his notebook, one he never intended to share and began to write a poem, not as a judge, but as a man breaking apart under the weight of years:

It's Tiring

Another chaotic day is finally over,

Body and mind feel crushed by a bulldozer.

Loyal friends of lonely evenings – whiskey and a bonfire,

And helpless brooding thoughts

about my wasted life, full of knots.

As the alcohol seeps into my veins,

Again comes your shadow floating on the flames.

Teasing me, humming and whispering,

the embers also rise and dance with you,

Exotic woman, this is the chaos caused by you.

Staring into the flames, my soul yearns,

Lusting for you, I continue to burn.

Broken stars above me flash and disappear into the endless universe

... and so is my desire.

My wanting you never seems to end,

Heady cocktail of lover and friend.

How I got so lucky, I cannot comprehend.

From the flashes, evil thoughts rise – how to snatch you.

The sinister smile cracks my lips,

The chess player will now make his move.

He stopped. Shut the journal. The fire snapped sharply as if in warning. He hated the man he used to be. Feared the man he could still become.

He closed his eyes, and the faces came.

Divya Bharti: A rising star, vibrant and young, gone in a blink. A fatal fall from a fifth-floor balcony. Decades later, the questions still lingered. Accident? Suicide? Murder? No one truly knew.

Jiah Khan: Brilliant, talented, found hanging from a ceiling fan. A note, a mother's grief, unanswered questions, and a legal system more interested in image than truth.

Sridevi: An icon. A woman adored by millions. Found lifeless in a bathtub in a foreign hotel room. Drowned? Cardiac arrest? The headlines changed daily. But the truth was lost somewhere between silence and spectacle.

Karan opened his eyes and stared at the swirl in his glass. If women like them, *celebrated, famous, watched by the entire country,* could disappear without closure, what chance did ordinary women like Sonia have?

Then more names crowded in, uninvited, but insistent.

Sunanda Pushkar: Her death was called unnatural, then natural, then controversial, until it faded into political noise.

Sheena Bora: Murdered, her body burnt and dumped, buried beneath the lies of a powerful family.

Aarushi Talwar: Just a girl, killed in her own room. Her murder trial turned into a media circus. Justice buried beneath bias and botched forensics.

Disha Salian, Ankita Bhandari, Jessica Lal, Shivani Bhatnagar, Geetika Sharma…

Each face distinct. Each voice silenced.

Each one a cautionary tale.

A list that could fill every wall of this room, if he dared to write them all down. Young women, brilliant, promising, full of dreams – just *gone*. Erased by love gone wrong, betrayal, power, lust, control, and the silence of those who chose not to see.

His breath got caught, and he choked.

Sonia was one of them now. Not famous. Not rich. Not politically connected. Just a receptionist in a hill-town hotel, who had dared to speak out. And for that, she was gone.

And Nisha?

She was still alive. But for how long?

His grip tightened around the glass. The system failed women like them, over and over again. Failed to protect them. Failed to prosecute their killers. Failed to remember their names.

But not this time.

Not under his watch.

He set the glass down with quiet finality, the echo of it a promise.

Sonia Verma would not be another cold file gathering dust in some backroom archive. She wouldn't be reduced to a few lines in a police report, or worse, a forgotten name.

Someone in this town knew the truth.

And Karan was going to find them. Drag it out into the light. Tear the veil off every lie, every accomplice, every silence that had enabled this murder.

He stood by the window for a long time, watching the fog curl around the street lamps outside. The night wore on. And when he finally lay in bed, sleep came, but only in fragments.

The faces wouldn't leave him. They never did.

But this time, he wouldn't turn away.

This time, he would finish what had started, with the truth, not just the verdict.

And he wouldn't stop until Sonia's story was no longer a tragedy but a reckoning.

He was certain that the pieces of the puzzle were close, but the connections were still too elusive.

The last thought on his mind before he drifted off was, *'Every time you miss a train or get trapped in traffic, you are delayed for a reason, redirected by the unseen. Be sure that you will end up where you are meant to be.'*

Chapter 9
Walls Closing In

Tell a lie 1000 times and it becomes the truth.

- Joseph Goebbels

A sudden knock on the door jolted Karan from an uneasy sleep. He sat up, rubbing his eyes as the early morning mist seeped through the cracks of the window. Another knock came, insistent, deliberate.

Half-awake, he opened the door to find his caretaker standing with a folded newspaper in his weathered hands. With a soft, respectful "*Namaste*, Judge *sahib*," he handed over the newspaper and quietly departed.

Karan shut the door, yawning as he flipped through the pages. Then, something slipped out: a small, folded scrap of paper that fluttered to the floor. Frowning, he bent down, picked it up and unfolded it. The ink was smudged in places, but the message, hastily scribbled in black ink, was unmistakable:

"You are chasing ghosts.

Stop before the forest swallows you, too."

No signature. No name. Just a threat, plain and clear.

Karan exhaled slowly, scanning the note again. This wasn't a warning; it was a message. A calculated effort to make him stop digging. Was it Rohan? Or someone with more to lose? Someone who had the power to erase people as easily as they erased evidence?

He carefully placed the note in his folder, alongside the photograph he had received earlier. If they thought intimidation would deter him, they were mistaken.

Karan wore his coat and stepped outside, the crisp mountain air biting at his skin. His driver and the constables were already waiting, the car's engine idling softly in the quiet morning. Without a word, he slipped into the backseat, the hum of the engine grounding his thoughts as they pulled onto the winding road toward the Royal Pelling Hotel.

As they passed the Pemayangtse Monastery, its ancient structure standing solemnly against the misty backdrop, Karan's mind replayed the note's warning.

His gaze drifted back to the newspaper sprawled on the passenger seat. The bold headline made his stomach coil:

"Another Tragic Death in Pelling – Sonia's Neighbour

Found Dead Under Mysterious Circumstances."

A sinking weight settled in Karan's chest as he reread the report in his hand. The neighbour he'd spoken to just two days ago, the old woman who had nervously whispered about seeing someone near Sonia's room the night she died, was now dead.

Slipped in the bathroom, they said.

No witnesses.

No foul play suspected.

Too neat. Too sudden.

It wasn't just a tragic coincidence. It was a message. The walls were closing in, and whoever was behind

Sonia's murder was eliminating anything or anyone that could lead back to them.

By mid-morning, Karan was at the Courthouse. The inquiry chamber, once cold and impersonal, now hummed with quiet tension. Leela, Priya, and Kumar were already gathered, poring over fresh files and transcripts. The weight of recent events showed on their faces.

"The neighbour is dead," Karan said, setting the report down on the table. "Head trauma. No witnesses. They're calling it a domestic accident."

Karan leaned over the evidence board on the wall. "They're cleaning house. Removing anyone who might link them to Sonia. We need to move faster."

Leela paced behind him. "We need a fresh angle. Something they won't expect."

"There is something," Karan said. "Nisha mentioned some missing CCTV footage. From the hotel. The night Sonia died."

Priya looked up. "Did she give specifics?"

"She hinted that someone wiped it. And she's scared, more than she's letting on. Said the answers might still be in that hotel."

"Then that's where we go," Kumar said.

Karan nodded. "Tonight. Quietly."

That evening, just as the fog began to settle over the ridges of Pelling, Karan stood outside the Royal Pelling Hotel, the façade glowing dimly in the misty twilight. It was a place that wore its luxury like a mask, polished brass, clean marble, and curated silence. But beneath the surface, there were too many holes in the narrative.

He stepped inside with casual ease, but his mind was razor-sharp.

Nisha's cryptic warnings echoed in his ears. *"People are watching. Some staff know more than they're saying. And the cameras... not all of them were broken."*

At the front desk, a well-groomed receptionist looked up, her expression neutral but her eyes observant.

"Good evening, sir. Can I help you?" Her voice was professional, clipped.

Karan offered a calm smile. "Where's the lounge?"

She gestured politely toward the left corridor. "Past the elevators, to your right."

"Thanks," he said lightly, but as he walked away, he caught her watching him just a beat too long.

As he walked through the corridor, past staff-only doors, Karan wasn't just looking for a drink; he was looking for answers. And tonight, he'd find them.

His eyes wandered across the lobby, observing the beautiful lounge of the hotel bustling with activity. A blend of murmured conversations, clinking glasses, and the occasional burst of laughter from tourists. His attention was drawn to the hotel's bar, tucked into a shadowy corner, away from the lobby. Karan walked up to the bar and leaned casually against it, scanning the room when a waiter passed by, balancing a tray of drinks with practised ease. His movements were precise, almost too precise, as if he had trained himself to remain unnoticed.

He carried himself with an almost unnatural precision, his white uniform spotless, his tray balanced perfectly in one hand. His smile was practised, polite, and impersonal. He was lean, his dark hair neatly combed back. His posture was upright, his movements were efficient yet unobtrusive. But something about him caught Karan's attention, perhaps it was the stiffness in his gait or the way he avoided lingering too long at any one table.

His nametag read: Suresh.

Karan pretended to study the menu while observing and piecing together the nuances of the man's behaviour. Suresh served an elderly couple first, his voice smooth and practised, his smile polite but not forced. He leaned in slightly, nodding attentively as the old man spoke, adjusting a napkin for them with meticulous care. There was warmth in his tone, a genuine patience that made him seem at ease.

Karan's thoughts wandered back to Nisha's words. Her hints about the staff being key to unravelling the truth now seemed more pointed. He needed to tread carefully.

But when he approached a table of wealthy guests – men in tailored suits, women draped in expensive shawls, something changed. His posture stiffened ever so slightly. The polite mask remained, but Karan caught a flicker of something dark in his eyes, resentment, maybe, or something colder. The moment was brief, gone as quickly as it had appeared, replaced once again by his effortless composure.

There was no overt hostility, no outward sign of rebellion, but Karan's instincts told him there was more to this man than met the eye.

Karan absentmindedly ordered a scotch, but his mind catalogued the details.

There was a tension in Suresh, a barely contained energy, like a coiled snake ready to snap. The way his lips tightened ever so slightly as he nodded deferentially to a demanding patron.

Then, without warning, Suresh looked straight at him.

Dark, piercing eyes met Karan's, holding something indecipherable. It wasn't fear or anxiety, but something colder, sharper. A flicker of recognition? A challenge? The moment was fleeting, vanishing behind a carefully constructed mask as he waiter disappeared through the kitchen doors.

Suddenly, he appeared next to him with his scotch, his dark, piercing eyes meeting Karan's filled with something Karan couldn't quite place. There was an odd intensity to his gaze, a fleeting glint, barely perceptible, before it vanished behind a smooth, friendly smile.

"Your drink, sir," Suresh interrupted, offering the drink.

Karan took a sip, studying him. "Busy place."

"Yes, sir," Suresh replied, his smile unwavering. "Guests come and go. Keeps us all on our toes."

Karan swirled his drink. "You must see a lot of people working here. Do you get to know the guests?"

Suresh chuckled softly, shaking his head. "Not really, sir. Just faces and orders. People come, people leave. That's the nature of the job."

Karan's gaze didn't waver, watching for any telltale signs. "Were you here the night that the receptionist was killed?"

For a fraction of a second, Suresh paused, barely noticeable. Then he resumed polishing a glass. "Yes, sir. A terrible thing. But I didn't know her well. She was quiet and kept to herself."

Karan leaned in slightly. "And Rohan Thakur? He's been seen around here often. You two close?"

Suresh's smile widened just a fraction, but his eyes told another story. "Oh no, sir. He's a guest. Like anyone else."

Before Karan could probe further, the manager appeared.

"Good evening, sir. Hope you're having a good time." The manager's tone was laced with rehearsed politeness.

Suresh bowed his head slightly in farewell, his polite demeanour firmly in place.

"Just here for a quiet evening." Karan matched his polite tone. "This is a fine place," he complimented, taking a sip. "You must have a dedicated team to keep everything running smoothly."

The manager beamed with pride. "Indeed, sir. Most of our staff have been with us for years. They know the importance of maintaining our reputation."

Karan nodded, his tone casual. "And the newer ones? They must bring fresh energy to the team."

The manager hesitated, a fraction of a second too long before replying, "Yes, we've had a few new hires recently.

But Suresh has been here the longest. Hardworking. Quiet but efficient."

"Hmmm..." Karan said thoughtfully, filing the information away.

Just then, the manager's phone buzzed in his pocket. He glanced at the screen, his expression shifting subtly before he cleared his throat.

"Excuse me, sir, I have to take this call," he said, offering Karan a quick nod. "Thank you for your time. Let me know if you need anything else."

The manager left, and Karan returned his attention to the waiter, who was now behind the bar, meticulously arranging glasses. His movements were precise, almost mechanical, but there was an air of detachment about him, as if his mind were elsewhere.

When Suresh disappeared into the kitchen, Karan rose from his seat and walked back towards the reception desk.

At the reception desk, Karan flashed his credentials to the receptionist. "I need access to your CCTV footage and records of your staff for the past month. Particularly your floor servers and dining staff."

The receptionist hesitated, her eyes darting nervously. "I'll have to check with the manager, sir. Please wait a moment." She disappeared into the back office, leaving Karan to survey the scene.

The receptionist came back and stood in front of Karan with a tight smile and hesitated. "We do, but access is restricted. You'd need management's approval."

Karan smiled faintly. "Of course."

The receptionist scurried away. The manager appeared, his face a practised mask of courtesy.

Suddenly, Karan felt a presence behind him. Turning, he saw Nisha in the shadows of the lobby, her red *dupatta* wrapped tightly around her. Her eyes darted toward the lounge.

"Meet me outside in five minutes," she whispered and vanished.

Karan stepped outside, the crisp night air wrapping around him as he adjusted his coat. He found Nisha leaning against the garden fence, her red *dupatta* fluttering in the breeze, and her eyes darting around, cautious and watchful. She glanced at him, her lips curling into a faint, almost teasing smile.

"You took your time," she murmured as he approached.

"You didn't exactly leave me an appointment card," Karan replied dryly. "What is it?"

"You were right," Karan said without preamble. "I think the CCTV footage is missing. Who has the most to gain from erasing it?"

Nisha's fingers played with the hem of her scarf, her voice low and sultry. "Who, indeed? You think the waiter knows something?"

"More than he's letting on," Karan replied, watching her closely. "What aren't you telling me, Nisha?"

She stepped closer, her perfume lingering in the air between them.

"Sometimes, the truth is in the whispers, not the screams. You're chasing the obvious, but there's a deeper web." Her voice dropped, and she leaned in, her breath warm against his ear. "The waiter is just a thread. Pull it, and you'll find the knot."

Karan's brow furrowed. "What kind of knot?"

Before she could answer, a loud voice interrupted them. "Nisha!" It was her husband, the principal, striding toward them.

Nisha straightened, her expression shifting instantly to one of benign innocence. "I was just admiring the garden, darling," she said sweetly.

The principal's gaze lingered on Karan, his eyes narrowing slightly. "Judge *sahib*, you seem to be everywhere in Pelling these days."

Karan offered a polite smile. "Just doing my job."

As Nisha walked away with her husband, she turned back for the briefest of moments. Her hand rested on her scarf, and she flicked her fingers subtly toward the hotel.

Karan turned on his heel and walked back inside the hotel. The receptionist flinched at his sudden reappearance but quickly composed herself.

"The manager will see you now, sir."

"Sir, how can I assist you?" he asked, his tone neutral.

Karan leaned in slightly. "I need to see the CCTV footage from the night of Sonia's death."

The manager's smile faltered. "Ah, yes, the footage… There seems to be a small issue."

Karan folded his arms. "What kind of issue?"

The manager swallowed, glancing around as if checking for listening ears. "Certain parts of the recording are… missing. There was a technical failure, and we lost some hours of footage from that night."

Karan's jaw tightened. "That's a convenient failure. And let me guess, the missing hours are precisely when Sonia was last seen?"

The manager spread his hands, looking helpless. "I don't control the system, sir. It was brought to my attention only after your inquiry. The hard drive is intact, but there are gaps, sections that simply aren't there anymore."

Karan studied him. The man was nervous, yes, but whether it was guilt or fear, he couldn't yet tell. "Who had access to the footage?"

"Only myself and the head of security," the manager admitted. "And… well, the IT technician, Arun Dey, but he hasn't been in since the day after Sonia's death."

Karan narrowed his eyes. "Where is he now?"

The manager hesitated. "He took sudden leave. Saying he's unwell. But hasn't returned."

Karan's instincts flared. Someone had erased that footage, and Arun disappeared right after? That wasn't a coincidence.

"Give me his address. I want to speak with him."

The manager scribbled the details onto a notepad and handed it over, his fingers trembling slightly.

"Judge sir, I swear, I don't know what's happening. I just manage the hotel. I…"

Karan cut him off with a sharp look. "Then I suggest you start paying closer attention to what happens under your roof. Because someone is making sure certain things stay buried. And if I find out you're part of that cover-up, I won't be asking next time."

The manager nodded quickly, stepping back as Karan walked towards the door with questions and frustration simmering beneath his calm exterior. The missing footage, the forced politeness of the hotel staff, and now the vanishing IT technician – Arun. Everything pointed to a cover-up. And yet, there were still too many gaps.

The moment he stepped out of the exit, a glint of metal caught his eye. Across the street, nestled between a tea shop and a small convenience store, was an old electronics repair shop. The peeling paint on its faded blue sign read *Singh Electronics – Repairs & Surveillance Systems*.

Above its shuttered window, a set of dusty security cameras pointed directly at the entrance and exit of the Royal Pelling Hotel.

Karan's pulse quickened. If the hotel's footage was missing, perhaps these cameras had captured something the culprits hadn't considered.

He crossed the street swiftly and pushed open the door to the shop, setting off a small bell that jingled above the entrance. Inside, the air smelled of soldered wires and dust. The room was cluttered, shelves stacked with outdated radios, tangled cables, and half-assembled circuit boards.

A middle-aged man with thinning hair and glasses perched on the tip of his nose looked up from behind a counter, his hands deep inside the open body of a dismantled television.

"*Namaste*, Judge *sahib*," the man instantly recognised Karan and greeted him, his tone wary yet respectful. "How can I help you?"

Karan was secretly elated and flashed a disarming smile. "I need to see the footage from your security camera outside. Specifically, the night of Sonia's death."

The shopkeeper hesitated, rubbing his chin. "I don't usually give out recordings, sir. Privacy and all..."

Karan reached into his pocket and produced his official credentials. "This is a legal investigation. If you cooperate, I can ensure your name stays out of any reports. But if you don't, I'll have to take this matter up formally."

The man sighed and nodded, walking over to a monitor connected to the CCTV system. He tapped a few keys, scrolling through footage. "It's an old system," he muttered. "Only keeps recordings for a week before overwriting."

Karan's heart pounded. "Just find that night."

Minutes passed before the grainy footage flickered onto the screen. The timestamp read 11:42 p.m. on the night of Sonia's murder.

Karan leaned in, watching as figures moved in and out of the hotel's entrance. A heated exchange caught his attention, Rohan Thakur and Sonia standing near the doorway, their body language tense. Rohan gestured sharply, his face twisted with anger, while Sonia's stance was defiant, her arms crossed. The grainy footage showed them arguing for nearly a minute before Sonia turned abruptly and stormed back inside. Rohan lingered for a moment, running a frustrated hand through his hair, then exhaled sharply before walking out towards the street.

Karan wondered – *what had she said to him? And why had she gone back inside alone?*

Then, something else caught his eye. A black SUV idled across the street, its headlights dimmed, partially obscured by the shadows of the narrow lane. Moments later, a man emerged from the hotel and hurried toward the SUV.

It was Suresh.

The waiter glanced around furtively before opening the vehicle's back door. Another shadowy figure stepped out, tall, broad-shouldered, wearing a long coat. The two exchanged a few words before Suresh handed over something small – a key card.

The SUV drove off into the mist, disappearing down the road toward the outskirts of town.

Karan straightened, his mind spinning. Why was Suresh involved? What was on that key card?

"Can you zoom in on the license plate?" he asked.

The shopkeeper squinted at the screen, trying to sharpen the image, but the footage was grainy – faces blurred into shapes, edges dissolving into static. Even so, a few details stood out: a figure slipping something small and rectangular into a pocket – likely a key card – and, just beyond that, the faint outline of a vehicle.

The plate was partly legible through the noise: WB02Z - .

West Bengal plates.

Karan exhaled sharply, rubbing his chin. West Bengal had long been a hub for human trafficking rings and illegal poaching networks operating through the border towns. Smuggling routes ran deep through the region, often protected by corrupt officials and influential figures. Could Sonia's murder be connected to something much bigger than he had imagined?

Karan stared at the CCTV monitor, jaw tight. He knew the law. Knew this wasn't how things were done. But there wasn't time to file paperwork or wait for officials who might already be compromised.

He unplugged the original hard drive from the DVR, pulled a tamper-proof evidence bag from his coat, and sealed it inside. It wasn't standard protocol, but it was all he could trust right now.

Turning to the shopkeeper, his voice was low and deliberate. "You never saw me. If anyone asks, your cameras weren't working that night. I may need a certificate from you later."

The man swallowed hard and nodded. "Understood, sir. But… be careful, Judge *sahib*. People around here don't like outsiders asking too many questions."

Karan narrowed his eyes. "That sounds like a warning. I will need to record a formal statement of your handover. Don't worry about Inspector Singh."

Karan stepped back outside, realising that the web was wider than he had thought. And Suresh was tangled deep within it. He contemplated and then pulled out his phone and dialled. "Inspector Singh? It's me. I have the original hard drive from the CCTV footage. You'll need to log it in and prepare to testify that you received it from me directly. You're going to have to make this official with a clean chain of custody, admissible in court."

There was a long pause on the other end. Then: "You're cutting it close, Judge. This could blow back."

"It already has," Karan replied, and hung up.

A shiver ran down his spine; not from the cold, but from the weight of realisation. This wasn't just a murder. It was a cover-up. A conspiracy. And he had just found the thread that could unravel it all.

His thoughts churned as he made his way back to the guesthouse, the weight of the evidence pressing heavily on his mind. The original hard disk and backup felt like a ticking bomb, one that could either expose the truth or put a target on his back.

Once inside his dimly lit room, he loosened his tie and poured himself a drink, the amber liquid swirling in the glass as he stared at the desk cluttered with notes, files, and the USB drive. This had become his ritual: one drink, just enough to settle his mind, to sift through the chaos and map out his next steps. Thank God, he had the constables with him all the time, working like shadows.

He kept his glass down and started writing in his leather journal – the missing CCTV footage, Sonia and Rohan's argument, Suresh's secret meeting, the West Bengal plates, the brutal leopard attack that seemed too conveniently timed, and the corrupt officers, especially Inspector Singh, who had obstructed the case at every turn. His hand moved mechanically as he jotted down notes in his worn leather journal, listing every piece of evidence, every suspect, every missing link.

His eyes grew heavier, his mind cycling through the sequence of events, but exhaustion was creeping in. Soon, the lines blurred, the words dissolving into the shadows of his mind as sleep claimed him.

But sleep brought no solace. Instead, it pulled him into a restless dream; a chaotic montage of flashes and whispers. He saw Sonia's lifeless body, her unspoken pleas frozen in her vacant eyes. Inspector Singh's smirking face loomed before him, his voice dripping with veiled threats. The leopard's growl echoed through the mist, blending into the distant screech of tyres from the black SUV disappearing into the night. Suresh's trembling hands, passing the key card to the shadowy figure, flashed before him. Then, suddenly, a gunshot rang out, and Karan woke with a start, his breath ragged, heart pounding in the silence.

The first rays of dawn filtered through the curtains, casting long shadows across the room. Karan wiped the sweat from his brow. The nightmare wasn't just a dream; it was his subconscious piecing together the truth. And the truth was damning.

He reached for his phone and dialled Priya. "Meet me at the courthouse in an hour. We're summoning Inspector Singh."

As he hung up, his resolve hardened. Today, they were going to shake the cage. And if Singh thought his threats would work, he was about to find out just how wrong he was.

Chapter 10
The Battle For Truth

The glow can't be dimmed if the source is from within.

The next morning, Karan wasted no time. He personally ensured that the pen drive containing the CCTV footage from the hotel and the shop was sent to the forensic lab for immediate analysis. The results could prove to be the missing piece in exposing the larger conspiracy.

He summoned Inspector Singh to the courthouse, the tension in the air almost suffocating as a storm brewed outside, thick clouds casting shadows through the narrow, dust-laden windows. Outside, a frenzy of reporters swarmed the entrance, their cameras flashing like relentless lightning. News vans lined the street, journalists shouting questions at anyone who passed. The case had become a media spectacle, and the public was hungry for answers. The courthouse staff struggled to control the chaos, while officers held back the press, their voices drowned beneath the clamour of speculation and accusations.

Amid the media frenzy, Rohan Thakur arrived under heavy police escort, his usual arrogance now masked behind dark sunglasses and a stiff posture. His father, MLA Thakur, followed closely behind, exuding quiet confidence as he spoke in hushed tones to his lawyer. They were here to observe, to gauge how much control they still had over the situation.

From another corner, Nisha Sharma and her husband, Principal Sharma, entered the courthouse as well. Nisha's face was carefully blank, but her hands trembled as she clutched the end of her *dupatta*. Her husband walked beside her, his grip firm on her elbow; a silent reminder of the control he wielded over her. Yet, as she sat at the back, her eyes found Karan. Unlike the others in the room, he radiated unwavering resolve, standing his ground against forces that would break a lesser man.

She admired his courage, the way he refused to be intimidated. A flicker of something she hadn't felt in years stirred inside her – hope. Hope that justice could still be served. Her husband's fingers pressed warningly against her wrist, yanking her attention back to reality, but her thoughts lingered on Karan's fearless defiance.

Inside, however, an eerie silence reigned, broken only by the rhythmic ticking of the grand clock on the courtroom wall.

Inside the old stone-walled courthouse, Karan sat behind his desk, flanked by Priya and Leela, his sharp-witted legal associates, and Kumar, the local expert assisting in the investigation. The wooden blinds cast slanted shadows across the room, adding to the ominous atmosphere. The weight of the confrontation ahead pressed against them all.

Inspector Singh arrived with slow, deliberate steps, his uniform crisp and his expression unreadable. His sharp eyes flickered with unreadable calculation, his lips pressed into a thin, controlled line. The polished leather of his boots echoed against the marble floor, each footstep amplifying the uneasy silence that had settled in the chamber. He strode in with calculated arrogance, barely glancing at Karan before taking a seat opposite them. He knew this wasn't a courtesy meeting.

Karan's voice was steely as he folded his hands on the desk. "Inspector, we need to talk about the compromised evidence in Sonia's murder case. Specifically, the CCTV footage."

Singh folded his arms, his expression unreadable. "I don't know what you mean, Judge Negi. The footage was lost due to a technical failure, nothing more. Evidence gets misplaced all the time, Judge. Maybe you should stick to your courtroom and let the police handle investigations."

Karan interjected, her voice sharp. "Misplaced? A witness is dead. The technician vanished, and the implicating footage, which shows Rohan and Sonia arguing, is apparently misplaced, and yet, there's no mention of it in your reports. That's not an accident. It's deliberate."

Singh arrogantly smirked, tilting his head slightly. "Judge *sahib*, you're making serious allegations. Be careful. The law applies to everyone, even you."

Karan leaned forward. "Don't insult my intelligence. Was the footage lost, or was it deliberately erased? And let's not forget that your department conveniently failed to secure the crime scene properly, leading to contaminated forensic samples. That's not negligence, Inspector. That's obstruction of justice. And under the law, for a man in uniform, that carries serious consequences."

Singh glared at Karan. "You're stepping into dangerous territory, all of you," he said, pointing towards Priya, Leela and Kumar, "Consider it friendly advice." This was war.

Priya scoffed, flipping through a file. "Your definition of the law is rather selective, Inspector. Several key witnesses in this case have disappeared or met 'accidental' deaths, including Sonia's neighbour. Care to explain?"

Kumar, who had been silent until now, placed a forensic report on the desk. "We also have evidence that warrants deeper investigation. You have not questioned the witnesses nor the hotel employees. Why?"

Singh's jaw twitched, a flicker of irritation flashing in his eyes as he looked at Kumar. "You think you're onto something, don't you? But let me give you a word of advice: there are forces at play here bigger than you, bigger than this courthouse. You poke too hard, you might find yourself buried under bureaucratic red tape... or worse."

Karan intervened, trying hard to control himself. "Was that a threat, Inspector? Because that sounded like criminal intimidation. Would you like me to draft a formal complaint?"

Singh realised he was going overboard, checked himself, but continued, his voice lowering. "I'm only saying you should know when to walk away. You might be a respected judge, but even you aren't untouchable."

For a brief second, it seemed as if things might turn physical. The air between them was charged with open hostility. Karan refused to flinch, meeting Singh's gaze with unwavering resolve. He wasn't going to be intimidated.

The room fell silent for a moment, the tension crackling like a live wire.

Across the room, Nisha sat stiffly, her fingers twisting the edge of her *dupatta* in her lap as she observed the confrontation. Her husband's presence beside her was suffocating, but she couldn't take her eyes off Karan. His unwavering confidence, the way he faced down powerful men without a shred of fear, stirred something in her, something long buried. She had seen too many people bow to fear, yet here was a man standing against it, unmoved, relentless. Her admiration was cautious, but undeniable.

She took a deep breath, hoping no one noticed the way her gaze lingered on him for a fraction too long. But Leela did. Seated nearby, she caught the fleeting expression in Nisha's eyes: a mixture of longing and unspoken hope. She made a mental note, filing it away along with the many unspoken tensions thickening the air in the room.

Kumar, sensing the heat rising, interjected. "We're not accusing you, yet. But if we find evidence linking law enforcement to the cover-up, you'll be looking at criminal conspiracy charges under various provisions of the *Bhartiya Nyaya Sanhita*. Now, I suggest you start cooperating before this escalates."

Singh's fists clenched at his sides. His face remained impassive, but the controlled breathing and tightening of his shoulders told a different story. He was cornered, and he knew it.

Singh gave a short, dry laugh – the kind that held no amusement. "Still walking the straight line, Judge?" he said quietly. "Just remember – around here, the straight path's the one that leads off the cliff."

The air in the room crackled with further tension, and the two men locked in a silent standoff. Singh's jaw clenched, but he said nothing. Priya let out a slow breath. "That man is dangerous," she whispered to herself.

Singh's smirk faltered for the briefest second. Priya let out a breath she hadn't realised she was holding. "He's rattled. That's a good sign. I can see beads of sweat on his forehead."

Karan clenched his fists. This wasn't just about Sonia anymore. It was about a system built to protect those who thought themselves untouchable. Tactfully, he abruptly stopped. Singh was asked to leave the room and wait outside. Singh stomped out, red-faced.

Next, Karan's gaze locked onto Rohan's. "We have a lot to discuss."

Rohan adjusted the cuffs of his expensive blazer, his gaze sweeping the room with mild amusement, as though the entire proceeding were a mere formality, an inconvenience to be brushed aside. Despite his carefully curated composure, there was something in his eyes: a flicker of calculation, of measured restraint, that hinted at the pressure closing in around him.

Rohan smirked as he settled into the chair across from Karan, leaning back and acting like a man with nothing to fear. "You really think you have something on me, Judge?"

Karan didn't flinch. "We have CCTV footage placing you at the hotel entrance the night Sonia was murdered. You were seen arguing with her. Care to explain what that was about?"

Rohan chuckled, shaking his head. "An argument? Is that a crime now? Sonia was always… difficult. She liked to make a scene."

Priya's voice was sharp. "Difficult? Is that how you justify what happened to her?"

Rohan's smirk faltered for just a second before he recovered. "Listen, I had nothing to do with her death. That girl had a lot of enemies."

Karan narrowed his eyes. "Enemies? Like who?"

Rohan shrugged. "Maybe you should look at her personal life. She wasn't exactly an angel."

Karan's patience was wearing thin. "We also have footage of Suresh handing off a key card to someone in a black SUV that night. Do you know anything about that?"

Rohan's smirk disappeared completely this time. "I don't think you know who you're dealing with, but you're making a mistake coming after me."

Karan leaned forward. "The only mistake would be letting you walk out of here without answering for what you did. The evidence is stacking up, and once forensics confirms the missing footage, there will be no place left for you to hide."

Rohan's hands clenched into fists on the table. He was losing his composure. MLA Thakur's jaw tightened as he glared at his son.

Rohan, catching the glance, straightened slightly, but made no effort to acknowledge his father beyond a fleeting look, one that carried the barest hint of defiance.

Inside, Karan kept his gaze locked on Rohan. "You think your father's influence will save you? Think again. Justice doesn't work that way."

Vinod stood at the side, watching the exchange with an unreadable expression. He turned to his lawyer and whispered something before stepping out of the room.

As the proceedings wrapped up for the day, the air inside the courthouse remained thick with unease. Karan quietly observed everyone dispersing.

Inspector Singh walked in abruptly, adjusting his belt, his expression unreadable. "We'll see where your so-called evidence takes you, Judge," he muttered before turning on his heel and exiting the room. The clatter of his boots against the floor echoed ominously, leaving an unspoken warning hanging in the air.

MLA Thakur's irritation with Rohan was barely concealed beneath his composed exterior. The Thakur father and son exchanged looks, a battle of wills that spoke louder than words. Karan saw the MLA look at his son as reckless, unpredictable, a liability. And MLA Thakur was growing weary of cleaning up his mess.

Without a word, the politician turned on his heel and strode out of the room, his movements brisk, final. Rohan watched him go, his smirk slipping just a fraction before he schooled his features back into their usual mask of indifference.

Karan glanced around the room. Nisha remained seated, her hands still gripping the fabric of her *dupatta*. Her husband's fingers dug into her arm, urging her to stand, but her gaze lingered on Karan for just a moment longer. There was something in her eyes, respect, hope, or perhaps the recognition of a man who refused to be cowed by power.

Leela, watching everything unfold, murmured under her breath, “This isn’t over.”

Priya snapped her file shut. “No. It’s just beginning.”

As Karan stepped out of the courtroom, the cacophony of the media storm hit him like a wave. Flashbulbs went off, reporters shoved microphones in his face, shouting questions about the inquiry. He raised a hand, signalling for calm, before giving a measured response. “Justice takes time, but we will not be deterred. The truth will come out.” The walls around the guilty were closing in, and soon, there would be no escape.

Singh deliberately walked past him slowly as he whispered, “If I were you, I’d leave this case alone.”

Karan met his gaze, unflinching. “I don’t respond well to threats, Inspector. I don’t back down from the truth.”

As he walked down the steps, Karan’s mind was already racing ahead to the next move. He had rattled them – Inspector Singh, MLA Thakur, and most of all, Rohan. But rattling them wasn’t enough. He needed to break them.

Leela joined him, flipping through her notes. “That went as expected. Singh won’t back down, and Rohan… well, he’s too arrogant to know when he’s cornered.”

As they descended the courthouse steps, Priya and Kumar caught up with them. Priya held her phone in one hand. “I just got word from the forensics team. They’re analysing the footage now, but they’ve already noticed something interesting.”

Karan stopped, turning toward her. "What is it?"

She glanced around, lowering her voice. "The timestamp on the footage we recovered from the shop across the street – it's off. Someone tampered with it. We're not just dealing with a missing segment of CCTV footage. We're dealing with a deliberate alteration of the timeline."

Leela frowned. "So didn't they just erase the footage? Why did they modify it to create a false narrative?"

"Exactly." Priya exhaled sharply. "If we can restore the original timestamps, we might find out what really happened that night."

Kumar nodded. "They're dangerous. If what we suspect is true, they're not acting alone."

"Which makes them even more dangerous," Karan replied, his tone measured. "But arrogance also makes people reckless. And recklessness leads to mistakes."

Before Priya could respond, they heard a sound of hurried footsteps. Karan turned to see Nisha walking towards him. There was a quiet grace to the way she moved, but beneath it, Karan sensed an unsteady tremor, as if she were caught in an invisible bind she couldn't break free from. Her slender frame was wrapped in a deep maroon *sari* that contrasted against her pale skin. Her dark eyes held an intensity that was both fearful and determined, darting between him and the looming figure of her husband, who stood a few steps behind her, watching with an unspoken warning. For a moment, their gazes met, and in that fleeting instant, he saw more than fear; he saw a woman weighing the risk of speaking against the cost of remaining silent.

She gathered her courage and approached. "Karan… sorry, Judge Negi," she murmured, correcting herself in a voice barely above a whisper. "There's something you should know."

Karan studied her carefully. Her hands trembled slightly, but she kept them folded in front of her, masking her nerves. Behind her, Principal Sharma shifted impatiently, his grip tightening on her arm.

"What is it, Mrs. Sharma?" Karan asked, keeping his tone calm and neutral.

Before Nisha could speak, her husband interjected. "My wife has nothing to say, Judge. We were just leaving."

For a fraction of a second, something flashed in Nisha's eyes. Was it frustration, or desperation? But it was gone just as quickly before Karan could decipher it. She cast Karan a fleeting look, something unspoken passing between them before she turned and followed her husband into the crowd.

Leela sighed. "She wants to talk. But she's terrified."

Karan's jaw tightened. "We need to find a way to reach her. She might hold the missing piece of this puzzle."

Leela, arms crossed, tapped her pen against her notepad. "The question is, how do we get her away from her husband long enough to do it?"

"We need to be careful," Kumar added, his usual analytical demeanour clouded with concern. "If we push too hard, she might shut down completely or worse, her husband might take drastic action. We all know how much control he has over her."

Priya exhaled sharply. "We also can't ignore the fact that Nisha's hesitation might mean she knows something about Rohan or even MLA Thakur. If she's connected to this in any way, she's in just as much danger as we are."

Karan nodded, his mind already formulating the next step. "We let her know we're listening. No pressure. Just an opportunity for her to come forward when she's ready. In the meantime, we focus on what we have."

Leela scribbled something in her notepad. "We also need to confront Vinod, and we need eyes on Rohan and his father. They're going to retaliate. They won't just sit back and watch while we dismantle their cover-up."

Karan met her gaze, determination hardening in his expression. "Then let's be ready for them."

Kumar nodded. "And Suresh. He's the weak link. He knows more than he's letting on. We need to meet him again, but in a way that doesn't put him or us at risk."

Priya tapped her phone. "I'll track the technician. If he's still in town, we need to get to him before they do."

Karan glanced toward the darkening sky. "We split up. Leela and I will try to arrange another meeting with Vinod and Rohan. Priya, you and Kumar find Suresh and the technician. If we can get them to talk, we might finally have enough to dismantle this whole operation. Both teams will have one constable."

Leela smiled. "Time to shake the nest and see what crawls out."

Priya held up her phone. "That includes the forensic analysis of the footage, the tampered timestamps, we need to find out what was altered and why."

As they walked toward the parking lot, Karan's phone buzzed. He pulled it out, looking confused as he read the message: 'We need to talk. Meet me at the old library, midnight. Come alone.'

No name. No sender.

Karan pocketed the phone, his mind already piecing together the possibilities. Someone was ready to talk. But was it a lead or a trap?

Also, was he going overboard in this inquiry?

Chapter 11
The Meeting at the Library

Cages aren't made of iron, they're made of thoughts.
- Albert Einstein

The message about the midnight meeting still lingered in Karan's mind as he sat in his chamber, reviewing reports with Priya and Leela. But before he could act on it, Kumar entered, looking scared.

"The hotel IT technician, Arun, who was unwell, is gone."

"Gone? What do you mean, gone?" Karan asked sharply, looking up from the file, his voice cutting through the eerie quiet of the dimly lit office.

Kumar ran a hand through his damp hair, the tension visible in the creases of his forehead.

Priya pulled out Arun's file. "Okay, I went through Arun Dey's file. He worked in IT at Thakur's hotel, but his records are clean, no criminal history, nothing suspicious."

Kumar leaned back. "Until now.

Kumar snapped his fingers. "Wait, wait... if Arun was accessing hotel records, he might have downloaded something before they got to him. If he stored backups..."

Leela sat up. "His email. His cloud storage. His USB drives."

"His house was found unlocked this morning. No sign of forced entry, and his belongings were untouched, except for his work laptop and external drives. Those are missing."

A gust of wind howled outside, rattling the old glass windows. Karan's fingers tightened around the edge of the desk. "That means someone took him and cleaned up after," Priya muttered, pacing, her heels clicking against the polished wooden floor.

"Or worse," Leela added, her voice grim. She crossed her arms, glancing at the swirling mist outside, where the looming shadow of Pemayangtse Monastery was barely visible through the shrouded mist.

Karan's mind was racing.

"Find out everything about his last movements. Who he met, where he went. If someone took him, they're tying up loose ends. We need to get to Suresh before they do."

A call interrupted their discussion. Arun had been found but barely alive.

They rushed to the hospital, weaving through the winding roads of Pelling as fog curled around their vehicle, swallowing the headlights. The silhouette of the Rabdentse Ruins loomed in the distance, its ancient stones barely visible through the mist, standing as a ghostly reminder of fallen empires. The faint glimmer of Khecheopalri Lake was swallowed in darkness, its sacred waters whispering secrets no outsider could hear. Even the otherwise bustling Helipad Viewpoint, known for its sweeping vistas, was desolate, lost in the shadows of the night.

Every landmark felt altered by the eerie silence, transforming Pelling from a picturesque retreat into a town harbouring unseen dangers.

The emergency room was a flurry of activity when they arrived. The fluorescent lights flickered weakly, casting eerie shadows along the linoleum floor. Arun Dey lay unconscious on a stretcher, his face swollen beyond recognition, his breathing laboured and uneven. Dark bruises marred his arms and ribs, and his fingers were bent at unnatural angles, showing signs of a struggle, of torture.

A doctor approached, his expression tight with worry. "He has multiple fractures, internal bleeding, and signs of blunt force trauma. We're shifting him to the ICU. He's lucky to be alive."

As the stretcher began to roll past them, Karan instinctively stepped closer, his presence looming over the battered man. The technician's eyelids fluttered weakly, his lips parting as if to speak. A raspy breath escaped, but no words came, only a faint, strangled sound of pain.

"He's trying to say something," Leela murmured urgently.

Karan leaned in. "Stay with me. Who did this?"

A flicker of recognition passed through the technician's swollen eyes. His lips moved again, trembling, forming syllables that refused to come out. Frustration, pain, and desperation swam in his gaze before his head lolled to the side, consciousness slipping away.

The doctor interjected quickly. "He's in no condition to speak. We need to stabilise him first."

Karan straightened, exhaling sharply. "Make sure he's protected. No visitors except authorised personnel. If they tried to kill him once, they'll try again. I'll put two constables day and night outside his room."

The doctor nodded, signalling to the staff as the Arun disappeared behind the ICU doors. Karan clenched his fists at his sides. Whoever had done this had wanted him silenced. And they had nearly succeeded.

Karan stared at the man's motionless body, his stomach twisting with a mixture of rage and helplessness. Someone had wanted him silenced, but not just killed.

The hospital corridors seemed to stretch endlessly as Karan and his team walked to the waiting area. The weight of what they had just witnessed pressed heavily upon them.

"Someone had beaten him within an inch of his life, stolen his laptop, and wiped his drives. He found something. And they didn't want him talking," concluded Karan.

Leela shuddered. "They left him alive, though."

"That's because they think they got everything," Karan said. "Or..." He glanced at Kumar.

Kumar finished his thought. "...Or they were in a rush. If he wakes up and remembers what he found..." He let out a low whistle. "They'll come back to finish the job."

Priya's grip on her phone tightened. "Do we even know what he was looking at before the attack?"

Karan shook his head. "Not yet. But it had to be something in the hotel's digital records; CCTV footage, guest logs, financial transactions."

Karan nodded. "If he wakes up, we ask him directly. If he doesn't..." He met Kumar's gaze, "Find his digital footprint."

Karan turned to Leela, his jaw set with determination. "Leela, you head to his house. Go through his files, see if he left any notes or encrypted data behind. If anything looks suspicious, flag it immediately. Take one constable with you."

Leela nodded, already reaching for her phone to call the driver. "We'll dig through everything. If they wanted to erase something, it means it was important."

Karan looked at Kumar. "We'll head to find Suresh. He's the last link we have. If they get to the technician, they won't stop there."

Priya hesitated, glancing between them. "Be careful, Karan. Whoever's behind this, they're escalating fast."

Karan gave her a reassuring nod before stepping toward the vehicle with Kumar. As they drove off into the mist-covered streets, the town of Pelling seemed to shrink around them, its quiet beauty masking the deadly game playing out in the shadows.

As the vehicle wound through the desolate roads of Pelling, the looming presence of Kanchenjunga stood ghostly in the distance, its snow-capped peaks barely visible under the thick shroud of fog. The narrow streets leading into the town's poorer outskirts were eerily silent, the occasional flickering streetlamp casting long, distorted shadows. The constable followed behind on a bike.

They arrived at the slums on the outskirts of town, where Suresh had been staying. His makeshift hut stood in eerie silence, the door ajar. Karan's instincts kicked in immediately.

"Careful," he murmured to Kumar as they stepped inside.

The inside of the hut was in shambles – clothes and utensils strewn across the floor, a chair split clean in half, and shards of glass crunching underfoot. The air was thick with the scent of metal – sharp, tangy, and eerily familiar.

Karan paused, nostrils flaring as a dull recognition stirred in him. It was only when Kumar gasped and pointed to the dark stains smeared across the dirt floor that the suspicion hardened into certainty.

Kumar gasped, pointing to the dark stains smeared across the dirt floor. "It's fresh."

He crouched beside the marks, touching the edge of one stain with the back of his hand – it was cool, sticky. "Whatever happened, it was recent. But where's the body?" He murmured.

They searched through the debris, eyes narrowing as Kumar found Suresh's nametag, torn and stained with blood. "They didn't just take him. They made a point."

Karan's mind was already connecting the dots. "They wanted us to find this. It's a warning. They know we're close."

Kumar exchanged a wary glance with him. "If Suresh is still alive, he won't be for long. We need to move fast."

Karan nodded. "Let's go. We'll find Vinod next, if anyone knows what's going on, it's him."

They climbed into the vehicle, the engine roaring to life as they sped away from the slums. The winding roads of Pelling felt narrower, the mist thickening like a suffocating veil. The town's usual tranquillity had turned sinister, every shadow stretching too long, every flickering streetlamp barely cutting through the darkness. He was grateful that they were provided with an expert driver to navigate these hilly roads.

As they pulled up to a rundown lodge on the outskirts, a cold dread settled in Karan's stomach. They had barely stepped out of the car when they spotted Vinod sitting hunched on the porch, a cigarette trembling between his fingers. His eyes darted around like a hunted animal, his usual swagger replaced by sheer terror.

"I… I can't help you anymore," he stammered. His hands trembled as he took a drag from a cigarette.

Karan studied him, noting the deep bags under his eyes, the way his knee bounced erratically. "You've seen something, haven't you?"

Vinod swallowed hard. "They got to Suresh. And the tech guy. They'll come for me next. Please… I just want to get out of here."

Karan's patience was thin. "Who's giving the orders? Is it MLA Thakur?"

Vinod hesitated, his eyes darting around as though expecting someone to be listening. "I… I don't know much. I swear. But there's something… Sonia had evidence. A secret file, maybe… she kept notes, evidence… things…"

Karan's gaze sharpened. "Where is it?"

Vinod swallowed hard, his fingers twitching. "I don't know. She never told me. But she was extremely careful.

She only trusted a few people. I know she had a heated argument with Rohan before she died. And… Nisha. Sonia used to talk to Nisha sometimes. That's all I know. I swear."

Kumar shot Karan a worried look. If MLA Thakur was afraid, that meant whoever was behind this was far more dangerous than they had anticipated. But now, they had a new lead and two names that could bring them closer to the truth.

As they left Vinod's hideout, Karan's mind churned with thoughts. The pieces were starting to align, but something didn't sit right with him. Nisha. Could she really be as helpless as she seemed? Or was she playing a careful game, one where both Rohan and he were unwitting pawns?

"You're quiet," Kumar noted as they got into the vehicle.

Karan exhaled slowly. "Something isn't adding up. Sonia confided in Nisha. She knew something, but she never came forward. Now, she wants to meet in secret? What if she's not just a victim in this? What if she's hiding something?"

Kumar considered this, his expression pensive. "You think she's involved?"

Karan shook his head. "I don't know. But I can't ignore the possibility that she might be playing both sides. I need to be careful."

As they drove through the winding roads back into town, the mist clung thick to the mountains, wrapping around the streets like a ghostly shroud. The library's warm glow stood in stark contrast to the night, beckoning him inside. Whatever answers Nisha had, he needed to hear them, but he had to be ready for the possibility that she was not just a frightened woman seeking help, but a woman hiding her own secrets.

The scent of old books filled the air as he found her standing by the large window, the golden glow of a desk lamp casting shadows across her delicate features. She looked smaller here, lost in thought, her fingers lightly tracing the edge of a hardcover novel. There was an exhaustion in her posture, but also a quiet strength.

"I shouldn't be here," she murmured, glancing over her shoulder nervously.

"But you came anyway," Karan said softly, stepping closer.

She inhaled sharply, nodding. "Because… you're the only one who's listening."

Karan studied her, the way her fingers trembled slightly as she ran them along the spines of books. "Your husband?"

Her lips parted, but she hesitated. Finally, she whispered, "He doesn't just control me, Karan. He… he hurts me."

Karan's hands clenched into fists. "How long?"

"Since the beginning," she admitted, voice barely audible. "I thought marrying him would save me. Instead, it caged me."

She exhaled shakily, looking past Karan, as though staring at something far beyond the walls of the library. "I was nineteen when I ran away. My father refused to send me to college, saying education was wasted on a girl. My brother was given everything: tuition, new clothes, and a future. But me? My only future was marriage. I wanted more. So I left. And when Ravi proposed, I thought I was securing my place in the world. But all I did was trade one prison for another."

Karan's jaw tightened as he absorbed her words. "Why didn't you leave?"

She let out a bitter laugh. "Where would I go? No family, no money. And he made sure I felt that way - isolated, dependent. Every bruise, every cruel word, it was always followed by a reminder that I was nothing without him."

Karan reached out, his fingers grazing her wrist lightly, reassuringly. "You deserve better than this, Nisha."

She looked up at him then, her dark eyes swimming with uncertainty and something else. Something neither of them dared to name.

The tension between them was undeniable. His thumb brushed against her wrist, and she didn't pull away. Instead, she stepped closer, the space between them narrowing until the only thing separating them was restraint.

"Karan..." she whispered, but before she could say anything else, he leaned in, his lips capturing hers in a slow kiss. She responded hesitantly at first, then with a quiet urgency, as though savouring something forbidden.

When they pulled apart, her breath was uneven, her gaze searching his. "This is dangerous."

Karan nodded, his own breathing unsteady. "I know. But so is staying silent."

For the first time, she smiled, a sad but genuine curve of her lips. "Then help me find my voice."

Karan nodded. He wasn't just going to find the truth; he was going to protect her.

She hesitated, glancing towards the window, gathering her thoughts. "I… I don't know who to trust anymore," she admitted, her fingers tightening around his. "But I know Sonia trusted me. And now she's dead."

Karan leaned forward, his voice calm but firm. "What did she tell you?"

Nisha exhaled shakily. "Not much directly. But I know she was afraid. She told me she had proof, something that could bring everything to light. She was meeting someone the night she was killed."

Karan's pulse quickened. "Who?"

She hesitated before finally whispering, "Rohan."

Silence stretched between them as the weight of her words sank in. Karan's mind raced. Rohan had been at the hotel that night. The CCTV footage had caught him arguing with Sonia. What was Suresh doing? But why had Sonia agreed to meet him if she knew she was in danger?

Nisha swallowed hard. "I overheard them talking once. Sonia warned Rohan that she wasn't afraid to go public. She said she had something that would ruin his family. Rohan told her she didn't understand what she was getting into. That she wasn't fighting just him, she was fighting people far more powerful."

Karan frowned. "Did she ever tell you what exactly she had? Where did she keep it?"

Nisha shook her head. "No. But..." she hesitated, her brows furrowing. "Before she died, she gave me a key. She said if anything happened to her, I should use it to find the truth. But I was too scared. I didn't know what it unlocked, and I didn't want to get involved."

"Do you still have the key?"

She reached into the folds of her shawl and slowly placed a small, ornate key onto the table. The brass gleamed under the dim light, its intricate design hinting at something far more significant than a simple lock.

Karan picked it up, weighing it between his fingers. "This could be what got Sonia killed."

Nisha's eyes met his, and for the first time, there was something more than fear in them; there was trust. A fragile, dangerous trust.

"What happens now?" she whispered.

Karan pocketed the key. "Now, we find out what this unlocks. And we find out just how deep this conspiracy goes."

As the rain continued to lash against the windows, Karan couldn't shake the growing unease settling in his chest. If Sonia had been willing to die for this secret, then they were all running out of time.

And Nisha... she was now more entangled in this than ever before.

Chapter 12
Key To The Truth

A ship is always safe at the shore, but that is not what it is built for.

Karan pocketed the small brass key as he met Nisha's gaze. Her dark eyes glistened with unspoken fear, and for a fleeting moment, he saw something else – trust. A fragile, dangerous trust.

Before he could speak, a muffled sound reached them, the unmistakable crunch of hurried footsteps outside the library.

Nisha's breath hitched. "Someone's here," she whispered.

Karan's instincts flared. He stepped forward, positioning himself between her and the entrance. The old wooden shelves cast long shadows in the dim light, and the faint scent of paper and dust seemed suddenly suffocating.

A second later, the library door creaked open.

A figure lurked at the threshold, silhouetted against the dim streetlight. Karan barely caught a glimpse of the man's shape before he turned and bolted.

"Stay here," Karan ordered, but Nisha grabbed his wrist.

"No!" she hissed. "They're watching me. If they see me with you, my husband…"

Karan hesitated for half a second, then nodded. "Lock the door behind me."

Without another word, he sprinted into the night.

The mist had thickened, wrapping around the streets like ghostly tendrils. The figure was already halfway down the street, a dark blur weaving through the fog. Karan pushed forward, his heartbeat hammering against his ribs. Whoever this was, he had been waiting for him and Nisha. They knew she was talking.

The figure turned sharply into a narrow alley between two shuttered tea shops. Karan followed, his breath coming in controlled bursts. The alley was damp, the scent of wet stone filling his nostrils. The man ahead of him slipped, scrambling for balance before vanishing behind a stack of wooden crates.

Karan slowed, ears straining.

A creak. A shift in the darkness.

And then, an ambush.

A second figure lunged from the shadows, swinging something heavy. Karan barely ducked in time. The iron rod whooshed past his head, striking the stone wall with a sharp clang. He pivoted, driving his elbow into the attacker's ribs.

The man grunted but recovered quickly, swinging again. Karan dodged left, catching the edge of the blow on his shoulder. Pain flared, but he didn't stop. He backed off just enough to lure the man in, then exploded forward, landing a brutal punch to the jaw. The man hit the ground, out cold.

Karan turned just in time to see the first man, the one he had been chasing, disappearing down another path.

Damn it.

He knelt beside the unconscious man, quickly patting down his pockets. No ID. No phone. But something glinted in the moonlight: a hotel keycard.

Karan turned it over. *Room 306. Pelling View Inn.*

Karan's grip tightened on the hotel keycard. The mist curled around him, thick and suffocating, as if the town itself were conspiring to keep its secrets buried. His shoulder throbbed where the iron rod had clipped him, but he ignored the pain. He had a lead, Room 306 at Pelling View Inn.

But first, Nisha.

He jogged back toward the library, moving swiftly through the deserted lanes. The old wooden doors were still shut, just as he had left them. He rapped twice, three quick knocks, one slow, the signal they had agreed upon. No answer.

A flicker of unease crawled down his spine. He knocked again.

Nothing.

His pulse quickened. He tried the handle – locked. He stepped back, scanning the street. No sign of the attackers. No sign of Nisha.

Then he saw it.

At the far end of the library's side wall, a faint trail of fresh footprints in the damp mud led away, disappearing into the mist. Smart. She hadn't waited for him; she had run.

Karan allowed himself a brief moment of relief. She was alive. And if she had followed their plan, she would have already made her way to safety.

Still, he had no time to waste. Room 306. That's where the answers were waiting. He rushed back to the hotel.

Pelling View Inn was the kind of place where anonymity was expected. A dimly lit lobby, a tired-looking receptionist, and a distinct lack of questions. Perfect for someone looking to hide in plain sight.

Karan approached the front desk, keeping his expression neutral. The receptionist, a wiry man with a thick moustache and bloodshot eyes, barely looked up from his newspaper.

"Need a room?" he mumbled.

Karan slid the keycard onto the counter. "Already have one. Room 306."

The receptionist's fingers twitched slightly before he recovered. "Ah. Right. Your friend's already up there."

Karan forced a casual nod. "Yeah. Thought I'd surprise him."

The man hesitated, then shrugged. "Go ahead."

Karan took the stairs two at a time, his body tense. On the third floor, he paused outside Room 306, pressing his ear to the door.

Silence.

His fingers tightened around the keycard. There was only one way to find out. Sliding the card through the reader, he pushed the door open, slowly, carefully.

The room was dark. The heavy curtains were drawn, blocking out even the faint glow of the streetlights. The air was thick with the scent of sweat and stale cigarettes.

Karan stepped inside, his gaze sweeping across the small space. A bed, unmade. A wooden desk littered with crumpled papers. A half-empty whiskey bottle near the window.

And then, in the dim light, he saw it.

A photograph was pinned to the wall above the desk. It was grainy, taken from a distance, but the subject was unmistakable.

Nisha.

His stomach twisted. Someone had been following her. Watching her. And now, they knew she had talked.

A creak came from behind.

Karan spun just as a shadow lunged from the darkness. The shadow moved fast, too fast.

Karan barely had time to throw himself sideways as the attacker swung a knife at him, the blade slicing through the air where his throat had been moments ago. He crashed into the small bedside table, sending the whiskey bottle shattering against the floor.

A second swing came, but Karan twisted, catching the attacker's wrist mid-strike. The dim light barely revealed the man's face: a scarred jawline, piercing eyes, and the stench of sweat and desperation.

They struggled, muscles locked in a brutal contest for control of the weapon.

Karan drove his knee into the man's ribs. A grunt. The attacker staggered but didn't let go of the knife.

Instead, he switched tactics, lunging low, trying to drive the blade into Karan's gut.

Big mistake.

Karan twisted his body, trapping the attacker's wrist between his arm and chest. Then, with practised precision, he wrenched the man's arm back, hard.

A sickening snap echoed through the room.

The attacker screamed, the knife clattering to the floor as he cradled his broken wrist.

Karan didn't waste time. He grabbed the man by his shirt and slammed him against the wall, pinning him with sheer force.

"Who sent you?" Karan hissed, breathing hard.

The attacker's face twisted in pain, but there was something else, too: defiance. "You have no idea what you're up against."

Karan's grip tightened. "Try me."

The man let out a bitter chuckle. "You think this is about a dead girl? It's bigger than that. You're already dead, Judge. You just don't know it yet."

Karan narrowed his eyes. Before he could push further, the man suddenly jerked forward, his eyes rolling back.

Karan barely managed to step aside as the attacker collapsed with a small dart protruding from his neck.

Someone had shot him from a distance.

Karan's instincts flared. Sniper.

He ducked low, keeping away from the window, heart pounding. Whoever was behind this didn't want their operative talking.

He grabbed the fallen knife and bolted for the door. Then his eyes landed on something else.

A burned envelope in the trash bin.

Karan pulled it out carefully, the edges singed, but some of the text was still legible. His eyes narrowed as he read the words stamped on the remaining scrap of paper: "*R. Thakur – CONFIDENTIAL*"

Rohan.

Karan's mind raced. What did this man want with Rohan? Was Rohan just another pawn, or was he deeper in this than he let on?

There was only one way to find out.

It was time to confront Rohan Thakur.

As he stepped out into the damp night air, he turned over Nisha's words in his mind. *If anything happens to me, use this to find the truth*, Nisha had said, handing over the key.

What truth had Sonia been so desperate to protect? And why had she trusted Nisha of all people?

The quiet streets of Pelling had never felt this hostile before; every flickering streetlamp, every shifting shadow in the mist, felt like a watching eye.

He adjusted his coat, pulling the collar up against the cold, but the chill wasn't from the mountain air; it was from the growing realisation that he had just crossed an invisible threshold.

A low hum of crickets and distant temple bells filled the silence, but Karan's mind was too busy dissecting possibilities. He had to figure out what the key unlocked and fast.

Nisha's confession had changed everything. Sonia hadn't just been in trouble; she had been hunted. And now, by taking this key, Karan had just painted a target on his own back.

His car was parked a few streets down, near an old tea stall that had long closed for the night. The constables were not to be seen. He regretted not taking the driver along. As he reached for the door handle, a movement in the reflection of the window caught his eye.

A shadow. Someone was watching.

Karan tensed, keeping his breathing steady. He didn't turn around, didn't react. Instead, he calmly opened the door and got inside, locking it.

His hands gripped the steering wheel, his pulse drumming in his ears. He took a slow breath before adjusting the rearview mirror.

There. A dark figure standing at the corner of the street, barely visible in the mist. Watching. Waiting.

Karan didn't hesitate. He started the engine, the low rumble cutting through the silence. Instead of driving away, he flicked his headlights on full beam, illuminating the figure.

A man. Medium build, dark jacket, partially obscured by the fog.

For a moment, neither of them moved.

Then, the man turned sharply and disappeared into a side alley.

Karan clenched his jaw. He could follow him, but he knew it was a trap. Whoever was after him wanted him to react. Not tonight. He had more pressing matters. Also, he was alone. He gripped the key in his pocket.

What had Sonia died for? And where did this key lead?

There was only one way to find out.

⚖

Back at his guesthouse, Karan locked the door, checking it twice before finally shrugging off his coat. His shoulder ached from earlier, a dull reminder of the night's chaos.

Whiskey first. Then thinking.

He poured a glass, watching the golden liquid swirl before taking a slow sip. The warmth spread through his chest, grounding him. A moment of solitude before the storm.

He sat by the fireplace, the dim glow casting flickering shadows across the wooden walls.

Then, he scribbled it all out in his leather journal:

The Puzzle So Far: Sonia's Key; what did it mean to unlock?, The Hotel Technician in ICU, Suresh's

Disappearance, Nisha's Role? What was her relation with Rohan? The Watcher Tonight?

Karan took another sip, exhaling slowly.

The pieces were coming together, but something still wasn't right. Sonia had been afraid of something bigger than Rohan.

Karan set the glass down and flipped through the pages filled with scribbled notes, contradictions, and unanswered questions. The flickering fire cast elongated shadows across the room, making the space feel smaller, more suffocating.

His mind churned through possibilities, the day's events swirling in his thoughts like a restless tide. The pieces were scattered, but he was getting closer. Too close.

Karan exhaled slowly, rubbing his temple with his free hand. His body ached from the fight at the hotel, from the weight of the case, from the exhaustion creeping into his bones. But his mind refused to rest.

He set the notebook beside him, his notes open to the list of agenda for the next day.

- F*ind out what this key unlocks.*
- *Ensure the technician's safety.*
- *Find Suresh before it's too late.*
- *Confront Rohan – again.*
- *The Attacker – the papers from room 306.*

The fire crackled softly, the room growing warmer, the whiskey settling in his veins.

That night, sleep eluded him again. He reached for the leather-bound journal again. The pages opened with a sigh, and the pen moved:

Promises and Dreams

Why can't you be as much mine as I am yours
Why can't you understand what my heart endures
That tug in my heart that you so beautifully create
With all these chains around us, oh, will it ever deflate?
Every word you say of your feelings for me, I do believe
But when reality and you just don't ever act accordingly, I grieve
I clamour for our happiness that is continually playing hide n seek
Then deftly into my own shell, I simply go, dejected and meek
So many thoughts and dreams that are shown by you
Will they ever see the aura of the morning dew
Are these just talks that will never see the light of day
Why are you ever so cautious and just wanting to have it this way??
I know, I know the guard is on, the security is paramount
But look, it's killing my fervour with its ghostly daunt
Even the instant pleasure of a date with my most desired mate
Is something I think I'll never be able to have on my plate?
With dejection and sorrow filled in my heart, I sit to wallow
Sometimes you offer me a bite which is more than I can swallow
The facts I face just weaken my resolve
And into the eerie darkness all my dreams dissolve.

When memories altogether flood my messed-up mind
They invoke an eerie experience of many a kind
Were they for real, or were they just a figment
Did I see them from up close or from a distance
Things that happened and all those that didn't
Few kept me satiated, many clamouring within
Were they all a real manifestation?
Or were they just a part of my wild imagination??
Some show me paradise with their simple allure
Some take me to the darkest of nadirs galore
Be it the crest or the fall of the eventful ride
I experience both, again, waiting for the feelings to subside
And as my thoughts bleed over the crucifix of the matter
I see there's less for me to cry over and more to flatter
They bathe me with happiness and immense positivity
I won't exchange anything to live in this memory
Thankful to those who took me to the heights of ecstasy
Ending up in the thorns of the game... in this life's fantasy
And as I have no choice but to go on with life, which is bitchy
I watch out for events that single out a strange synchronicity
Whatever they are, these treasured memories of mine
This flood eventually transports me into another place and time...
My heart aches in sadness & secret tears still flow,
What it means to have you and still to lose you, will U ever know?

Every time U conform to the "should be's", I lose you
I've lost, lost you
as the moments pass, I sadly realise.
Is it really only the chains that hold and bind you sore
Or perhaps it is just that you are not wanting any more
Cheated and hurt, I hold those scarring thoughts,
My life seems to be ending in conspiratory knots.
Today, I thought, I saw a rainbow lurking in that domain
Can that come alive? Will we ever dance in the rain??

He kept the pen and journal aside and leaned back against the chair. Picking up the key and clutching it between his fingers, he sat still.

After a while, his eyelids grew heavy as the thoughts tangled together, twisting into fractured images: Sonia's bloodstained face, Nisha's trembling hands, the shadowy figure in the mist, and the weight of the key pressing into his palm like a silent accusation.

His breathing slowed.

The brass key gleamed in the firelight one last time before sleep pulled him under.

And in the darkness of his dreams, the puzzle pieces kept shifting, refusing to fit.

Chapter 13
The Puzzle Pieces

My pain is my motivation.

The morning mist clung to Pelling like a suffocating veil, shrouding the mountains and muffling the usual sounds of the waking town. Inside the inquiry room, the air was thick with tension as Karan Negi reviewed his notes.

The courthouse office had never felt so claustrophobic. The heavy wooden beams overhead, the damp scent of old paper and ink, the faint hum of clerks moving about outside, but all of it blurred into the background as Karan surveyed his team. They weren't just investigating a murder anymore. They were navigating a battlefield where the enemy held all the cards.

Today was critical.

Rohan Thakur had been summoned for questioning, and Karan was about to test the strength of his alibi.

Yesterday's events were still on his mind, which he would discuss after the meeting. Leela was already at her desk, furiously scribbling in her notebook while Kumar leaned against a cabinet, sipping tea with his usual nonchalance, except his eyes betrayed a sharp awareness.

"Boss, I'll give you a hundred rupees if Rohan doesn't walk in here today with that smug, 'do-you-know-who-my-father-is' look," Kumar remarked, shaking his head.

Karan smirked but didn't look up. "Save your money, Kumar. We both know that's exactly what's going to happen," then looking at Leela, Karan asked, "How's Arun doing?"

"He is still in ICU and under sedation," replied Leela, "We should be able to speak with him once he is conscious."

"Let's hope that's soon," said Karan and looked at the door as it creaked open.

A constable led in Rohan Thakur, followed by his high-profile lawyer, Arvind Mehta. As expected, Rohan strutted in with the arrogance of a man who believed himself untouchable.

"Judge *saab*," Mehta greeted, his tone clipped but courteous. "My client is here as per your summons."

Karan nodded, his expression unreadable as he gestured to the chair opposite him.

"Mr. Thakur, thank you for joining us."

"Not that I had a choice," Rohan scoffed, slouching back into the seat.

Mehta placed a folder on the table and pushed his glasses up the bridge of his nose. "Let's keep this brief, shall we?"

Karan ignored the lawyer and focused on Rohan.

"You claimed you were at a party the night Sonia Verma was murdered, Mr. Thakur," he said calmly, tapping his pen against the table. "So, write down the exact time you left the hotel and every place you went after."

Rohan blinked. "What? Why?"

Karan pushed a blank sheet toward him. "Go ahead. I'll verify it against the traffic cameras and phone records." Karan leaned back into his chair. His piercing eyes drilled into Rohan's.

Rohan hesitated, then forced a smirk. "Around 10:30 p.m. Plenty of people saw me. And yes, I can give names."

Karan tapped his pen against the desk. "Good. Then I assume you won't mind if we verify their statements?"

"Go ahead," Rohan said lazily. "I have nothing to hide."

Karan slid a photograph across the table. "This CCTV footage from a gas station places your car on the road leading to the forest at 11:45 p.m. Can you explain that?"

For the first time, a flicker of uncertainty crossed Rohan's face. Mehta, however, remained impassive.

Mehta interjected smoothly. "My client isn't required to recall every minor detail of his movements. He often takes late-night drives to clear his head. That in itself proves nothing."

Karan leaned forward, locking his gaze on Rohan. "Then explain why your phone records show that you called Sonia multiple times that night."

Leela tapped a report. "And that the last call lasted exactly 47 seconds."

Rohan's jaw tightened, his fingers twitching slightly. Quickly regaining his composure, he said aloud, "I HAVE NOTHING TO DO WITH HER MURDER!"

Silence. The words hung in the air like a slow-burning fuse. Leela sucked in a breath, and Kumar's smirk vanished.

Karan remained unfazed. "Then why were you meeting her?"

"She needed help. But I refused," Rohan snapped.

"We heard that you forced yourself on her."

Rohan's lips curled into a sneer. "No. I didn't."

Mehta sat forward sharply. "With all due respect, Judge Negi, unless you have conclusive evidence, you cannot make such accusations."

Karan held up another document.

"I don't need accusations, Mehta. The forensic report is clear: Sonia was strangled before her body was staged to look like an animal attack." Karan nodded. "But even without them, Mr. Thakur, you had a clear motive."

Rohan scoffed. "A motive for what? A leopard killed her. The whole town knows that."

Karan smiled coldly. "A very convenient theory, Mr. Thakur. Unfortunately, the forensic evidence doesn't support it. Sonia was strangled before her body was staged to look like an animal attack, before she was burnt."

Rohan's smirk faltered.

Karan slid another file across the table. "I'd be careful what I say next, Mr. Thakur. Lying under oath during this inquiry is a punishable offence."

Mehta was about to interject, but Karan raised a hand.

"Let's cut the performance. You and Sonia argued that night. You left the hotel. Your car was spotted near the crime scene. And now, we have proof of the CCTV footage. The question isn't whether you were involved, but how deep."

Mehta stood. "I believe we're done here. My client has answered enough."

Karan studied Rohan for a long moment, noticing sadness and fear in his eyes, then nodded. "For now. But this is far from over."

Just before leaving, Mehta mumbled. "This interrogation was highly inappropriate…"

Karan cut him off. "Then file a complaint."

As Rohan and his lawyer left, Kumar let out a low whistle.

"That," he said, "was the first time I saw Rohan Thakur actually shut up."

Leela, still processing everything, whispered, "He's hiding something. And I bet his father knows."

Karan exhaled. "Something doesn't seem to fit in."

Inside his makeshift office, his team gathered for the day's developments and charted the further plan of action. Priya stood by the window, arms crossed, her sharp eyes scanning the street outside, ever watchful. Kumar was at the long table, slumped over a pile of files, scribbling notes with half-drunk *chai* beside him. Leela, normally poised, sat stiffly, her hands wrapped around a steaming cup, dark circles betraying a sleepless night.

"Now, coming back to yesterday's developments."

He adjusted the brass key in his pocket. The weight of it was oddly heavy, as if Sonia's last breath was still trapped inside it. Whatever this unlocked would expose the truth. Or get him killed, but he knew that courage does not mean you get afraid. It means that fear cannot stop you.

Exhaustion clung to them all, but none of them were ready to stop. Stopping anyways wasn't an option anymore. Stopping meant losing.

"We have a problem," Karan announced, shutting the door behind him. "And we don't have time to play catch-up."

Kumar scoffed. "A problem? Sir, we have about six."

Karan didn't disagree.

He moved to the head of the table, rolling up his sleeves. "Let's start with what we know."

The weight of the case pressed down on Karan as he leaned over the table, his hands resting on the cool wooden surface. The room felt smaller, more claustrophobic, as if the walls themselves were absorbing the tension.

Priya, Kumar, and Leela sat around the table, their faces taut with exhaustion and determination. Karan placed the brass key in the centre of the table. A small object, yet the biggest question mark in the investigation.

"This is what Sonia died protecting," he said. His voice was steady, but there was an edge of restrained frustration. "Whatever this unlocks, someone wanted it buried."

Kumar let out a low whistle. "You realise how many doors there are in this town, right? We're looking for a needle in a haystack."

Leela shot him a sharp look. "This is serious, Kumar."

"Look at the ridges. It's not standard for apartments or offices. It's older, custom-made."

Priya leaned forward, her brows knitted together. "It could be a locker. If Sonia knew her life was in danger, she wouldn't have kept it somewhere obvious."

Karan's voice was measured. "Sonia worked at Thakur's hotel. If she had anything valuable, she wouldn't have kept it at home. Too easy to access. It had to be somewhere only she knew."

Kumar nodded, catching on. "And Nisha said Sonia was scared; paranoid, even. If she had a key, it means she locked something away."

"Exactly," Karan nodded. "She passed it to Nisha, which means she was running out of time. She knew someone was coming for her."

Leela hesitated before speaking. "Sonia wasn't reckless. If she took precautions, then the key must lead to something incriminating, something she thought could protect her."

Kumar leaned back, rubbing his temples. "Unless it's a dead end. What if she left it as a red herring to throw off her killers?"

Karan's jaw tightened. "Then why did she give it to Nisha? Why not just destroy it?"

Silence filled the room. The only sound was the distant murmur of clerks shuffling outside.

They all knew the answer.

Sonia had intended for this key to be found. It wasn't just a clue - it was her final message.

Priya picked up the key, examining it closely as she traced the grooves with her fingertips, thinking. “It looks antique. Could be for something old; a locker, a safe hidden in a wall, or even an old storage unit.”

“We start with the places she frequented the most.” Karan added, “We need to cross-reference this with every storage facility, bank, and hotel where Sonia had records.”

Kumar pulled out his notebook. “I’ll start with the banks and registered storage lockers in town. But what if it’s something more obscure? A hidden compartment?”

Leela, deep in thought, suddenly spoke up. “Sonia was meticulous, right? What if she used a personal safe? Maybe a hidden compartment in her apartment or workplace?”

Karan’s gaze sharpened. “Then we start with the obvious, her apartment. If she hid something, that’s where we’ll find our first clue.”

Kumar slid a stack of photos across the table. A ransacked hut. Blood stains. Broken furniture. Signs of a struggle. “This one is bad, sir. Suresh’s hut looked like a goddamn crime scene. Blood on the floor, door left open; it was a message.”

Priya clenched her jaw. “Either they killed him, or they’re using him as leverage.”

Karan exhaled. “If he’s alive, they’re trying to break him. If he’s dead, we’re out of time.”

“They didn’t just take him,” Kumar muttered. “They wanted us to know.”

Priya studied the photos. "That means he was valuable."

Karan concluded. "Which means he knew something. Either he told them… or they're making sure he never does."

Leela hesitated. "If he's still alive… what are they doing to him?"

"And if he's dead?" Priya added.

"Then we find him, or his body. And the people who put him there." Karan clenched his jaw. "There's something else," he said, his voice steady but cold.

Priya, who had been flipping through a file, stopped mid-turn. Kumar raised an eyebrow, and Leela, who had been quietly sipping her *chai*, finally looked up.

Karan leaned forward, bracing his hands against the wooden table. "Last night, Nisha and I were ambushed. Twice."

Kumar's pen froze in the air. "What?"

Priya's jaw tightened. "Ambushed? Where?"

"The library first," Karan said, scanning their reactions. "We heard someone outside while I was talking to Nisha. I went after him, but he was fast. Slipped into the alleys before I could get a good look."

Leela's fingers tightened around her cup. "They were watching her."

Karan nodded. "And when they weren't sure if she had talked, they tried again."

Priya's voice dropped. "How bad?"

"I traced the guy back to Room 306 at Pelling View Inn," Karan continued. "The place was a mess. Papers everywhere. A bottle of whiskey was on the table. And…" He hesitated for just a second. "Photos of Nisha. Someone has been watching her for a long time."

Silence.

Leela paled. "That means she's been a target even before she came to you."

Kumar let out a low whistle. "So, what, this isn't just about what she knows now? Someone was tracking her long before Sonia died?"

"Looks that way," Karan muttered. "And then, while I was going through the room… someone attacked me."

Priya straightened. "Attacked you?"

Karan's voice remained steady. "Came at me with a knife. He knew what he was doing, so he was trained. But I managed to shake him off. He got away."

Kumar scoffed. "And you're telling us all this now?"

"I needed to confirm what we were dealing with first," Karan said, eyeing him. "And now, I know. This isn't just about Sonia's murder anymore. We're in the middle of something much bigger."

Priya crossed her arms. "Bigger than Rohan Thakur?"

Karan replied. "Maybe even bigger than MLA Thakur."

A heavy silence settled over them.

Finally, Priya leaned forward. "So, what's the plan?"

Karan looked at each of them before speaking. "We split up. We move fast."

Priya met his gaze. "What do you need me to do?"

"You go through Arun's things and the papers from Room 306," Karan instructed. "Whoever was staying there had files on Nisha. I want to know what they were tracking and for how long."

Priya nodded. "I'll get started right away."

Karan turned to Kumar. "You're handling Sonia's key. Check banks, storage units, rental properties... anything that might be connected to her."

Kumar ran a hand through his hair. "And what if we find nothing?"

Karan's jaw tightened. "Then we dig deeper."

Leela, still looking shaken, finally spoke. "And me?"

"You're staying at the hospital with Arun Dey," Karan said firmly. "If he wakes up, get his statement. Find out what he saw before they tried to silence him."

Leela hesitated. "And if they come back?"

Karan's gaze darkened. "Call me first. Make sure no one goes near him."

Leela looked worried and nodded.

Kumar leaned back in his chair. "And you?"

"I'm going after Rohan and Suresh," Karan said. "He's the missing link. If he's alive, he knows something. If he's dead... we find out who made him disappear."

Priya tapped her fingers against the table. "And what about the guy who attacked you last night?"

Karan's lips pressed into a thin line. "We find him too. No more ghosts. No more running."

Priya squared her shoulders. "Alright. And Karan – not alone anymore, please."

Kumar chuckled and cracked his knuckles. "Time to break some rules."

Leela swallowed, but her voice was steady. "I'll leave immediately and ensure Arun makes it."

Karan exhaled, knowing the next 24 hours would change everything.

"Then let's get to work."

And with that, they scattered into the mist-covered streets of Pelling, walking straight into the storm.

Karan adjusted his coat against the cold as he stepped outside the courthouse. The sky was still grey, the morning mist curling around the narrow lanes like ghostly fingers.

He was halfway to his car when his phone rang. It was a blocked number. He hesitated for just a second before answering.

"Karan Negi."

There moment of static. Then, a voice, low, breathless, ragged voice came through. "Judge *saab*..."

Karan didn't waste time. "Who's this?"

"It's me. Suresh." Another rustle of movement on the other end. A distant creak, like an old wooden door.

Karan stopped cold. "People are looking for you." He said, his grip on the phone tightened. "Where the hell have you been?"

A sigh. "I'm alive, but won't be for long."

Karan asked, "Where are you?"

Another pause. Suresh whispered, "I have proof... Rohan killed Sonia."

Karan's breath stilled. "What? You're sure?" he pressed, voice measured.

There was a long pause. Then a soft, muffled noise. A shuffle. A chair scraping against concrete.

Karan's instincts screamed at him. Something wasn't right.

"Where are you?" Karan asked.

"I can't say," Suresh whispered. *"They're looking for me,"* Suresh continued in a hoarse whisper. *"Rohan and his father – they want me dead."*

"Suresh, listen..."

"I'll give you the proof," Suresh cut in. *"Meet me at the old tea factory. Midnight."*

Karan frowned. "That place has been abandoned for years."

"Exactly."

"Suresh, if you really have proof, you need to..."

"No time, sir!" Suresh cut him off, panicked. *"If I don't make it..."*

A loud thud on the other end. A metallic clatter.

Karan sat up straight. "Suresh?"

A heavy silence.

Then, a sharp click. The line went dead.

Karan stared at his phone, his gut twisting. This was either a desperate plea for help or a carefully set trap.

He set the phone down, his mind already calculating. If Suresh was there, he didn't have much time left.

Before Karan could process the call, his phone buzzed again. This time, it was Leela.

"Karan… we have a problem."

"What now?"

"Arun is dead."

"WHAT! HOW?"

"The moment I reached, the constables received a call and we were informed that they were called off duty from the hospital on the pretext of a sudden departmental reshuffle," Leela said, "but let's be honest, it smells like someone higher up didn't want them here."

Leela continued, "Also, Priya called and informed that the CCTV footage has been retrieved. It shows Rohan and Sonia fighting, then later Suresh coming and handing a USB to a man."

Karan's blood ran cold.

Chapter 14
Trap At The Tea Factory

Minds are like parachutes.

They only function when open

- Thomas Dewar

The drive back to Karan's guesthouse through the narrow, winding roads was slow, and the headlights barely cut through the thick night air. The scent of damp earth and pine drifted through his open window. Despite its mysteries, Pelling had transformed. Now, it was a hub for mountain bikers, rock climbers, and trekkers, a town that thrived on adventure. It had resorts for the wealthy, homestays for the spiritual, and narrow paths that led to views so breathtaking they seemed almost unreal. Karam enjoyed the drive, the crisp mountain air brushing against his face, clearing his thoughts with every mile. Yet tonight, Pelling didn't feel like a tourist paradise.

As he drove past the Royal Pelling Hotel, his mind replayed every moment from the interrogation with Rohan. The arrogance, the flickers of doubt, the barely concealed fear.

He pulled into the driveway, and he sat in the car for a moment. Before getting out of the vehicle, he looked at his reflection in the rearview mirror. The dim glow from the porch light illuminated the dark circles under his eyes, the exhaustion pressing against his temples like an unwelcome guest. The constables were a real solace. He had developed a habit of always checking their presence.

He had too many loose ends and not enough time. With each step, he replayed the sequence of events in his mind. Sonia Verma's murder had set off a chain reaction of betrayals, lies, and hidden agendas. The original claim that she had been killed in a leopard attack had been debunked; the forensic report had made that clear. Why had she been strangled before her body was burnt? Who needed to cover up her death by burning the body in such a theatrical manner?

Rohan's alibi was shaky at best, and while his lawyer skilfully dodged direct accusations, the cracks in his story were widening. The CCTV footage and a witness placed his car near the crime scene. His phone records revealed repeated calls to Sonia. And now, with the hotel technician dead, Suresh had suddenly surfaced, claiming to possess crucial evidence.

Yet something didn't sit right with Karan. The trail felt too clean, too convenient. It was as if Rohan's guilt had been meticulously staged; packaged and presented, just waiting for someone to uncover.

And then there was the technician, Arun Dey. The man had uncovered something damning before he was beaten within an inch of his life. His laptop, his drives were all wiped clean. And now, someone had silenced him permanently.

Karan pushed the door open, stepping into the dimly lit guesthouse. As he entered his room, the wooden floors creaked under his weight as he tossed his coat onto the chair near the window and reached for the whiskey bottle on the shelf. He poured himself a drink, letting the amber liquid swirl in the glass before taking a slow sip as his thoughts went to Nisha.

The woman whose presence in this case felt more and more like fate. She had been friends with Sonia, trusted enough to be given a key that likely held the final piece of the puzzle. But in doing so, she had unknowingly become a target.

Karan exhaled sharply. None of this was a coincidence. Someone was orchestrating every move, making sure that certain truths never saw the light of day. And now, he was about to walk into a meeting that could either bring clarity or be his last mistake.

He needed to clear his head, to think through his next move before heading to the abandoned tea factory.

Everything fit together too perfectly, like a puzzle designed for him to solve. His instincts screamed at him, this meeting wasn't just about evidence. Someone wanted him to go there alone.

A soft knock at the door interrupted his thoughts.

Karan turned sharply, his muscles instinctively tensing as his fingers brushed against the holster at his waist.

He wasn't expecting visitors. Not tonight.

He moved toward the door cautiously, unlocking it just enough to peer outside.

"Nisha..."

She stood there, shivering slightly, her shawl wrapped tightly around her small frame, dark eyes wide and searching. The dim hallway light cast shadows over her cheekbones, but even in the poor lighting, Karan saw the fresh bruises.

"Karan..." she whispered. "Can I come in?"

He stepped aside.

She hesitated for half a second, like a caged bird testing freedom, before slipping inside, her scent drifting past him, warm and soft, tinged with something floral and faintly musky.

"Are you okay?" Karan said quietly.

Nisha nodded. "I had to meet you."

The way she said it, slow, deliberate, sent an almost imperceptible shiver down Karan's spine.

He looked at her, really looked this time. The dim light caught the faint bruise blooming along her jawline, a thin cut near her lip that hadn't fully healed. Her posture was composed, almost defiant, but her shoulders carried the kind of stiffness that came from too many nights spent guarding herself.

The tension between them crackled like a live wire. Nisha's gaze lifted, searching his face, something unreadable flickering in her eyes – fear, defiance, maybe even longing.

Nisha lifted her gaze, searching his face. A flicker of something unreadable; fear, defiance, longing, danced in her expression.

But something in his stance must have given him away because she took a step forward. Close enough for him to feel the heat radiating from her. He didn't move back.

"Suresh called me and wants to meet."

Her palm pressed lightly against his chest, just over his heartbeat.

The fabric of her shawl brushed against his shirt, and the light touch sent a slow burn through his body. His knuckles flexed at his sides, a battle raging beneath his skin.

"When? Now?" she murmured.

"You're going, aren't you?" she whispered.

Karan nodded. "Midnight. Tea factory."

She swallowed. "It's a trap."

His hand tightened over hers, pressing her palm to his chest; his heartbeat fast, erratic, vulnerable in a way she hadn't seen before. Their eyes locked, the silence between them heavy with everything unspoken.

"I don't plan on getting trapped," he said, voice low, almost a whisper.

She didn't pull her hand away. Instead, she stepped closer, her breath mingling with his. And then, as if drawn by an invisible current, he cupped her face gently and kissed her; tentatively at first, as if asking permission. She answered with a soft gasp, deepening it, her fingers curling into his shirt. The world blurred, and time paused. It was raw, tender, and filled with everything they'd held back for far too long.

When they finally broke apart, breathless and dazed, he rested his forehead against hers.

"I'll see you soon," he murmured.

They left together in silence, a different kind of understanding between them now.

He dropped her outside her home, their fingers lingering just a second longer before he turned and drove towards the tea factory.

Karan drove in silence. The constables had been instructed to stay just outside view but within earshot, close enough to respond if they heard a shout. His gun was loaded, holstered. His team was informed and ready.

The tea factory loomed ahead. The moonlight barely illuminated its skeletal frame etched against the dark canvas of the hills.

It had been abandoned for nearly a decade. Vines had crept over the broken walls, reclaiming what man had left behind. The iron gates hung loose, creaking softly in the cold wind.

The perfect place to disappear.

As the road curved into darkness, his phone buzzed with messages.

Priya: *"Karan, don't do anything reckless."*

Kumar: *"We're nearby. Give us a signal if things go south."*

Karan parked his car a few meters away and stepped into the fog. The factory stood in ruins, silent, watching.

He killed the engine, sitting for a moment, listening. Not a sound. Not even the chirp of night insects.

His gut clenched. *Something was wrong.*

Then, a faint shift in the shadows near the entrance. Karan reached for his gun.

A few meters ahead, a heavy iron door stood slightly ajar. The hinges had long rusted, leaving jagged orange stains along the cement walls. The rusted metal door groaned as Karan stepped inside.

His footsteps echoed ominously in the vast, empty space.

The air was thick with dampness, the scent of rust and decay mixing with the faint, lingering smell of tea leaves from decades past. A dim shaft of moonlight filtered through a broken skylight, casting fractured beams across the floor, highlighting the swirling dust that moved in the cold night air.

He pulled his coat tighter against the chill and checked his surroundings. No movement. No sounds except the distant hooting of an owl.

He reached for his gun, keeping it close, but hidden beneath his coat. If this was an ambush, he wasn't going to walk in blindly.

His phone buzzed. A single message from an unknown number: *Inside. Alone. No tricks.*

Karan realised, they were watching him.

A faint shuffling noise. The factory's massive machinery was still intact; hulking metal beasts frozen in time, their gears covered in dust, their pipes whispering in the wind.

Then, a shadow moved near one of the old conveyor belts.

"Suresh?" Karan called out.

A figure staggered forward from behind a rusted column.

Suresh – the man looked like a ghost – his clothes tattered and stained, his eyes sunken due to lack of sleep. His face was covered in sweat, and his hands trembled as he clutched a small black bag tightly against his chest as though it were the only thing keeping him alive.

His eyes darted around the space, wild with paranoia.

"Judge *saab*," he whispered. "You came."

Karan didn't lower his guard. Something about Suresh's body language was off. "You said you had proof. Where is it?"

Suresh swallowed hard and took a shaky step forward. "I have it… I have everything." He raised the bag slightly. "This will prove Rohan killed Sonia."

Karan didn't lower his weapon. Why did this feel rehearsed?

Suresh's eyes flickered toward the entrance. "I couldn't. They'd kill me."

Karan took a slow step closer. "Who? Rohan? Or someone else?"

Suresh hesitated. His breathing grew uneven.

A footstep. Then, a metallic click. The distinct, chilling sound of a gun being cocked.

Someone else was here.

Karan reacted instantly, pulling his gun and spinning around.

Then, gunfire erupted. Karan dove sideways behind an overturned crate as bullets tore through the factory, shattering glass and sending metal fragments flying.

He needed to even the playing field. Karan pulled his gun from the holster, waited for the briefest pause in the gunfire. Peeking out from cover, he fired.

CRACK!

He spotted three... no, four figures moving between the old machinery.

Silencers. Trained killers.

His first shot found its mark, hitting one of the gunmen in the shoulder, making the attacker grunt as he stumbled back, knocking over a rusted pipe. The loud clang echoed through the hollowed-out factory.

The second attacker lunged out of the shadows, gun raised.

Karan spun, kicked a metal chair toward him, knocking the man off balance just long enough to fire again.

CRACK!

A second shot.

The gunman jerked backwards, clutching his thigh, his weapon clattering to the ground.

Then, a third figure rushed him from behind. Karan barely had time to turn before a hard elbow crashed into his ribs, knocking the air from his lungs. Pain exploded through his side. He stumbled, catching himself against an overturned crate.

The attacker grabbed him by the collar, trying to drive a knife into his side. Karan twisted sharply, using the momentum to slam the man's wrist against the rusted edge of a conveyor belt. The knife clattered to the floor.

Karan grabbed a rusted pipe from the floor and swung it hard. The metal connected hard with the attacker's jaw. A sickening crunch. The man collapsed instantly, unconscious.

Without pausing, Karan hurled the pipe again – this time at the exposed bulb overhead. The glass burst, showering sparks as the room plunged into darkness.

The glass shattered. Darkness swallowed the room.

But the fourth attacker was still standing. And he had Suresh by the throat. The man had grabbed him in a chokehold, using him as a human shield, his gun pressed firmly against Suresh's temple.

"DROP YOUR GUN!" the man shouted.

Suresh gasped, his legs kicking weakly.

Karan froze. His mind was racing.

The man's finger hovered over the trigger. One wrong move and Suresh was dead.

Karan's eyes darted around the room. He needed a distraction.

Then, he saw it. A hanging metal chain swayed slightly above them.

If he could just...

Suddenly, there was noise outside – loud, commanding.

"POLICE! DROP YOUR WEAPONS!"

Constables stormed in, guns raised. Too late. Flashing lights flooded the factory's entrance.

The gunman hesitated for a fraction of a second. And that was all Karan needed. He lunged forward, grabbing the hanging chain and yanking it hard. A metal beam above came loose, crashing down between them with a deafening CLANG!

The attacker flinched as Karan fired. One shot. Straight to the shoulder.

The gunman staggered back, dropping Suresh in the process.

Suresh let out a panicked scream as a bullet grazed his leg, sending him sprawling onto the cold factory floor. He hit the floor, gasping for air.

The constables stormed in, weapons raised.

But it was too late.

The remaining attackers had already vanished into the mist, slipping away like ghosts, leaving only Karan, a wounded Suresh, and the echoes of gunfire.

The constables secured the scene, but Karan was already on his feet, grabbing Suresh by the collar.

"Who set this up?" Karan demanded, dragging Suresh toward the side exit, moving fast.

Suresh was shaking violently. "It's them… Thakur's people… They don't want me talking!"

Karan stood in the dim light of the factory, chest heaving, the scent of gunpowder and rust thick in the air.

Suresh lay on the ground, clutching his bleeding leg, his face contorted in pain. A constable rushed forward, helping him up.

Karan turned to the officer in charge. "What took you so long?"

One of the constables hesitated before speaking, "Sir... we were ordered to hold back until we heard gunfire."

Karan's stomach sank. Someone had held them back on purpose. Someone had delayed them on purpose. Someone wanted him to face this ambush alone.

His mind raced, piecing it together. This wasn't just a cover-up. This was a set-up. And whoever was pulling the strings was still out there.

He turned back to Suresh. "You said you had proof."

Suresh, still gasping for breath, reached for the black bag. "I do," he wheezed.

Karan took it from him, opening it. Inside was a USB drive, marked with the words *'Rohan Confession.'* A bloodstained scarf – Sonia's. CCTV stills of Rohan and Sonia arguing at the hotel. A crumpled piece of paper, seemingly handwritten by Sonia, with one chilling line: *'If anything happens to me, Rohan is responsible.'*

Karan stared at the contents, his heartbeat heavy against his ribs. It was everything the case needed. Everything pointed perfectly to Rohan's guilt. The way it was presented. The way it was wrapped up, almost neatly delivered into his hands. He should've felt relief. Instead, a cold thought slid through his mind.

It was all too perfect. Too staged.

But he couldn't dwell on it now.

Suresh looked up at him, his eyes desperate. "This is it, sir... this is the truth. He killed her."

Karan snapped out of his thoughts and knelt beside him. "Get the first-aid kit, now!" he barked at one of the constables.

As gauze was pressed against the wound and antiseptic dabbed hastily, Karan pocketed the USB.

"We'll find out soon enough," he said, voice low but resolute.

He stood and turned to the officers. "Take him to the courthouse. He's to be placed in judicial custody until the hearing tomorrow. No press. No visitors. Tight security."

"Also, secure the unconscious one," Karan ordered, pointing to the man still lying motionless.

"Check his vitals. If he's alive, cuff him and call in a medical unit. I want him in custody and guarded around the clock."

As they carried Suresh away, Karan looked at the evidence one last time. This was it. The missing puzzle piece.

Or so it seemed.

Karan and his team sat in his dimly lit office at the Courthouse, the black USB drive lying motionless on his desk like a snake coiled in waiting. It was marked with two words: *'Rohan Confession.'*

Across from him, Priya leaned against the filing cabinet, arms crossed, her brows furrowed in deep thought. Kumar, hunched over a laptop, sipped his now-cold tea while scrolling through the data Suresh had provided. Leela sat on the edge of the desk, notebook in hand, watching the USB, like it might explode.

Karan exhaled, rubbing his temples. "This is it, the final nail in Rohan's coffin."

Priya's sharp eyes flickered toward him. "Let's see what's in it."

Karan tapped his fingers against the desk. "That's what's bothering me." He picked up the USB, flipping it between his fingers. "Suresh delivered this like a wrapped gift. Sonia's scarf, CCTV stills, and now a digital confession? It's strategically misleading."

Kumar cracked his knuckles. "Only one way to know if this is real."

She plugged the USB into his laptop.

A single file appeared on the screen. 'Rohan Confession.'

"Play it," Karan said quietly.

The video was grainy, like it had been filmed in secret. The footage showed the dimly lit corridor outside Sonia's hotel suite.

Rohan entered the frame. His movements were hurried, his head swivelling as if making sure he wasn't being followed. He knocked. Sonia opened the door, her arms crossed. The conversation had no audio, but subtitles ran at the bottom.

Sonia: "You can't keep running from this, Rohan."

Rohan: "I told you to stay out of it. You don't know what you're getting into."

Sonia: "I know exactly what I'm getting into."

Rohan: (pauses) "You're making a mistake."

Sonia: "You don't have the courage to fight them, do you?"

Rohan: "I can't!"

Sonia: (shaking her head) "Then I'll do it without you."

Rohan: "Sonia, if you go public, they'll..."

The screen glitched. Then, a sudden cut.

The next scene was outside the hotel, where Rohan's hands were gripping her shoulders. The angle made it impossible to tell if he was pulling her or pushing her near the black SUV.

Sonia's lips moved quickly. She seemed to be struggling.

Then, another cut.

The final scene was a close-up of Rohan, pacing near the window, breathing hard. The subtitle read: *'I didn't mean to kill her.'*

The screen froze. Silence filled the room.

Kumar let out a low whistle. "Damn. That's... convincing."

Leela frowned. "Too convincing."

Karan replayed the footage, pausing at key moments. His eyes narrowed.

"The cuts," he muttered. "Look at the way the scene jumps. It's not continuous."

Priya leaned closer. "And why are the subtitles so... precise? The video has no audio, yet someone conveniently added text?"

Leela frowned. "Exactly. Who wrote them? The only person who would've known what they were saying is Sonia. And she's dead."

Kumar typed furiously. "I'll check the metadata." His fingers danced across the keyboard, pulling up the file's details. He stopped suddenly.

His face darkened.

"Karan… this video was edited. The timestamp has been altered."

Priya straightened. "Edited how?"

Kumar turned the laptop around. "The footage was stitched together from different clips. The confession at the end? The voice doesn't even match the lip movement. Someone edited and merged the words together to make it look like a confession."

Karan's fingers tightened around the desk. "So it's fake."

Leela's brows knitted together. "That means someone wants Rohan convicted so badly that they manufactured evidence."

Priya's voice was quiet but firm. "Who benefits the most from his conviction?"

Karan drew a long breath. "Whoever the real killer is."

A heavy silence fell over the room.

Karan leaned back, staring at the screen. His mind ran through the possibilities.

If he exposed this now, it would dismantle the case before it even reached the courtroom. But then, whoever was orchestrating this setup would get away, slipping back into the shadows.

But if he played along, let the inquiry unfold, he could see who pushed the hardest for Rohan's conviction. He had to chart the path forward.

His jaw clenched. He needed to see the bigger picture.

He closed the laptop. "We don't say anything. Not yet."

Leela hesitated. "You want to let this play out?"

Karan nodded. "We need to see who's pulling the strings. If we reveal the truth now, they'll just try another move. But if we let them believe they've won…"

Karan exhaled and added. "It's time I visit the lion's den and visit Rohan, his father."

Priya crossed her arms. "Are you sure it's safe? They have already threatened and attempted so many attacks."

Karan's gaze hardened. "Let's see. I have my constables with me, and I don't think they will attack me in their own house. Meanwhile, can you, Leela and Kumar ensure all evidences are authenticated so we can create a watertight case? My report has to be precise."

He stood up, handing over the USB to Leela. "Send this for a forensic test and decryption to get the authenticity checked."

Karan stepped out of the courthouse and headed to his guesthouse.

Tonight, he sat on the floor by the fireplace as a storm brewed inside him; not the kind that demanded action, but the kind that twisted your insides with things left unsaid.

He opened his worn leather journal, flipped to a blank page, and began to write without thinking.

Grief Stricken

Love's true form… will take its shape,

Come on, love, we'll make our escape.

We don't have to conform to convention.
We'll break the rules.
Splashes of colour, fabric of silk.
Occult fascinates, and horror suddenly thrills
Just groping around and going through these hills
Millions of Havens under a sky that's blue.
You are the love of my life... and it's true
Nature and music entwine as one
Dreams, hopes, ambitions still undone
When you misunderstand... that's what I can't stand
Why don't you accept me as I am?
I am a rebel, but with a just cause
Will change all within me that is flawed
Please tolerate me... it's not that hard
Emotions play a very big part
Thoughts of mine fly like colour in time
Trying to sing the song of harmony that falls in rhyme
Be my shrink, that's all I ask
Trouble, it seems now, but this too shall pass.

Maybe this wasn't just poetry. Maybe it was a letter never meant to be sent. Either way, it was him; laid bare on paper. He stared at the final lines before he drifted off to sleep.

Chapter 15
Face to Face with the Devil

People do not insult us; they simply express their opinions.

Their opinions reflect their upbringing, not us.

- Epictetus

The next morning, Karan drove to MLA Thakur's mansion, flanked by two armed constables. The mist from the Himalayan foothills curled around the road, pressing on the air and his thoughts. Each bend tightened the knot in his chest. The mansion rose ahead – towering white pillars, a sprawling garden, luxury cars gleaming under the cold sun. But beneath its polished grandeur, Karan knew, it was nothing more than a monument to greed, corruption, and secrets that could swallow him whole.

Two guards flanked the grand iron gates, their expressions indifferent, their hands resting on their belts, where guns were likely holstered. Karan stopped at the gate, and one of them stepped forward, giving Karan a blank look before nodding slightly.

"Judge *saab*," he said curtly, tilting his head. "*Sahib* is expecting you."

That was surprising. Karan hadn't called ahead. Thakur already knew he was coming.

The wrought iron gates creaked open slowly, deliberately, as if even they took their time deciding who deserved entry.

Karan drove inside, his eyes scanning the estate. Karan stepped out of his car, eyes narrowing as he took in the imposing estate before him. MLA Thakur's mansion wasn't just a home; it was a symbol. A fortress of power built on blood money, its high walls and security cameras a reminder that only the wealthy could afford to be untouchable.

Inside, a butler led him through a hallway lined with antique paintings, expensive sculptures, opulent chandeliers and ornate wooden carvings. Everything was meant to showcase wealth, influence, and legacy. The house had the grandeur of a king's palace, but it felt cold, devoid of warmth.

As Karan entered the grand study, he nearly choked on the air that was thick with the scent of expensive cigars, imported alcohol, and power. A massive chandelier loomed above, and polished marble floors reflected Karan's worn shoes, a stark contrast to the opulence around him. As he walked toward the sitting area, he wasn't surprised to see MLA Thakur lounging on a silk-covered sofa, a half-filled whiskey glass in hand, legs crossed like a king holding court. His expression barely shifted as Karan entered.

"Ah, our crusader of justice from the opposition, Judge Negi." Thakur's lips curled into a smirk as he swirled his drink. "To what do I owe this uninvited pleasure?"

Karan's jaw clenched. "I'm not here because of politics, Thakur. I'm here because Sonia Verma is dead."

Thakur smirked. "Ah, yes. The tragic young woman who got involved in things she shouldn't have." He sighed, feigning disappointment. "It's sad, really. She didn't know how the world worked."

Karan's hands tightened into fists. "She knew exactly how it worked. That's why she wanted to expose it."

Thakur chuckled, shaking his head. "You're persistent. I'll give you that. But persistence doesn't change reality. And the reality is, Negi, that people like you deal in morality, while people like me deal in results."

Karan took a step closer. "Then let's talk about results. Sonia Verma is dead. Her neighbour is dead. Arun Dey is dead. Suresh is missing. Your son was the last person seen with Sonia before she was murdered."

Thakur raised an eyebrow, amused. "You really have no idea what you're up against, do you?" He let out a slow chuckle, shaking his head. His eyes, dark and calculating, held the cold amusement of a predator.

Karan's gaze remained steady. "I know enough."

Thakur moved closer, his expression turning colder. "Then you know how things work. I have money, I have power, and I have the right people in my pocket. The police, the judges, even some of your friends in the media." He took a slow sip of his whiskey before placing the glass down. "You see, justice isn't about truth. It's about control. And I control everything here."

Karan clenched his fists. "Not anymore."

Thakur chuckled. "Ah, yes, the noble warrior. Tell me, Karan, do you really think you're the first man to come after me? The first man to stand here and demand justice?" He leaned back, lazily watching him. "You won't be the last. And you will lose."

Karan took a slow step forward, his voice like steel. "Let me tell you something, MLA Thakur. I've met men like you before. Powerful. Wealthy. Arrogant. And do you know where they are now?"

Thakur's smirk faltered slightly.

"They're either behind bars," Karan continued, "or dead in the gutters, betrayed by the very people they thought they owned."

A dangerous silence filled the room.

For a moment, Thakur just stared at him. Then he exhaled sharply and shook his head. "You've made a mistake coming here, Karan."

"No, you made the mistake of underestimating me."

Thakur's eyes darkened, "You should be careful, Judge. Men like me don't just make enemies disappear. We make them suffer first."

Karan held his ground. "I'll take my chances. Now, where is Rohan? He's involved in an ongoing murder investigation."

Thakur sighed theatrically. "Oh, for god's sake, Negi. Do you honestly think this pathetic circus will touch me?"

Karan's jaw clenched. "Murder isn't a game, Thakur."

Thakur smirked, but his fingers tightened slightly around his glass.

"My son," he said slowly, "is a disappointment."

Karan narrowed his eyes. "You don't seem too broken up about that."

Thakur sat back, exhaled dramatically, and set his glass down. "Rohan is a disappointment, I won't deny it. Weak, undisciplined, reckless. But he's my blood.

"He was never strong enough. Never ruthless enough. He was supposed to follow in my footsteps, continue my legacy. Instead, he became… soft." He scoffed. "A boy who detests the very name that feeds him."

Karan felt a flicker of something; pity? No, understanding.

Thakur continued, his tone colder. "But he's still my blood." Then,, his voice dropping as he continued. "And I protect what's mine."

Karan studied him. "Even if he's guilty?"

Thakur smirked. "Guilt is subjective, Negi. It's not about what's right. It's about what can be proven."

Karan's fists tightened. "The law is bigger than you."

Thakur's laughter was slow and deliberate. "That's adorable. You still believe in the law."

The MLA leaned back, his fingers tracing the rim of his whiskey glass. "You see, justice is a game, my friend. And I know how to play it better than anyone."

Then, in a quieter, more deliberate tone, Thakur added, "You're stepping into a snake pit, Negi. Do you really think you'll walk out of this unscathed?"

Karan didn't blink. "I don't care what happens to me."

Thakur studied him for a long moment, then sighed theatrically before standing up and walking slowly to a nearby cabinet where a row of expensive liquor bottles stood like trophies. Pouring himself another drink, he turned back to Karan with a smirk.

"You see, Judge *saab*," he continued, and raising his glass slightly, "the system is mine. The courts, the police, the press... they all answer to power. And power, Negi, is not in the hands of idealists. It belongs to those who can buy it, break it, or bury it."

Karan's fists clenched. "You can't buy the truth."

Thakur sipped his drink. "But I can bury it," he said, letting out a short laugh.

Karan held his gaze. "If you're so confident, then again, let me speak to Rohan."

Thakur studied him for a long moment, then let out a low, humourless laugh. For a second, Karan thought he would refuse.

Silence stretched between them.

"Fine," he said, waving his hand. "If you insist on this foolishness, go talk to my useless son."

Then, with an exasperated sigh, He snapped his fingers, and a servant appeared out of nowhere, somewhere through the corridor. "Take him to my son." Thakur looked back at Karan and warned, "But watch yourself, Negi. Family matters should stay within the family. If you're going to dig through mine, expect to be buried with it."

Karan turned and followed the guard. Behind him, Thakur's smirk never faded.

As Karan walked away, he could still feel Thakur's eyes on his back. A warning. A threat. A promise.

Rohan's room was nothing like the rest of the house. The bookshelves were neatly arranged, the furniture untouched. The room had the cold precision of a curated exhibit rather than a home. While the rest of the mansion was draped in wealth and arrogance, his space was suffocating. The curtains were drawn, the furniture expensive but unwelcoming. It was a stark contrast to the opulence outside; a prison disguised as privilege.

The walls were lined with expensive books he probably had never read, and the furniture was perfectly arranged, as if untouched. It didn't feel like a young man's living space. It felt like a luxurious prison.

Rohan stood by the massive glass window, arms crossed, his gaze lost in the fog-covered hills. He didn't turn when Karan entered.

"You came all this way just to play detective?" Rohan's voice was flat, his fingers playing with the cigarette in his hand, but he wasn't smoking it.

"I came for the truth," Karan said simply.

Rohan scoffed. "Then you came to the wrong place."

Karan took a step forward. "You hated Sonia."

Rohan's body stiffened slightly. "I never said that."

"You argued with her. You were the last person seen with her before she was killed."

Rohan turned, and for the first time, Karan saw the exhaustion in his face. "You think I killed her?"

"I think you're hiding something."

Silence.

Rohan exhaled sharply, raking a hand through his hair. "You wouldn't understand."

Karan's gaze sharpened. "Try me. I feel you didn't kill Sonia."

Rohan let out a bitter laugh. "Took you long enough."

Karan asked, "Then tell me what really happened."

Rohan exhaled. "It doesn't matter. You'll never be able to touch my father."

Karan's eyes didn't waver. "Then help me."

For the first time, Rohan looked at him properly. His fingers tightened around the cigarette, his jaw clenching. There was something in his eyes; fear, regret, something deeper than the arrogance he usually wore like armour.

Rohan walked to the couch, sat down, and hesitated before speaking. "Sonia wasn't blackmailing me." He admitted. "She… wanted me to help take my father down." His voice was quieter now.

Karan felt a shift in his gut. "And you refused."

He let out a hollow laugh.

"She thought I had courage. She thought I wanted justice. But I didn't. I just wanted to survive."

Karan watched him carefully. "Survive what?"

Rohan let out a bitter laugh. He turned to face Karan fully, his expression raw. "Everything I do is watched. Every word I say gets reported back. Suresh was always there, lurking, waiting to inform my father if I so much as blinked the wrong way."

Karan narrowed his eyes. "So you played along."

"You think I had a choice?" Rohan's hands clenched into fists. "What else could I do? Sonia thought I had courage. But I didn't." His voice dropped. "And now she's dead because of it."

Rohan's gaze darkened as he continued. "You don't know what it's like growing up here. My father doesn't raise sons. He breeds puppets. He owns people, and the moment you try to cut your own strings, he makes sure you regret it."

A heavy silence stretched between them.

"She told me she had proof," Rohan continued. "Something that would bring him down. But I knew better. No one brings him down. So I acted distant. I ignored her. I… pretended I didn't care."

Karan studied him. "But you did care."

Rohan swallowed. "I did. But it was too late.

"She wasn't just after my father's money laundering." He hesitated. "She found something worse."

Karan's pulse quickened. "What?"

Rohan's fingers tapped against the armrest. "Human trafficking. Poaching. Girls have gone missing for years. You think my father just dabbles in politics?" He let out a bitter laugh. "He owns people, Judge. And he sells them too."

Karan felt the weight of those words settle deep in his chest.

"And Sonia?" he asked.

Rohan's jaw clenched. "She wanted me to help her expose it. I was being watched, so I kept my distance. But she kept pushing."

He looked away. "And then… she was dead."

Rohan's expression darkened. "I don't know the full details. But it's real. My father's empire isn't just about power; it's about money. And people are his currency."

Karan took a slow breath. This was bigger than he had imagined.

Karan sat quietly, processing. Rohan wasn't just some privileged brat. He was a prisoner in his own home. And Sonia had died trying to free him, too.

Karan finally stood. "You said she had proof. Do you know where it is?"

Rohan hesitated. "No. But she mentioned a key."

Karan's heart stopped for half a second.

"A key?"

Rohan nodded. "She said it was the only way to the truth."

Karan felt the weight of the brass key in his pocket.

He had a mansion full of enemies behind him, but now, he had his first real ally in front of him.

The war wasn't just coming. It had already begun.

"Thank you, Rohan. Your truth shall set you free."

Karan turned and left the room. His mind was still processing Rohan's words as he stepped out of the Thakur mansion. Human trafficking. Poaching. Sonia's proof.

It wasn't just political corruption anymore. It was a criminal empire.

His phone vibrated with a message. It was Nisha: *I know what the key opens. Also… I think Sonia was scared of Suresh. She never trusted him.*

Karan stopped in his tracks. Sonia's key. Suresh. Fear. The pieces clicked together like a lock turning.

Sonia's biggest fear wasn't Rohan. It was Suresh. He remembered the trap at the old tea factory. It was all clear now.

He immediately dialled Nisha.

She picked up on the second ring. Her voice was tense, urgent. "Karan, I need to see you tonight at the ruins."

"What do you mean you know what the key opens?" he asked, already heading toward his car.

"I think it's connected to the Monastery in Pelling. Sonia and I went there once, and she acted strange, nervous. I didn't think much of it back then, but now..." She hesitated. "She said something about a hidden place where she kept important things."

"And Suresh?"

"Sonia never trusted him," Nisha said. "She always looked wary around him. I didn't question it before, but now... I think she knew something about him that we didn't."

Karan tightened his grip on the seat. He wanted to rush to her right now, but took a deep breath and said, "I need to run a background check on him. Immediately. I'll meet you at the ruins tonight."

Nisha agreed and disconnected the phone. It was time for him to call the only person that he could trust with Suresh's background check – Anya, his niece.

Chapter 16
A Cyber Trail of Blood

The more we simplify our desires, the more we amplify our peace.

Karan hit speed dial. The phone rang three times before a woman's voice answered.

"Uncle K?"

Far from the chaos unfolding in Pelling, Anya sat in her dimly lit apartment in Kolkata, fingers flying across the keyboard. Anya. His niece. A cyber forensic expert and one of the sharpest minds he knew. Anya's expertise in cyber forensics made her invaluable. She had hacked into restricted databases before, but something about this request sent a chill through her.

"I need a background check," Karan said without preamble.

She chuckled. "No 'hello'? No, 'how's my favourite niece?'"

"This is urgent, Anya."

The teasing disappeared from her voice. "Who's the target?"

"Suresh," Karan said. "Sonia's murder case. I've sent you all the details, including his photograph. I need everything on him. His history, ID records, and known Associates. And check for anything unusual – name changes, government red flags."

A pause. Then the sound of rapid typing. Lines of code scrolled down the screen as her AI-assisted program dissected the data extracted from Suresh's digital footprint. The room was silent except for the rhythmic tapping of keys and the occasional beep from Anya's system.

"This might take a couple of hours, I'll have to bypass three levels of encryption. I'll call you back as soon as possible," she said. "If he has skeletons, I'll find them."

Karan exhaled. "Make it fast."

He hung up and moved back in his seat, rubbing his temple. If Sonia had feared Suresh, it wasn't just paranoia.

A few keystrokes later, she was inside the National Crime Registry. His biometrics flagged an old case. She found his real identity. Her eyes widened as she stumbled upon a flagged report with Suresh's image.

Name: Mohd. Ismail – Wanted in Delhi. Serial rapist. Suspected murderer. Fugitive.

Anya's pulse quickened. She cross-referenced old missing persons reports and crime scene evidence. DNA samples from multiple unsolved murders matched Suresh. He had been operating under false identities for years, slipping through the cracks of the system. The results were chilling.

Fifteen minutes later, Anya called back. Her voice was dead serious.

"Karan Uncle, you need to hear this."

"Go ahead."

"Suresh isn't who he says he is," she said.

Karan's blood went cold.

"His records are fake. His ID, his employment history – all fabricated. He's living under a false Aadhaar card," Anya explained.

Karan reconfirmed. "The ID, the employment records, everything about him in Pelling? It's fake?"

"I ran his biometrics through old police databases and… Uncle, I found his real identity."

The pause before she spoke again felt like a death sentence.

"Uncle, he's a wanted serial rapist and murderer from Delhi."

Karan's grip on the phone tightened.

She took a breath and continued. "Suresh Kumar is actually Mohd. Ismail. Wanted in Delhi. Serial rapist. Suspected murderer. Three confirmed rape cases. Two missing women and two murders. All young women. He went underground after escaping from police custody three years ago."

After a long silence, Karan finally spoke, his voice quiet but lethal. "And MLA Thakur brought him to Pelling?"

"Yes," Anya confirmed. "He wasn't just any employee," she said. "He was handpicked. Thakur put him on the payroll under a different name and made sure no one questioned his background. He was the enforcer."

Karan inhaled sharply. "Are you sure?"

Anya didn't hesitate. "One hundred percent. No one knew where he went."

Karan exhaled slowly. So, Suresh wasn't just working for MLA Thakur; he was the one making sure no loose ends survived. Thakur's problem solver. His watchdog. For things the MLA didn't want his own hands dirty with. Suresh handled 'problems.' He silenced people. He watched over Rohan. He made sure no one got in MLA Thakur's way.

Karan's free hand clenched into a fist. A serial predator had been living under their noses, and nobody knew. Karan exhaled sharply, stepping away from the courthouse steps, where two junior clerks were walking past. He closed his eyes briefly. Everything was making sense now.

And Sonia? She had found out. And that had gotten her killed.

Karan opened his eyes, his decision already made. "Send me everything you have. I need to end this."

As Anya dug deeper, Suresh's past unfolded in chilling detail.

Born in a Delhi slum. The youngest of five. Raised by an alcoholic father. A mother too broken to protect him. Beatings. Starvation. A childhood steeped in violence. He was a product of something much darker – a man shaped by trauma. Karan had first learned about the Lucifer Effect in university, a term for how ordinary people can commit evil under certain circumstances. Now, looking at him, he saw the theory come alive. Suresh's childhood had been a relentless cycle of violence and deprivation. He grew up watching his father beat his mother into submission, learning from an early age that power belonged to those who took it by force.

As a boy, he was often locked in a dark, windowless room for hours, sometimes days at a time, as punishment for disobedience. Hunger gnawed at his belly, and the screams of his mother just beyond the thin walls became the lullaby of his childhood. He watched how his father viewed women: weak, disposable, meant only to serve. Suresh internalised those lessons.

But what shaped him the most was envy.

There were girls in his neighbourhood who had suffered just as much as he had, yet somehow, they found a way out. Some excelled in school, defied their circumstances, and built lives outside the slums. He despised them for it. He resented their strength, their courage to break free, to defy fate, while he remained shackled to his past. He began to see them as a personal insult, as proof that he had failed while they had succeeded.

As a teenager, he learned to blend in. Manipulate. Lie. Local thugs noticed him. He started working under local thugs, eventually making his way into MLA Thakur's network. He learned that control over others was the closest thing to real power he could attain. It was during these years that his hatred for strong, independent women festered into something monstrous. He didn't just want to silence them; he wanted to destroy them. Thanks to the toothless and corrupt judicial system, making him bolder over the years, he managed to get away every time.

His victims followed a pattern: courageous, ambitious women who had fought against all odds to carve a better life for themselves. In the past years, he had targeted and killed many, including a schoolgirl who wanted to study to have a better life, the journalist who had exposed many wrongdoings, and the teacher who stood up to local criminals. The old lady, Sonia's neighbour, wanted to tell the truth to the police. And finally, Sonia, the woman who had dared to threaten the entire operation.

Suresh saw her as another woman who had dared to defy the system.

Anya clenched her jaw. The forensic reports told a clear story. Different cities. Different methods. Same signature.

Then she found the missing link: a flood of documents, mugshots, and police reports. A blurry surveillance image from Delhi. Suresh, sitting inside a run-down bar. And beside him?

Inspector Vikram Singh.

The corrupt inspector had been working with Suresh before they both came to Pelling.

And that meant the entire case had just exploded into something even bigger.

And worst of all? He had almost gotten away with it.

Looking at Suresh's track record, Inspector Vikram Singh and MLA Thakur were quick to recognise the deep-seated rage within Suresh. They saw the perfect pawn in a man who harboured such violent hatred, yet was cunning enough to carry out his orders without question. Thakur fed into Suresh's darkness, reinforcing his belief that strong women needed to be put in their place, twisting his trauma into a tool of control.

The inspector and Thakur gave Suresh the power he had always craved: money, protection, and most importantly, an outlet for his rage. Every time a woman stood up against the MLA's illegal activities, Suresh was sent to 'handle' the problem. He was given a free hand, no consequences, no questions asked. His crimes were covered up, his victims erased, and in return, he became Thakur's most loyal enforcer.

When Sonia began investigating the trafficking ring, Thakur knew she was dangerous. He had seen her kind before; fearless, relentless, unwilling to back down. But this time, he had Suresh. He knew Suresh wouldn't hesitate. He didn't need to be ordered. He would see Sonia as just another woman who had dared to challenge the system.

And so, Suresh did what he always did. But this time, Sonia had been prepared.

Suresh wasn't just a fixer for MLA Thakur. He was a serial rapist and murderer, targeting women who embodied everything he hated: strength, resilience, defiance.

Anya's hands trembled as she pieced all the proof together. This wasn't just another criminal in Thakur's empire; this was a man who had turned his own trauma into a weapon. A man who had made it his life's purpose to break women who refused to be broken.

She ran VigilantAI – an advanced forensic system scanning police archives to scan through hundreds of case files, analysing patterns, facial recognition, and metadata.

Her screen flashed. A match.

Anya called up Karan again, and quickly shared her screen with Karan, her tone clipped with urgency. "The AI flagged these discrepancies in Suresh's records," she said, highlighting the data in rapid strokes. "See this? His employee ID – registered under two different birthdates. And here - five online accounts tied to the same encrypted IP address." She paused, her voice dropping. "That's not a mistake, Karan. That's deliberate. Classic identity fraud."

Anya straightened in her chair, absorbing the data. VigilantAI had mapped out connections between missing persons cases, flagged inconsistencies in police reports, and even uncovered deepfake images used to create false alibis.

"Three confirmed rape cases. Two missing women. Two murders," Karan murmured. "He's been hiding in plain sight."

Anya nodded grimly. "And there's more. I ran an AI-generated linguistic analysis on his police reports. The phrasing is eerily similar across multiple reports, suggesting he wrote them himself or dictated them."

Karan clenched his jaw. "That means he's had inside help."

Anya's fingers flew across the keyboard. "I cross-referenced the locations of the victims with cell tower pings. Suresh's phone was within a one-kilometre radius of every crime scene, but never directly at the location; always lurking nearby. He's careful, but not careful enough."

Suddenly, her screen flickered.

A notification popped up: *Unauthorised Access Attempt Detected*

Anya's breath hitched. "Someone's trying to breach my system." She immediately activated a counter-surveillance program. VigilantAI sprang into action, tracing the intruder's digital footprint.

"It's a masked IP, rerouted through multiple servers, but…" Anya frowned, eyes darting across the data stream. "They slipped up. The AI traced the signal to a local network - uh, something called Lower Bojoghari Road." She glanced up at Karan. "Does that mean anything to you?"

A chill ran down Karan's spine. His voice was barely a whisper. "Yeah," he said. "That's where the police headquarters is."

Anya exhaled shakily. "He knows we're onto him."

Karan stiffened. "Back up everything you've got and don't leave a trace. Get out of there. NOW," he said before the line got cut.

Anya's phone buzzed. A blocked number.

She hesitated before answering. A distorted voice came through. "You should stop digging, Miss Cyber Genius. Or you'll be the next missing person."

Karan grabbed the phone and redialled Anya's number, but got no reply. He said a quick prayer for her safety.

Meanwhile, Anya's AI system beeped again, finalising its latest scan. A new match appeared on the screen: a car, captured by a traffic camera just three blocks away. Someone was watching them.

She needed to get this to Karan before it was too late. She immediately called him. No answer.

Her heart pounded. Something was wrong.

Anya grabbed her car keys and her laptop, forwarding everything she found to a secure drive. She needed to get to Pelling. She needed to warn Karan.

She ran and got into her car and slammed her foot on the accelerator. Whatever she had uncovered, it was worth killing for. And she wasn't about to let them win.

As she sped down the highway and stopped for a minute to activate a secure VPN on her laptop, her fingers flew over the keyboard, tapping. If they were onto her, she had to act fast. She dug deeper into the MLA's records, bypassing multiple firewalls.

Then she found it.

A ledger with hidden transactions linking him to offshore accounts, bribery payments, and classified documents mentioning Sonia's name.

Her stomach turned. This wasn't just a cover-up. This was an organised network of corruption at the highest level in the system.

A flashing alert popped up again on her screen – *Unauthorised access detected*. System breach logged.

She had been spotted.

Cursing, she shut her laptop, gripping the wheel tighter. They were coming for her. Her only option was to reach Pelling before they did. Would she make it in time?

Headlights appeared in her rearview mirror, gaining fast. A black SUV, unmarked but menacing, swerved into her lane.

Anya's grip tightened on the wheel. She floored the accelerator, the speedometer climbing. The highway stretched endlessly ahead, but she wasn't naïve. They wouldn't let her reach Pelling alive.

The SUV rammed into her bumper, the impact nearly sending her off the road. She gritted her teeth, steering hard to maintain control.

Then, a second vehicle appeared ahead of her, blocking the road.

A trap.

Anya yanked the wheel left, skidding onto a dirt path that led into the dense forest. The SUV followed, tyres kicking up dust and gravel. Branches scraped against the windows as she navigated the winding trail. She needed an opening, an escape route.

Up ahead, a small bridge loomed. It was old, unstable. Too risky. But she had no choice. She gunned the engine, the car hurtling forward as gunshots rang out behind her. The bridge creaked under the weight of her vehicle, splintering as she sped across.

A final gunshot shattered her rear windshield just as she reached the other side.

Then…

The bridge collapsed, taking her pursuers with it.

Anya gasped for breath, her hands trembling. She wasn't safe yet, but she had bought herself time.

She pressed her foot to the pedal. Pelling was still miles away. And Karan was running out of time.

⚖

Chapter 17

Betrayal, Confession and a Night of Reckoning

Fall is not always a loss. Fall gives rise to new growth.

Meanwhile, in Pelling, Karan was looking forward to meeting Nisha tonight.

He entered his guesthouse and asked for dinner before heading to the ruins to meet Nisha. The lights in the guesthouse flickered once and steadied as Karan sat by the window, the ink bottle uncapped, a single candle dancing in the corner. He wasn't sure what drove him tonight – restlessness, guilt, desire, or maybe all three.

He reached for a fresh sheet in his journal and began to write. This wasn't evidence. This wasn't memory.

It was just truth – ugly, soft, forbidden.

Forbidden Love

I love you with a love that's forbidden, yet I can't stop.

I dream of your arms around me, your lips on mine.

When you look at me...

My soul shudders with joy...

My heart skips a beat...

In my dreams, I am sexy to you, and there's no end to the pleasure I can give you

I am loving you with a soft, gentle love
that would shake you to the core.
In my dreams, I feel you near me...
around me, I am in you...
I want to love you openly
Without fear or reservation,
But this is a forbidden love,
So I hide it,
keep it in secret and love you only in my dreams.
For only in my dreams I am acceptable to you,
In the surreal, my fantasies can be realised...
I close my eyes – it's you I see,
Hoping that you'd lie with me,
Give me a lethal dose,
Of that love, that shall never die
Give in, show me that side,
Let those feelings be your guide,
Don't question them, never ask why.
Heart to heart, beat to beat,
My cheeks flush, my hands tremble
At your touch, kiss and hugs
In my heart, this really tugs
The pieces of me reassemble
I open my eyes and look

There beside me where you should be
But it's only darkness that I see...
Silent tears streaking my cheeks
I reach over where you should be
But I know you're far away from me.
I hit my knees, hoping you will hear my cries
As a part of me slowly dies
Wishing you weren't just in my dreams
I shriek and I scream
But will fate allow this?
Look into my eyes
To see how they glow
Through them, read my thoughts
For my words, you can't know.
Touch me in secret
From the world we will hide,
Use the wind for your whispers,
To know our love hasn't died.
Cry with me in the shadows,
Smile so they don't see,
All that goes on behind the scenes
When you and I are free.
There will come a day
When they all will know,

That for this life I was yours,

Even if we could not show.

And on that day I will find you,

Our love no longer a crime,

And on that day I will blend in you,

Until the end of time.

He placed the pen down. No law could rewrite that kind of truth. And no inquiry could silence it.

He couldn't wait to meet her tonight.

At around 1:00 a.m., Nisha shut the door with a trembling hand, her back pressing against the cool wood. Every inch of her body throbbed from fresh bruises, and each breath felt sharp, shallow.

The dim light from the hallway cast shadows along the cracked walls, her husband's angry voice still echoing in her mind.

Her husband sat in his usual chair, his eyes sharp with suspicion. He had been watching her too closely over the past few days, his paranoia growing like a storm on the horizon.

"You think I don't see it?" Sharma had snarled earlier that night, gripping her wrist so tightly that it bruised instantly.

"The way you look at him? At that bastard Karan? Do you think I'm a fool? You think I don't know?" he said, his voice low, dangerous.

Nisha froze. "Know what?"

His jaw tightened. "That you're sneaking around with Karan Negi."

She forced herself to remain calm. "You're imagining things."

Ravi stood abruptly, knocking his chair back. In two strides, he was in front of her.

A sharp slap across her face sent her crashing to the floor.

"You think I don't notice the way you look at him?" His grip on her wrist tightened, cold and deliberate. "You think I haven't figured out why you keep bringing up Sonia's murder?"

The words hit harder than his painful grip on her skin. She tried to pull back, but his hold only deepened. Her pulse hammered against his fingers. For a second, she thought of speaking – denying, explaining, *something* – but his eyes warned her it wouldn't matter. The truth or a lie, either could cost her. So she stayed silent.

Then the shift came – sudden, feral. His composure cracked. The chair behind her toppled as he lunged, his movements raw and unrestrained, more beast than man. Nisha stumbled back, the wall cold against her spine.

"You forget your place, Nisha," he snarled. "You're mine. You always have been."

Fear clawed at her chest, but she forced herself to look up, refusing to cower. Her voice trembled, but her words cut clean.

"And yet," she said, holding his gaze, "you're the one who's afraid."

He paused, then rose, every movement brittle. "You don't get to look at another man."

Rage flared in his eyes – pure, unfiltered jealousy – and something in him was unravelling. He was spiralling, and Nisha knew the truth of it: if she misstepped, he would kill her.

She let the realisation harden into a plan.

He prowled the room like a caged animal, nostrils flaring, jaw working. Nisha moved with the calm of someone who'd rehearsed this a thousand times in her head. She crossed to the kitchen as if to make tea, hands steady though her insides trembled.

At the ornate wooden dining table, she poured the steaming liquid into a porcelain cup, fingers a little unsteady as the steam rose. She didn't hesitate. When he reached for the cup, she pressed it into his hands as if offering peace.

He watched her, suspicious for a heartbeat, then lifted the cup. She stirred once, slow and casual, watching the dark swirl hide the extra drops she'd been hiding for weeks – the contingency she'd promised herself she'd never need.

"You're tired," she said, her voice smooth despite the racing of her heart. "Drink."

She kept her expression blank as he raised the cup and took a sip.

She watched him drink it.

Ravi hesitated, his arrogance overriding his paranoia. He took a sip, then another. Within minutes, his eyes began to droop.

She watched as his words slurred and his body swayed. She stepped back as he collapsed onto the chair, his breathing slowing.

She grabbed her phone, her shawl, and sent a message to Karan.

And then, she ran.

She waited for Karan, listening to the wind howling through the ancient ruins, leaning on cracked stone walls which were worn by centuries of history. The night was cold, unforgiving, and eerily silent. She saw Karan pulling his coat tighter around himself, scanning the area. No one in sight.

Then, a soft rustling from the shadows.

He turned sharply. "Nisha?"

Karan's eyes ran all over Nisha – over her bruised arms, her torn sleeve, the faint trace of blood at her lip. She stepped forward from behind a broken archway, her shawl wrapped tightly around her battered body. Her face was bruised, her lip split, but defiance burned in her eyes.

"What happened?" he asked, trying to keep calm.

She hesitated, then met his eyes. "My husband knows. I had to sedate him to get here."

His jaw tensed. "You need to leave him, Nisha. He'll..."

"I didn't come here to talk about my marriage," she interrupted.

He resisted the urge to ask if she was okay. He already knew the answer.

"You're late," she murmured, not turning around.

"You're cryptic," Karan countered, stepping beside her. His fists were clenched as he took in the bruises she tried to hide. Trying to keep his voice calm and steady, he said, "Why did you call me here?"

Nisha glanced over her shoulder, as if expecting someone to appear. Then she whispered, "Because everything you think you know is a lie."

Karan's pulse quickened. "What do you mean?"

She turned, eyes flashing. "Suresh is lying."

Karan's pulse quickened. "Suresh was her colleague."

"And the last person to see her alive," Nisha added.

Silence stretched between them.

"Then why pin this on Rohan?" Karan asked.

Nisha let out a bitter laugh. "Because it's easy. Because he's already guilty in the court of public opinion. Because no one wants to dig deeper."

Karan nodded slowly. "But we have no proof."

Her jaw clenched. "We do. Remember the key she gave me. Do you have it with you?"

"Yes."

Nisha stepped closer, her voice urgent. "I remembered – the secret hiding place."

Karan's heart pounded. "Tell me everything."

Nisha inhaled sharply. He tightened his grip on the key.

"Last night I remembered, Sonia's last words to me, '*If anything happens to me... remember where we spent our afternoons.*' It took me some time to piece it together."

She continued, "Sonia loved books," Nisha whispered. "If she hid something, it had to be somewhere safe, somewhere sacred. The old library vault beneath Pemayangtse Monastery; it's the only place no one would question."

"Monasteries keep records," Karan murmured. "Sometimes, old storage rooms. Secret compartments. If Sonia wanted to hide something, she wouldn't have chosen a place where anyone could look."

Karan exhaled, understanding dawning on his face.

"She always loved that library," she whispered, remembering Sonia. "She said it was the only place in Pelling that felt untouched by greed. That's where we spent our afternoons – reading books."

Karan nodded. "Then that's where we start."

Nisha hesitated. "I think she has hidden it in the old library vault, hidden beneath the Pemayangtse monastery."

Karan felt the pieces fall into place. If they found it, they'd have everything they needed.

But before he could speak, Nisha suddenly grabbed his arm. Her voice dropped to a whisper. "We're being watched."

Karan's body tensed. His instincts kicked in immediately. He turned slowly, his gaze flicking to the shadows.

There. A dark figure, lurking near the stone pillars.

"Go," Karan murmured. "Now."

They slipped away into the ruins and lost the stalker.

Karan tightened his grip on his concealed gun as they ran and slipped into his car, where the constables were waiting.

They drove silently towards Pemayangtse Monastery. The ancient monastery loomed ahead, its golden rooftop barely visible under the thick fog that clung to the hills.

Karan and Nisha moved cautiously, their footsteps muffled by the soft, moss-covered stone path leading to the monastery's forbidden archives in the library.

"Are you sure about this?" Nisha whispered, her voice barely audible.

Karan glanced at her, his expression unreadable. "No. But we don't have a choice."

She swallowed hard but nodded. They had come too far to turn back now.

The monastery's archives were located at the farthest wing of the temple, a place few outsiders were ever allowed to enter.

Karan traced his fingers along the wall, feeling for any irregularities.

Then, he found it.

A small engraving, almost invisible in the dim light. A symbol, matching the symbol on the key. He pressed it. A faint click echoed in the stone corridor.

Nisha's breath caught. "What was that?"

Karan pushed against the wooden bookshelf before them, and it shifted.

With a soft creaking sound, the shelf moved, revealing a narrow staircase leading underground.

"Sonia knew this place existed," Karan murmured.

Nisha swallowed hard. "Then we're walking straight into her last secret."

They descended, leaving the constables who were following them behind.

The vault was suffocatingly small, the air thick with dust and the scent of old parchment. Scrolls and forgotten books rested in chaotic heaps, their secrets sealed by time.

But in the centre, on a stone pedestal, sat a single metal lockbox; modern and out of place, among the relics of history.

Karan's heart thumped. "This is it."

Nisha moved forward, reaching into her shawl. "The key…"

She pulled out the small, ornate key Sonia had left her. With trembling hands, she inserted it into the lock.

Click.

The box snapped open. Inside was a bundle of documents, a leather-bound journal, and a USB drive.

Karan carefully lifted the journal and flipped through its pages. Sonia's handwriting filled every inch. There were financial records and details with all the names.

'Suresh is hiding something. He's always meeting MLA Thakur's men at the hotel.

'There's an entire network involved. Trafficking. Poaching. Blackmail. The hotel is a front.

'I think Rohan is trapped. He's being watched by Suresh. He's scared, but he wants out.

'If I disappear, it will be because of Suresh and MLA Thakur. He's dangerous.'

Karan gritted his teeth. Suresh had killed Sonia and framed Rohan. But what was on the USB?

He slid it into the port. Folders and files flooded the screen – documents, photos, audio clips. One video stood out: Confession.mp4.

He clicked it open. The screen crackled to life, revealing a grainy, shaky feed. In the corner, the timestamp read June 13, 2023 – the night Sonia was murdered. The location tag confirmed it: the Royal Pelling Hotel. The footage came from a hidden camera, its angle slightly tilted, the room dimly lit.

Sonia appeared on screen, her expression weary but determined. She sat facing the lens, voice trembling yet fierce.

"If you're watching this," she began, "I'm probably dead. I found something. Something big. MLA Thakur isn't just running a trafficking ring – he's involved in poaching too, and he's corrupted the entire system."

Karan's blood ran cold.

"No..." Nisha whispered, eyes wide.

The screen flickered again, cutting to a different angle – a hidden pen camera this time. The timestamp and location were the same: the night of Sonia's murder, the

Royal Pelling Hotel. Sonia was arguing – but not with Rohan.

With Suresh.

The image broke into static, the last few seconds warped and distorted, but the voices were unmistakable.

Nisha's hand flew to her mouth. "Oh my God."

The video's audio was distorted, but clear enough.

Sonia (angrily): *"I know what you're doing, Suresh. I have proof."*

Suresh: *"You have nothing. "*

Sonia: *"The trafficking, the poaching, the money laundering, which you do for the MLA, all goes through the hotel. And I have names and all the details."*

Suresh (smirking): *"You think anyone will believe you?"*

Sonia: *"I already sent backups to someone I trust."*

Suresh tensed, *"You better mind your own business or I will kill you, and if you don't stay away from Rohan, he will be killed too."*

The image fell into static and stayed there. For a long beat, nothing moved but the tiny white noise on the screen.

Karan and Nisha sat frozen, the light from the monitor painting their faces in ghastly hues. The truth lay bare between the interruptions: Rohan had been framed, and Suresh – Suresh had murdered Sonia. The threat to Rohan. The backups Sonia swore she'd sent.

"We need to duplicate this and get it off the premises," Karan said, voice tight. He reached for the keyboard with shaking fingers. "And we find where Sonia sent the backups. Now."

She began copying the video files, every second a small war against time and those who would bury the truth.

Karan exhaled. "I need to call my niece, Anya, to do a full background check on MLA Thakur. If Suresh is lying, we need to know why."

"And if it's worse than we think?" Nisha asked.

Karan's jaw set. "Then we make sure he never lies again."

The ruins were silent for a moment. Then Nisha stepped closer.

"Thank you for believing me," she murmured.

Karan looked down at her, seeing the exhaustion, the fear, and something else – trust.

His fingers brushed against hers. "I always will. But we need to get out of here. Now."

As he closed the lockbox, he felt it. That unnerving sensation.

They were being watched.

A faint creak echoed in the distance. Karan's hand went to his gun. "Nisha, stay behind me."

The shadows shifted. A figure emerged - tall, deliberate. A man in a black coat, face hidden under a hood. A silencer glinting in his gloved hand.

"You should have left the past buried, Judge."

The muffled gunshot rang out, piercing the sacred silence of the monastery vault.

Karan instinctively pulled Nisha down behind a stone pillar as the bullet slammed into the ancient wooden beam above them. Dust rained down in a fine cloud, the sharp echoes of the gunfire bouncing off the vaulted stone walls.

Footsteps. The gunman was closing in.

Karan clenched his jaw, his grip tightening around his own weapon. He signalled for Nisha to stay low. She nodded, her breath coming in quick, shallow gasps.

Karan dove forward, tackling him. A brutal struggle ensued with fists colliding and bodies slamming into stone walls. Karan landed a hard punch, sending the gunman staggering.

"Run!" he yelled at Nisha.

She hesitated, then bolted toward the exit.

Another shot.

This time, it barely missed Karan's shoulder, embedding into the cold stone beside him.

No time. They had to move.

Karan fired a shot in the attacker's direction; not to hit, but to force him back. The moment the assailant ducked for cover, Karan grabbed Nisha's wrist and pulled her toward the stairs. "Stay down!"

Then he reached for his own gun, but the attacker had vanished into the shadows.

They raced up the narrow passageway, their footsteps thundering against the ancient stone steps. Behind them, the gunman cursed, his heavy boots pounding after them.

The moment they reached the top, Karan shoved the bookshelf back into place, sealing the entrance to the vault.

It wouldn't hold him for long.

They bolted through the monastery, past prayer halls and deserted corridors, the scent of incense thick in the air. Statues of deities loomed in the dim glow of candlelight, silent witnesses to the chaos unfolding.

A monk appeared at the far end of the hallway, startled by the commotion. Karan barely had time to shout, "Stay inside!" before they barrelled past him, heading for the courtyard. The main doors were in sight.

Nisha was panting, shaken. "Who the hell was that?"

Karan's face was grim. "Someone who doesn't want this truth to come out."

He grabbed her wrist, urgency burning in his gaze. They weren't safe yet.

"We have to go public with this. Now."

Nisha's lips parted in shock. "But…"

He held up the USB drive. "This is bigger than just Rohan's case. This is about everything Sonia died for."

Suddenly, a burst of torchlight cut through the trees up ahead.

"Sir! Over here!" a constable's voice rang out.

Two constables emerged from the shadows, rifles raised, eyes scanning the treeline.

"You're late," Karan snapped, dragging Nisha down behind a boulder as another bullet sliced through the branches overhead.

More gunfire erupted behind them; their pursuers were closing in, using the terrain to their advantage. Nisha ducked, covering her head, her chest heaving.

"Cover fire! Now!" Karan ordered.

The constables opened fire, short controlled bursts lighting up the trees. The attackers scattered, ducking into the shadows. For a moment, it gave them breathing space.

Karan checked the USB in his pocket. Still there. Still intact.

He turned to Nisha. "You good to run?"

She nodded, jaw clenched. "Let's finish this."

"We move in formation!" Karan barked to the constables. "One in front, one rear. We head to the south access road. There's a safe house in the next village."

They moved fast, slipping through the forest, low to the ground. The air was damp with mist and dew. Every rustle behind them sounded like death.

Another gunshot cracked; a constable ahead took a hit in the shoulder, dropping with a cry. Karan and the others dragged him behind a tree.

"Bullet went clean through," Karan said, tying a cloth around the wound. "You'll make it."

The wounded constable gritted his teeth, blood staining the bark behind him. "Go, sir. I'll slow them down."

“Not a chance,” Karan muttered. “We all go.”

He turned to Nisha. “Can you hold this pressure?” She nodded, taking over the makeshift bandage while Karan lay down, avoiding another volley of covering fire.

More voices rose behind them; search lights now flickering through the fog. Whoever was behind this had resources, training, and a kill order.

But Karan had the one thing they didn’t.

Proof.

He locked eyes with Nisha. “This ends today.”

Together, with the injured constable supported between them and the other covering their flanks, they disappeared into the forest’s thick underbrush. Behind them, the gunfire faded. The truth was still alive and moving. Now they just had to survive long enough to expose it.

Karan and Nisha sprinted through the dense undergrowth, their breath ragged, feet pounding against the uneven terrain. Gunshots echoed through the ruins, bullets biting into stone and tree bark as their pursuers closed in.

“This way!” Karan pulled Nisha towards a narrow path leading deeper into the forest. The thick foliage provided some cover, but it also meant they were running blind.

A sharp crack sounded; a bullet grazed a tree just inches from Karan’s head. He cursed under his breath, veering sharply to the right.

The monastery ruins vanished behind them, swallowed by the darkness of the forest. They had to keep moving. They couldn’t let themselves be cornered.

After what felt like an eternity, Karan spotted the faint silhouette of his SUV tucked behind a cluster of trees, partially camouflaged by moss and shadows.

Karan gave a terse nod. "Let's move."

Karan helped Nisha into the back seat, then slid in beside her while one constable took the wheel and the other rode shotgun, scanning the rearview mirror. The SUV hummed to life and began descending the winding trail away from the ruins.

The drive down the mountain was quiet, tense. Fog slithered across the road, swallowing everything around it. Nisha clutched her arm, bruises dark against her skin. Karan glanced at her fingers, still trembling.

By the time they reached his guest house, tucked against a hillside away from prying eyes, dawn was just beginning to break. The two constables got out first, checking the perimeter with flashlights drawn.

"Clear," one called back.

Karan ushered Nisha inside. After getting first-aid, the constables remained outside, setting up post at the front and rear entrances of the cottage.

Inside, their shadows moved along the wooden floors, cast by the flicker of the fire crackling in the hearth with wide windows that framed the Himalayan forest like a painting.

Karan bolted the door and turned to Nisha. She was leaning against the wall, her shoulders sagging with exhaustion, her breath uneven, and her cheeks stained with the memory of flight and fear. But her eyes, her eyes held fire.

"That was too close," she whispered.

Karan's gaze dropped to her wrist. The bruises were clearer now under the soft light. He stepped closer, gently taking her hand, pulling her to him.

"Did he do this to you? Because of me?" His voice was low, tightly controlled.

"Don't worry," she said, meeting his eyes. "I gave him sleeping pills before I left."

He exhaled sharply, brushing his fingers over the bruises. She shivered; not from fear, but from the way he touched her. Carefully. Deliberately.

"You shouldn't go back."

"And what do you suggest?" she asked. "That I vanish?"

"Yes," he admitted after a pause. "I can't protect you if you're not with me."

Her breath hitched. "Is that the only reason?"

He stepped in closer. "No. It's not."

His fingers brushed a strand of hair from her face, his touch reverent. Then he cradled her cheek with one hand, his eyes searching hers for permission. And she gave it.

Their lips met; tentative at first, uncertain, as if crossing a line neither had dared to acknowledge until now. But once it broke, the kiss deepened, slow, searching, desperate, as if something long locked away had finally been permitted to breathe.

His mouth moved over hers like a question, and her response came in the way she pressed into him, fingers sliding up into his thick hair, anchoring herself to something real for the first time in what felt like years. As her hands moved up to grip his shoulders, her shawl slipped from her shoulders, pooling silently at her feet. The soft fabric revealed bruises blooming across her collarbone, delicate and dark like storm clouds against porcelain.

Karan stilled. His jaw clenched. He reached out, his fingers brushing the marks with a tenderness that made her shiver.

"You're safe now," he murmured, voice hoarse.

Her eyes didn't waver. "I know."

The air between them thickened, scented with woodsmoke and want, suspended in something too fragile to name, too potent to ignore.

He broke away just long enough to whisper, "Are you sure?"

Nisha nodded. Then, in a voice barely audible, she whispered, "I need this. I need *you*."

That was all it took.

He simply lifted her into his arms, cradling her as though she were fragile. As he carried her to the soft-lit bedroom, she traced his jaw with her fingers, studying the man beneath the armour, disciplined, composed, always in control, now slowly unravelling. She pressed her face into his neck, breathing him in, earth and smoke and something unmistakably him.

She gasped softly as he lay her down on the bed.

Clothes slipped away like whispered secrets, falling to the floor unnoticed, irrelevant. He knelt beside her, and his fingers traced the outline of her collarbone, down her arm, over the curve of her waist, lingering over the fading bruises. His touch made her shiver, not from pain, but from the reverence in it.

As he bent down and kissed each mark with aching tenderness, she closed her eyes and let herself fall into the kiss, into his warmth, into this moment that felt carved out of time.

Their bodies came together slowly, achingly, like waves drawn to the shore after a storm. She lifted her hand and let her fingers thread through his hair, anchoring herself, as waves of sensation pulled her into the moment.

While Karan's fingers traced her like she was something sacred, committing to every curve, every scar, every tremble to memory. Every kiss was soft, tender, a question and a confession all at once.

There were no more words. They moved in perfect rhythm, languid, urgent, then soft again. Gasping, she reached for him, guiding his hand over the curve of her waist, her body humming with anticipation. Her hands caressed him, curious and open, down the ridges of his chest, the soft dip of his waist and below. He shivered beneath her touch. She arched beneath him, fingertips dragging over his back, her heart rising to meet his with each breath. It was about everything they were shedding: pain, fear, restraint. It was something that felt whole.

Slowly, deliberately, he let his hand rest beneath the gentle curve of her breast, then continued downward, skimming the line of her waist, mapping her contours like a sculptor rediscovering his finest work. His thumb brushed across her, and she arched instinctively. An invitation, a wordless plea. That was all the permission he needed.

His lips followed, slow and reverent, pressing warm kisses along her neck, then across the swell of her chest. The trail he left behind felt like fire laced with tenderness. His tongue circled, teased, then sucked gently, pulling her deeper into the moment, grazing her soft, delicate skin.

She trembled beneath him, not from fear, but from the ache that pulsed through her, urgent and sweet. He took his time, each movement precise, every flick of his tongue was like fuel to the fire that had already started inside her. Her back arched, hips lifting slightly as her body responded to his hungry desire.

She moaned, not just from the sensation, but from the sight of him – wild, focused and utterly consumed by her.

His strong hands gently slid down her thighs, coaxing them open as he kissed her stomach, her hips, her inner thighs and everywhere but where she needed him most. Teasing. Worshipping. Learning her. Tasting her skin like he might never get the chance again.

She was breathless now, her lips parted, heart racing, toes curling under the sheets. She felt like she might unravel if he didn't touch her where she needed him most.

And he knew it. He could feel it in the way she moved, in the way she whispered his name like it was the only word that existed.

Still, he took his time.

His fingers skimmed along the inside of her thigh, teasing and deliberate until she was squirming beneath him, her breath caught somewhere between a plea and a moan.

Then finally, he touched her. A soft brush. A slow stroke. A low, pleased sound from his throat as he felt how wet she was for him.

She moaned, her hips lifting toward his hand, and he smiled against her skin.

"You want more?" he murmured, his voice a gravelly whisper against her ear.

She nodded, eyes half-closed, lips parted, "Yes... please."

Then he slowly slid his hand between her thighs, fingers brushing through slick heat, teasing, circling, just enough to make her hips buck up, seeking more.

"Please," she whispered, her voice cracking open with raw need.

Karan smiled against her skin. "Not yet," he murmured. "I want to taste you first."

She barely had time to protest before he lowered himself, kissing his way down her body with reverent, deliberate slowness. When he reached the soft curve of her inner thigh, he paused, his breath warm, his hands steady as they held her gently in place.

Nisha's breath caught as he looked up at her once, his eyes dark and full of meaning, before he dipped his head and touched her with his mouth; softly at first, like he was learning her rhythm. A gasp escaped her lips, one hand clutching the bedsheet, the other tangling in his hair.

He moved with quiet intensity, exploring and tasting her with patient devotion, each motion drawing another whisper of her name from the back of her throat.

She gasped, fingers clutching the sheets, thighs trembling as the sensations rolled through her in waves; sweet, deep, undeniable as her body arched towards him. The sensation was exquisite. Intimate. Electric.

Just when she thought it couldn't go deeper, he added the pressure of his fingers; skilled, intuitive, finding her most sensitive places and coaxing her gently toward the edge again. His rhythm remained controlled, even as her breath quickened, even as she bucked and shuddered beneath him.

Her release came like a tide breaking, sudden, overwhelming, and complete. Her body tightened, trembled. Her voice broke in a moan as the tension within her snapped and melted into release, leaving her shaking, breathless and overwhelmed as her body gave in to everything he was giving her.

She reached for him, pulled him into a kiss that was full of gratitude, wonder, and something deeper, tasting her own release on his lips and not minding at all.

She whispered his name again, not out of necessity, but because in that moment, there was no other word her heart could form.

And then, with a playful smile and a gleam in her eyes, she rolled on top of him. It was her turn now.

With a slow, teasing smile and a gleam in her eyes, she shifted. With graceful confidence, Nisha rolled him onto his back, straddling him. Her hair fell forward like silk curtains, brushing his skin. As her bare form met his, her breasts grazed his chest, as she kissed her way down his body, along the sharp line of his collarbone, over the ridges of his abs, finally reaching the hardness between his thighs.

She gripped him, stroking slowly his length as her tongue teased the tip, then slid all the way down. He let out a guttural sound, his fingers fisting the sheets as she took him into her mouth, her tongue tracing lazy circles, her pace unhurried but wickedly effective.

"God, Nisha... You make me forget everything," he said into the hollow of her throat.

"Then forget," she whispered, threading her fingers into his hair again, urging him on. "Just be here. With me."

When she pulled away, leaving him slick and swollen, he couldn't wait any longer.

She guided him in, slowly, completely, a soft gasp escaping her lips as he entered deeper, watching him unravel above her with his eyes shut, lips parted, muscles taut. They moved together, rising and falling like tide and shore; hard and slow, then building into something faster, urgent. Their bodies drenched in sweat and want.

He flipped her beneath him, lining himself up and pressing into her in one slow, deep thrust. She clung to him with her arms wrapped around his shoulders. A gasp tore from her throat, her nails raked down his back as he filled her completely. Holding on to each other in the storm they'd created together.

A soft cry left her lips, muffled against his neck, as she came apart beneath him, as he held her through it, his body moving with hers, slowly.

He followed soon after, a whispered groan against her ear, as if even in release, he was afraid to let her go. They lay next to each other, half asleep yet unsatiated.

The room had grown still again, save for the faint crackle of the fireplace. Nisha stirred first, shifting under the soft weight of Karan's arm. The fireplace crackled again, louder this time, a warm pop echoing through the quiet. Outside the window, mist clung to the trees like a veil. But inside, the warmth between them still burned, slow and steady.

Karan brushed his fingers along her nape, trailing down her back, pausing at her waist. This time, his touch wasn't asking. It was claiming.

Nisha shifted once more, sliding over him, the bedsheet slipping from her back. The firelight danced across her skin, highlighting the golden curves of her body, the softness of her gaze. Karan's hands moved instinctively up her thighs, over her hips, along the curve of her back.

Their lips brushing again, lazy, teasing, lingering.

"I don't think we're finished," she whispered against his mouth.

Karan responded by sitting up, wrapping an arm around her waist and pulling her closer. "No," he murmured, "we're just getting started."

"We'll never sleep," she whispered back, her voice like silk.

"Then we won't," he said, breathless, eyes dark with affection, "Just one more time."

He stood, lifting her effortlessly into his arms, and she wrapped her legs around him, arms around his neck, soft laughter escaping her lips as he carried her across the room.

He set her down gently against the wide windowsill, just beside the fireplace, where warmth met the chill of the air seeping through the old panes.

Karan lowered her gently onto the window seat cushioned with wool throws, her back now framed by the glass pane and the flickering fire beside them. She gasped when he pressed her gently against the cool glass behind her. The contrast of heat and cold, firelight and morning frost, sent a thrill down her spine.

"Here?" she asked, breathless.

He kissed the corner of her mouth. "Yes."

He dropped to his knees before her. She looked down, breath shallow, heart thundering. There was something disarming about seeing him like this, powerful, controlled Karan, willingly brought to his knees for her.

His hands gripped her thighs gently, his thumbs stroking soft circles into her skin, brushing a kiss just above her hip bone. She gasped, as anticipation coiled in her belly like fire waiting to catch.

"I want to worship you," he said softly, voice gravel-edged. "Let me."

She nodded, wordless. Trusting.

His mouth followed the curve of her inner thigh, lips parting to press heat into the most sensitive places. Her breath trembled. She arched toward him instinctively, guided by need and the tension his touch left in its wake.

He looked up at her, studying her for a moment, her flushed cheeks, tousled hair, eyes filled with longing, before coming up for a kiss again. This kiss was deeper, darker, sweet and searing. His tongue tangled with hers, and she melted into him. His warm breath and his stubble grazed her skin in the most delicious way. His hands slid behind her, supporting her lower back as she arched toward him, hips rolling forward instinctively. "I can't stop touching you," he whispered, his voice frayed.

"Then don't," she replied, lips barely parting as waves of sensation rippled through her. She murmured his name, not pleading, offering. Trusting.

Her lips found his temple, his cheekbone, the corner of his mouth. "You're still with me," she whispered against his skin.

"Always," he breathed, eyes locked on hers.

Each roll of her hips was met with his gentle guidance, his hands framing her like he couldn't quite believe she was real. Their bodies whispered secrets, their eyes held stories too long buried.

Her body curved forward, and they moved in the glow of the fire, silhouetted against the glass. Each movement was bold now, confident, unafraid. Their breath fogged the window behind her, their sighs and gasps mixing with the crackle of the fire.

It was wild, but not rushed. Hungry, but not careless. Like they had something to prove, and nothing left to hide.

They moved faster now, the pace building, tension tightening like a drawn bow. When release came, it was quiet, but devastating, her body clenching around him, his grip tightening, both of them falling together into something vast and unspoken.

They lost count of how many times, how many positions, and how many gasps and growls were shared in the dark. Each time more intense, more raw, more necessary. The bed creaked softly beneath them.

When finally they collapsed, breathless and trembling, the room was soaked in heat, and they lay tangled in a slow, sensual rhythm that burned and soothed all at once, fingers locked, breath mingled, hearts completely unguarded.

Their whispers filled the room, words unspoken in daylight, now confessed in darkness.

And as the hours passed, they rediscovered each other over and over again, until there was nothing left to give but everything. And when they finally collapsed together, their bodies slick with sweat, skin flushed, chests rising in sync; it wasn't just exhaustion, or just physical release.

It was something more. A surrender. A transformation. A sealing.

A silent vow whispered between kisses and held in the beat of two hearts racing in unison. They clung to each other through the aftermath, neither willing to let go.

As they slowly sank back down onto the mattress, tangled together, beneath the soft sheets, skin warm, hearts finally steady, a soft laugh escaped her lips.

"What?" he murmured, brushing his thumb over her cheek.

"I think we're going to be very, very tired today," she said sleepily.

Karan smiled, pressing a kiss to her forehead. "Worth it."

"Every second," she whispered, and curled into his chest.

Eventually, sleep came for them. And only when the first streaks of dawn kissed the horizon did they drift off, wrapped in each other.

Spent. Changed.

Later, when the room was still and only a solitary birdsong filled the morning air, Nisha stirred.

Karan was already watching her, eyes heavy with thought.

She brushed a hand through his dishevelled hair. "It's 6 a.m. We need to go."

"There's still a lot to be done," he said, "before we can finally be together, for good."

She smiled, soft, unguarded.

He cupped her face. "I won't let anything happen to you."

And she believed him, lying in his arms, which were still wrapped around her like armour. In this stolen morning, she felt something she hadn't felt in years.

Safe.

And for the first time, she whispered the words they'd both been afraid to say.

"I love you."

Karan froze. His breath caught. Then he kissed her again, hard, deep, desperate.

Because now, he knew. He wouldn't let her go. Not ever. They parted only to fight again. And they'd fight side by side.

Chapter 18
Unmasking

Patience is also a form of action.
- Auguste Rodin

Anya arrived at the courthouse just in time for the inquiry. Every muscle in her body ached, exhaustion pulling at her limbs, but she couldn't afford to stop now. She sprinted up the courthouse steps, weaving through the crowd of journalists, police officers, and spectators who had gathered outside, her breath coming in sharp gasps.

Cameras flashed, microphones thrust forward, voices overlapping in a chaotic symphony of questions and speculations.

Ignoring them, Anya pushed through the heavy wooden doors and stepped inside.

Across the hallway, she spotted Karan. He was battered but standing, his face marred by bruises, his expression unreadable. Their eyes met, and a wave of relief washed over her.

"You're alive," she breathed, her chest tightening.

Karan gave a curt nod, gripping her shoulder. "And you made it. Tell me you found something."

Anya didn't hesitate. She reached into her pocket and pressed the small USB drive into his palm.

"More than something," she whispered. "It's everything."

Karan's fingers curled around the device, his mind racing. If what she said was true, if this drive contained undeniable proof, then the true mastermind was about to be exposed. Thakur had orchestrated everything from behind the scenes. The inquiry was a success.

He exhaled sharply, the weight of the moment settling over him. Without another word, they moved toward his office.

Inside, Leela looked up from a pile of case files, her sharp eyes widening in surprise.

"Karan?" she asked, her gaze flicking between him and Anya.

Karan shut the door and turned to his team. "Meet Anya, my niece. She's been working with me as a cyber forensic expert, along with us. She did a background check on Suresh, and she just brought us the missing piece of the puzzle."

Anya stepped forward, placing the flash drive on the desk. "It's worse than we thought."

Leela's brows furrowed as she picked up the drive. "What's on this?"

"The missing piece of evidence." Anya's voice was low but firm. "The proof we needed. Suresh isn't just a murderer. He's a serial predator. And Inspector Singh, he's been covering for him all along."

Before anyone could react, a court officer stepped into the room and announced, "Judge *saab*, we're ready for the inquiry."

Karan turned to his team. "Gather all the evidence: the hotel footage, the shop's CCTV, Sonia's USB drive, the forensic reports, evidence of the murder, and finally the printout of all the forensic evidence brought in by Anya. We're bringing everything in."

Anya nodded, her pulse hammering.

Karan asked the officer. "Check if Suresh has been brought in."

The officer saluted. "Yes, sir. He's here, waiting and secured in holding. The Commission of Inquiry resumes in ten minutes."

Karan instructed Anya, his voice low. "Stay close. This isn't over yet."

They stepped into the outer chamber of the courtroom, where the inquiry proceedings were set to begin. Karan adjusted his tie, his fingers betraying none of the nerves simmering beneath his composed exterior. He had prepared for this moment meticulously, anticipating every counterargument, every possible diversion the opposition might attempt.

The atmosphere was full of anticipation; every seat in the gallery was occupied; journalists, political figures, Sonia Verma's grieving parents, and a sea of curious onlookers, hungry for justice.

Karan had allowed the media and the public to attend, ensuring complete transparency and safety. At the front, a row of cameras and microphones was set, their lenses trained to capture every detail of the historic and dramatic finale to the inquiry proceedings and ready to broadcast every second of it for the world to dissect.

On one side, the prosecution team, led by Special Public Prosecutor Harsh Bhatia, sat with their stacks of forensic reports, CCTV footage, and witness statements.

Opposite them, Rohan Thakur sat at the defence table, expressionless, his eyes staring straight ahead, almost resigned to his fate. His new lawyer, Arvind Mehta, one of Delhi's finest defence attorneys, accompanied by his previous lawyer, Sunil Tiwari, was cool and collected.

Unlike a criminal trial, this was not about guilt or innocence; it was about uncovering the truth. The Commission, chaired by Karan, had the authority to summon witnesses, review evidence, and make recommendations for further prosecution. But Karan had deviously planned the whole sequence as if it were a courtroom proceeding for the full effect in front of the media.

MLA Thakur, his expression unreadable, was flanked by his high-profile legal team. His once-imposing presence was reduced to a shadow of arrogance barely holding itself together. His legal team, hand-picked to protect him from any liability, whispered furiously amongst themselves as this rumour of damning new evidence threatened to burn their carefully constructed defence to the ground.

Karan's gaze flicked to Nisha, sitting at the back of the courtroom. Arms crossed. Face unreadable.

Watching. Waiting.

Karan kept a file on the table. Inside, Suresh's real identity, his past crimes, and the forensic proof linking him to Sonia's murder.

Karan struck his gavel. "This Commission of Inquiry has been convened to investigate the murder of Sonia Verma and the alleged cover-up. The proceedings shall begin."

The lead prosecutor, Harsh Bhatia, stood. "We begin today's proceedings with witness examination."

Priya, in the gallery, exhaled slowly, her eyes darting between the prosecution and the defence. Then she came towards Karan, whispering, "MLA Thakur's lawyers just filed a motion to dismiss any new evidence."

Karan sighed. Predictable. Ill-advised.

"Motion denied," he said flatly. "We proceed."

Rohan looked nervous, unaware of what to expect.

Nisha sat in the back of the courtroom, her fingers curled into fists on her lap. Her jaw tightened, but her expression remained impassive; a mask carefully held in place. Only her eyes, dark and stormy, betrayed the turmoil within her.

Karan glanced at her and felt something wasn't right.

Harsh Bhatia walked towards the front of the room, buttoning his suit jacket and commenced in his sharp voice, his tone commanding.

"This was not an act of impulse. It was premeditated murder. The prosecution will establish, beyond a reasonable doubt, that Rohan Thakur not only had motive but also the opportunity to eliminate Sonia Verma. We will demonstrate through forensic analysis, digital evidence, and eyewitness testimony that the accused is responsible for this heinous crime."

Karan nodded. "Proceed. Call the first witness."

The bailiff called out: "Jatin, hotel staff member at Pelling View Inn."

A young, nervous-looking man took the stand.

Bhatia wasted no time.

"Where were you on the night of Sonia Verma's murder?"

The witness gulped. "I was at the hotel, sir. In the corridor near the terrace."

Bhatia braced his elbows on the table. "And what did you see?"

Jatin hesitated, then spoke. "I saw Mr. Rohan Thakur... arguing with Ms. Sonia Verma."

A murmur rippled through the courtroom.

Bhatia nodded. "And did you hear what they were arguing about?"

Jatin fidgeted. "I... I only heard bits and pieces... but Sonia was yelling. She said, '*You don't have the courage to stand against him, do you?*'"

Bhatia turned dramatically toward Karan.

"Your Honour, this clearly indicates that Sonia Verma had damaging information about the accused or his father, MLA Thakur. She was pressuring him. And what happened next?"

Jatin's voice dropped. "Rohan grabbed her wrist. She pulled away and stormed off. This is also seen in the CCTV footage retrieved."

The prosecution then played a grainy CCTV clip.

Bhatia paced. "And what did you see after that?"

Jatin looked down. "A few hours later... she was dead."

The next witness was Dr. Meena Iyer, chief forensic examiner.

Bhatia stepped forward.

"Dr. Iyer, what did your autopsy reveal as the cause of death?"

Dr. Iyer cleared her throat. "Ms. Verma died due to blunt force trauma to the skull. The impact suggests that she was struck with a heavy, blunt object and then burnt."

Bhatia held up an evidence bag. Inside was a *kukhri* and a rope, wrapped in plastic.

"This, your Honour, was found near the crime scene." He turned to the forensic expert.

"Yes. The *kukhri* has a partial fingerprint matching the accused, Rohan Thakur."

A collective gasp rippled through the courtroom.

Bhatia's expression hardened. "So, to summarise: Rohan Thakur's fingerprint is on the murder weapon. CCTV footage from the shop is proof of him having an argument. And an eyewitness saw Rohan near the forest clearing before she died, and his car was seen by the tea stand lady."

He turned to the Karan.

"Your Honour, we have already established a timeline. The evidence is overwhelming. And now, we will hear from the one man who can confirm, beyond doubt, that Rohan Thakur murdered Sonia Verma."

The heavy oak doors of the courtroom creaked open. All eyes turned toward the entrance.

A young man in his early thirties limped inside, his face gaunt, his skin sallow from years of hardship. His dark, sunken eyes flickered with something between fear and defiance. He adjusted his wrinkled shirt, trying to mask his nervousness.

The bailiff's voice rang clear. "State's witness, Suresh Kumar."

Murmurs rippled through the courtroom. Journalists whispered urgently, pens poised over notepads. The defence team exchanged quick glances.

Karan's eyes locked onto Suresh. *This is it. The final piece of the puzzle. If he cracks, everything unravels. Hope the plan succeeds*.

Karan kept his features neutral, but inside, his mind was racing.

Bhatia, the lead prosecutor, stepped forward, his voice steady, commanding.

"Mr. Kumar, you are testifying under oath. You understand that any attempt of a false statement to mislead this Inquiry Commission will be treated as perjury?"

Bhatia gestured grandly. "Mr. Suresh, please tell the court what Rohan told you the night of the murder."

Suresh licked his dry lips and, in a shaky voice, said, "Yes… sir."

Bhatia nodded. "Tell the court what you told the police."

Suresh's fingers tapped against the wooden railing of the witness stand. Finally, he exhaled, lowered his eyes and spoke. "That night… Rohan Thakur came to me. He was panicking. I'd never seen him like that before."

Bhatia stepped closer. "What did he say?"

Suresh hesitated. His eyes flicked toward Rohan Thakur, sitting rigid at the defence table.

Bhatia pressed. "Speak, Mr. Kumar."

Suresh swallowed hard. "He said… *'I didn't mean to hurt her. It wasn't supposed to happen like this.'*"

A gasp swept through the courtroom like a wave. The sound of pens scratching hurriedly on notepads filled the air.

Rohan Thakur clenched his fists on the table, his face blank but his knuckles white, while his father, MLA Thakur, shifted in his seat, his expression unreadable behind dark sunglasses.

Bhatia turned to the media persons, his voice slow, deliberate. "You heard that, ladies and gentlemen. A direct confession. Not hearsay. Not speculation. The accused, Rohan Thakur, confessed to the main witness."

Karan's jaw tightened. The tension in the room thickened. He watched the room carefully. Some looked shaken. Others sceptical.

Bhatia wasn't done. "Mr. Kumar, what else did Rohan say?"

Suresh hesitated again, rubbing his fingers together as if trying to steady himself. "He said…" He cleared his throat. "He said, *'She was threatening to expose us. I had no choice.'* He said this gloatingly."

Another collective gasp.

Bhatia's expression hardened. "Expose *who*, Mr. Kumar?"

Suresh glanced at MLA Thakur again. His throat bobbed as he swallowed. "I... I don't know."

Bhatia's eyes narrowed. "You don't know, or you're afraid to say?"

Silence.

Bhatia turned to Karan. "Your Honour, the prosecution submits that Sonia Verma was murdered because she had information that could bring down Rohan Thakur's truth."

Karan's voice was level. "The Commission will consider this testimony."

Arvind Mehta, the Defence Attorney, shot up from his seat, his tone sharp. "Objection! The CCTV footage doesn't show the murder. It only shows my client and the victim arguing. It only proves that my client was there. It does not prove he killed her. That is not evidence of homicide."

Karan nodded. "Sustained. However, the Commission will weigh the credibility of Mr. Kumar's testimony."

Mehta pressed on. "Your Honour, this witness is a known criminal. His words cannot be taken at face value."

Bhatia was ready. "The defence is correct, Mr. Kumar has a criminal record. But let me remind the court that criminals *often* work with those in power. The truth does not become invalid just because it comes from a less-than-perfect witness."

Mehta scoffed. "A convenient argument, Prosecutor. You expect all of us to believe the words of a man who has lied his entire life?"

Bhatia smirked. "Oh, I don't *expect* them to believe him, Mr. Mehta. I expect them to believe the *evidence* that backs his claims."

With that, he gestured to the bailiff, who placed a plastic evidence bag on the prosecution table. Inside it was the *khukri*, its metal gleaming under the fluorescent lights.

Bhatia's voice was razor-sharp. "This weapon was found near the crime scene. It has Sonia Verma's blood… and Rohan Thakur's fingerprint."

More whispers.

Mehta's jaw tightened. "Circumstantial."

Bhatia chuckled dryly. "*Circumstantial*? A recorded altercation, a murder weapon with his fingerprint, a witness hearing a confession; if that's not evidence, then what is?"

Karan held up a hand. "Enough. The commission will decide."

Bhatia again turned toward the media. "Motive. Forensics. Digital trail. A confession. The prosecution rests."

Karan nodded. "Sustained. However, the commission may weigh the credibility of the witness."

Bhatia folded his arms. "Your Honour, the evidence is overwhelming. The motive, the forensics, the digital footprint, and now a confession. There is no doubt that Rohan Thakur murdered Sonia Verma. I rest my case."

Arvind Mehta strolled toward Suresh with slow, deliberate steps. "Mr. Kumar, did Rohan explicitly say, 'I strangled Sonia Verma'?"

Suresh hesitated. "Not those exact words, no."

Mehta nodded as if satisfied. "No further questions."

Mehta had just let the most damning testimony slide by without a fight. He then turned to the forensic report.

"Dr. Iyer, were there any other sets of fingerprints found near the crime scene?"

A brief hesitation. "Yes."

Mehta pounced. "And were they tested?"

Dr. Iyer shifted in her seat. "Not all."

Mehta's eyes narrowed. "Why not?"

Bhatia cut in. "Objection. This is irrelevant."

Karan leaned forward. "Overruled. Answer the question, Dr. Iyer."

Dr. Iyer cleared her throat. "Some prints were deemed inconclusive due to partial smudging."

A ripple of doubt spread through the courtroom.

Now, Mehta turned to the people of the media, his voice calm but firm. "We have a witness who admits Rohan never confessed explicitly. We have fingerprint evidence that was selectively tested. And we have no CCTV footage showing the actual murder."

A pause.

"So I ask you, is this proof really beyond a reasonable doubt?"

Bhatia smirked, stepping forward again. "Your Honour, at this point, we request the commission to consider the overwhelming evidence presented. We have CCTV footage, forensic proof, and now a witness confirming the accused's confession."

He turned to Karan, voice dropping to a persuasive rhythm. "This is not a case of reasonable doubt. This is a case of justice finally catching up to power.

"Your Honour," Bhatia continued, his voice dripping with finality, "the prosecution rests."

But Karan wasn't done. Now that everyone was done, it was his turn to question. His fingers tightened around his pen.

"I have questions for Mr. Suresh – or should I say Mohd. Ismail?"

Suresh frowned. "Who? What?"

A ripple of confusion stirred in the room.

"Silence."

Karan's gaze was cool, unwavering.

"Mohd. Ismail aka Suresh, the evidence you provided… has been verified as fabricated."

The air seemed to be sucked out of the room.

Suresh's smirk faltered for the first time, "What?"

Karan's voice quiet but cutting, he pressed on. "You ran from Delhi because they were closing in on you, weren't they? You thought Pelling was a safe hideout. And then, you got greedy.

"The forensics team re-examined the prints. They weren't *Rohan Thakur's*. They were *yours*."

Gasps.

Bhatia spun around. "That's not possible. What the hell?"

Karan's lips pressed into a thin line. "Oh, but it is. The fingerprints on the handle were lifted after the fact. Planted. By *you*."

Suresh's fingers twitched against the wooden railing.

Karan didn't let up. "You worked for MLA Thakur. You arranged disappearances. You cleaned up his messes. And when Sonia became a threat, you..."

Suresh cut him off, his voice sharp. "NO!"

Karan didn't blink. "Then who did?"

Silence.

"You're a fixer, Suresh. But Sonia – she was different. She was too smart. She *knew* something."

Sweat trickled down Suresh's temple. His breathing quickened. The crescendo was getting unbearable.

Karan pressed. "She had something big enough to scare even MLA Thakur, didn't she?"

Suresh's hands curled into fists. "SHE SHOULD HAVE WALKED AWAY."

Karan slammed the file shut. "But she didn't. Because she believed in justice."

A tense pause.

Then, Suresh let out a cold, humourless chuckle. A bead of sweat trickled down his temple, and he shifted in his seat. "You think you know everything, don't you?" he whispered.

"I know enough," Karan shot back. "Enough to put you away for life."

Suresh scoffed, but it lacked conviction. His voice was barely above a whisper. "You're forgetting one thing, Judge *saab*." He leaned forward, his voice a low growl. "I'm not the only one in this."

Karan narrowed his eyes. "Who else? MLA Thakur?" Karan said, his voice dangerously low. "The trafficking ring, the cover-ups, Sonia's murder and you were his fixer."

Suresh let out a slow exhale. His head was swooning in circles, his eyes were rolling upwards, and his confidence was waning. "I had no choice," he muttered. "You don't say no to Thakur."

Karan tilted his head and looked directly at Suresh. "You had a choice the moment you killed Sonia."

Suresh's jaw tightened. "She was going to ruin everything. She found out too much."

Karan's fists clenched. "And now, you're going to pay for it."

Karan's eyes locked on Suresh as he picked up the file and showed it to him. "This isn't just paperwork," he said, flipping open the folder. "It's DNA evidence. Forensic and financial transactions. CCTV footage placing you at the scene of Sonia's murder."

"Who else?" Karan asked.

Suresh gave him a cold, toothy grin. "You already know. You just don't want to believe it."

Karan's stomach twisted. "Inspector Vikram Singh?"

"You're too late," Suresh sneered. "You take me down, and they will make sure you never leave this courthouse alive. You've already lost, Judge *saab*."

The shockwaves created a tidal wave of gasps in the court. The world was watching.

Karan clenched his jaw. "We'll see about that." He turned to the bailiff and ordered. "Place Mr. Suresh under protective custody. And summon Inspector Vikram Singh."

Suresh's smirk wavered, but he quickly masked it with indifference. He shifted in his chair, the chains betraying his nerves, as they rattled against the steel chair. "You think you've won, Judge *saab*?" he sneered, but his voice had lost its edge. "You think a few files and a dead woman's video will change the system?"

Karan said nothing. His steady gaze didn't waver – and more than the words, Karan's gaze unnerved Suresh.

He shifted, eyes darting to the officers at the door. The cold glint of their holstered guns, the quiet buzz among the spectators, the sharp eyes of the press – it all pressed in on him. For the first time, he didn't feel powerful; he felt trapped.

Suresh's fingers twitched. He opened his mouth, closed it, then exhaled sharply – a long, shaking breath that carried the sound of a man cracking. His eyes, once mocking, were now rimmed with a strange mix of fear, rage and defeat.

He exhaled sharply, his smirk now fully erased "I killed her," he muttered.

The courtroom froze.

The clerk dropped his pen. A reporter gasped. Somewhere at the back, a woman stifled a cry. The murmur of disbelief spread like wildfire through the chamber.

Mehta blinked as though he hadn't heard correctly. "Your Honour – did he–?"

"Yes," Karan said quietly, eyes locked on Suresh. "We all heard him."

A muscle in Suresh's jaw twitched.

Bhatia's knuckles turned white as he gripped the table edge. Mehta straightened, face drained of colour. The court stenographer hesitated, then resumed typing – her fingers trembling on the keys.

Karan's voice rang through the silent courtroom.

"This isn't just about Sonia Verma's murder. This is about *justice catching up to power*."

At the back of the courtroom, MLA Thakur's jaw tightened. His lips barely moved as he leaned toward his aide. "Handle it," he whispered.

Outside, thunder rolled across the sky – low, threatening, as if the heavens themselves were taking note.

Inside, the walls of power were beginning to crumble. Karan had presided over many hearings, but none carried the weight of this one. This wasn't just about justice; it was about exposing the rot that had festered beneath the surface for too long.

"This Commission has reviewed extensive evidence linked to MLA Thakur," Karan began, his voice firm. "Testimonies, forensic reports, and financial transactions all point to his involvement in human trafficking, illegal wildlife trade, and multiple homicides, including the murder of Sonia Verma."

Mehta smirked. "Mere allegations."

Karan remained unshaken. "The evidence speaks for itself."

Then he looked at Leela, and she played the final piece of evidence left by Sonia – the footage on the projector screen; grainy yet damning. Clips of Suresh meeting with Thakur's associates, black money transactions, and footage of Sonia's last known movements before her murder filled the screen. Gasps repeatedly rippled through the crowd. Reporters scribbled furiously, phones buzzed as social media exploded with real-time updates.

Phones buzzed. Journalists scribbled. The truth was now viral.

Thakur's lawyer smirked. "Mere allegations. Circumstantial at best, Your Honour."

Karan didn't flinch. "Let's put that to the test."

He gestured toward Anya, who had compiled an airtight digital dossier. Anya stood, her presence sharp and commanding. She activated a live forensic audit, the screen displaying undeniable proof of transactions funnelled into offshore accounts. Bribes to officials. Payments to known traffickers. Blood money.

And then, the final blow.

Suresh screamed, "Thakur used me. Gave me power, protection. Told me to get rid of women like Sonia who stood in his way. And I did it. I did it all for him."

A murmur rippled through the courtroom. News anchors whispered into microphones. Twitter exploded with real-time updates.

Even Thakur's legal team shifted uneasily.

Karan banged the gavel. "Silence!"

He turned his gaze back to Thakur. "Sonia Verma was about to expose you, wasn't she? That's why you sent Suresh after her."

For the first time, Thakur's smirk faltered. But he recovered quickly, leaning forward, his voice dripping with venom. "You have no idea who you're messing with, Judge *saab*. You have no idea the reach the system has."

Karan met his stare with an unwavering gaze. "And you have no idea how far justice is willing to reach."

"Record this: MLA Thakur, you are going to be subjected to a criminal trial for human trafficking, conspiracy to commit murder, and corruption, and immediately are being placed under judicial custody."

Karan's gaze shifted toward the uniformed man standing rigidly at the edge of the courtroom.

"Inspector Vikram Singh," he said, his voice cutting through the chaos. "You are hereby placed under arrest for suppressing evidence and intimidating witnesses."

A ripple of shock swept through the room. Vikram froze, his jaw tightening as two constables stepped forward.

Karan turned then, his eyes finding Rohan. "Based on newly uncovered evidence and the confession of Suresh

Kumar, this Commission declares Rohan Thakur not guilty."

The words landed like thunder and travelled like a forest fire.

On every live broadcast, banners flashed across every news channel: *"Breaking: Rohan Thakur Acquitted."*

Rohan slumped in his chair, as if the strings that held him upright had been cut. A breath he'd been holding finally escaped. Freedom. But also, grief.

The room erupted. Applause broke out from Sonia's supporters. Journalists shouted into phones. Thakur stood frozen.

Inside the courtroom, the MLA sat still, his face observing everything in disbelief.

He snapped. "You fools! You think I'll rot in a cell like a common criminal? I built this city!"

His hands flailed as he fought back, snarling, shouting curses.

"This isn't over!" he roared, but this time, his voice was drowned by the sound of justice crashing down around him – no one listened.

Judge Karan Negi remained still, watching the man who had controlled Pelling for years, losing control over himself as he knew that the moment he walked out of this room, they would come for him too.

The gavel came down again.

A tense silence hung between them.

Karan adjusted his glasses and spoke with the cold clarity of someone who had reached the end of an inquiry. "Mohd. Ismail, also known as Suresh Kumar – based on the evidence presented, this Commission finds you responsible and recommends immediate prosecution for the death of Sonia Verma."

As the officers moved toward Suresh, he lunged forward in one quick motion, grabbed a pen from the table and drove it deep into his throat.

Gasps turned to screams.

Blood spilt like ink, soaking the wooden table. Blood spurted as he convulsed, his breath gurgling. Officers rushed forward, but it was too late. His body slumped forward, lifeless, a dark crimson pool spreading across the table.

Leela covered her mouth. Priya turned away, tears in her eyes.

Karan stared at the scene, his heart pounding. It was over.

Or so he thought. A commotion filled the room.

But Karan knew this fight wasn't finished. Not yet.

"This Commission of Inquiry will now submit its findings to the government for conducting a criminal hearing. Let justice take its due course against all remaining accused."

The gavel came down. Once and then twice.

Journalists scrambled toward the front doors of the courthouse, camera flashes illuminating the evening sky like lightning. News vans lined the streets, their engines running, anchors live on air.

The Courthouse front exploded in media frenzy. News banners screamed: "*MLA Thakur Arrested in Sensational Murder Inquiry*", "*Suresh Kumar Dead in Courtroom - Suicide or Silencing?*", "*Justice or Conspiracy? Nation Divided After Verdict*", "*The End of Political Privilege? MLA's accused of High-Profile Killing!*", "*Justice for Sonia Verma or Political Conspiracy?*"

The moment the MLA walked toward the exit, news reporters shouted questions, their voices overlapping into a deafening roar.

"Mr. Thakur, will you challenge the report?"

"Do you maintain your innocence?"

"What do you have to say to Sonia Verma's family?"

"Sir, we need to leave," a nervous advisor urged. "The situation is escalating."

The verdict sent shockwaves across the country.

News channels ran heated debates, social media exploded with hashtags, and every political party had something to say.

Televisions across the country blared with breaking-news debates - in homes, offices, and roadside tea stalls alike. Passionate anchors demanded answers, their voices rising above the studio noise. "Why was Rohan Thakur framed?" one shouted, as rival panellists argued over motives and cover-ups. Every channel had its own headline, its own outrage, and the nation couldn't look away.

"The Inquiry Had Glaring Inconsistencies – Why Did No One Stop It?", "Who Really Killed Sonia Verma?"

By nightfall, the nation was glued to its screens. Every major channel had gone into overdrive, dissecting the Inquiry's shocking climax from every possible angle. Studio lights glared, anchors spoke over each other, and the words *justice* and *conspiracy* echoed across airwaves.

On *IDTV Prime,* the anchor's voice carried a mix of awe and disbelief.

Anchor: *"Today, we witnessed what some are calling a historic conviction," she began. "Suresh Kumar, also known as Mohd. Ismail, the puppet of powerful MLA Aditya Thakur, was proven guilty of the murder of receptionist Sonia Verma. But was this truly justice... or is there more to the story? Why did he kill himself before the world, right inside the Inquiry Room?"*

"Was this a political witch hunt or a landmark moment in India's judicial history?"

The debate erupted.

Advocate Ramesh Talwar: *"The Commission relied on verified evidence. This isn't about politics. It's about law."*

Faye Ahuja: *"And yet, the cyber evidence conveniently appeared at the last minute. Who benefits?"*

Ajay Rathore: *"This is classic political cleansing before elections. Make no mistake, this was engineered."*

TV Panel Discussion – IDTV Prime

Anchor: "Today, we witnessed what some are calling a 'historic conviction' – Suresh Kumar, aka Mohd. Ismail, the puppet of powerful MLA Aditya Thakur, was proven guilty of the murder of receptionist Sonia Verma. But was this truly justice, or is there more to the story?

Why did he kill himself in front of the whole world in the Inquiry Room?"

Panellists Debate: At 9 p.m.

Senior Advocate Ejaz Ahmed: "The evidence against MLA Thakur is overwhelming. The judiciary has proven that no one is above the law."

Investigative Journalist Rohini Razdan: "I disagree. There are glaring inconsistencies in this case. Why was there no forensic timeline presented? Was this inquiry manipulated?"

Political Analyst Raghu Yadav: "This is nothing but a political hit job. The opposition has been waiting for a chance to take down MLA Thakur for years! This is a conspiracy, not justice!"

Sonia Verma's former colleague, Vidhi Saxena: "Are we seriously saying that Sonia, a hotel receptionist at Thakur's Royal Pelling Hotel, wasn't murdered by Thakur? She knew something dangerous, and MLA Thakur silenced her. Let's not pretend he's innocent."

Hashtags were trending on Social Media: #JusticeForSonia – Trending at #1, demanding the maximum sentence for Rohan, #FramedByTheSystem – At #2, #FramedThakur – Trending at #3, claiming he was framed, #MLAExposed – At #4, #WhoReallyKilledSonia? – A conspiracy thread gaining traction.

A tweet from @TruthUncovered went viral:

"Where was the forensic audit before the Inquiry? How did a corrupt cop like Vikram Singh stay hidden for so long? Something stinks. We're not done yet. #WhoReallyKilledSonia"

Karan watched from the courthouse steps as the aftermath unfolded.

Rohan's name was cleared. Though the weight of his father's sins would always linger, he was free to carve out a future of his own. He left the courthouse without a word, stepping into a life that was finally his to control.

Sonia's parents, however, were left with nothing but memories of their daughter. They walked out clutching a faded photograph of Sonia as her father stared blankly ahead. The verdict brought justice, but not their daughter back. The silence between them was heavier than the gavel's final strike.

Karan went back to the guesthouse. The night was too quiet. The kind of quiet that makes every heartbeat sound like thunder. Karan sat at the edge of his bed, the dim lamp casting long shadows across the room. The bottle sat half-empty on the table. The loneliness sat full in his chest.

He opened his journal again. No courtroom, no argument, no mask, just the ache of absence, distilled into words.

Frustrations Galore...

You were on my mind when I woke up this morning – I was remembering your smile

I guess the next time I'll see your face will take a little while

I was remembering your arms around me

How I loved the way I felt wrapped up in them

I was remembering your voice

It made my heart skip a beat

How the very sight of you made my day – it was such a treat

Remembering your eyes

how they always met mine

remembering all the little things you said – to make it all seem worthwhile

I was wondering when we'll be together – just the two of us...

I guess I'm missing you more than I usually do.

Tonight...

I'm lying here again, staring at the stars, thinking of you!

I feel so alone when you're not around.

It feels as if the walls are coming down.

I close my eyes, and you're here.

I see your face, feel your touch, and taste your kiss.

I'm constantly thinking of you...

When something goes wrong, and I'm down,

Thinking of you always brings me around.

I've pondered over it time and again

It's a bittersweet feeling that causes a bittersweet pain

I thought it might be loneliness, but realised that's not what it really is

It's just a feeling of solitude – and in this solitude, I might even begin to find bliss.

He closed the notebook and leaned back, and looked out the window. The stars outside were hidden tonight, but in his mind, she still stood under them, smiling.

Epilogue
A New Beginning

Don't cry because it's over. Smile because it happened.

- Dr. Seuss

The next couple of days, back at the guesthouse, Karan had many a peaceful night's sleep after a long time.

He stood by the window, suitcase by his side.

The newspaper headlines screamed:

"The Fall of Thakur: Justice Has Spoken"

"Pelling's Dirty Secrets Finally Exposed"

"One Girl's Death Shook a Nation"

He looked older today; tired, not from lack of sleep, but from carrying the weight of justice for far too long. This inquiry hadn't just been about one man's crimes. It had become something bigger. A reckoning.

MLA Thakur was arrested within hours. The trafficking ring was dismantled, its web of corruption exposed. His properties were raided, bank accounts frozen, every connection and ally he had spent decades cultivating vanished like smoke.

On his last day at his office, Karan looked at his legal team with admiration and thanked a formidable group of women who had worked tirelessly to dismantle Thakur's empire.

Leela, a sharp-minded prosecutor who had built the case brick by brick. Meena, the forensic analyst who had ensured every piece of evidence was airtight. And Priya, who had fought relentlessly for the victims who never got their day in court. They were warriors in their own right – Shakti, the embodiment of power, determination, and justice.

And Kumar. Reliable, street smart, soft-spoken, and always a step ahead, Kumar had been Karan's quiet pillar. He had navigated bureaucratic labyrinths, followed trails no one else would've spotted, and offered unwavering loyalty during the most uncertain moments. Where others saw walls, Kumar found doors.

The constables were life-savers.

It was the relentless pursuit of truth that had brought down the powerful men who had long believed themselves untouchable.

Anya, Leela, Priya, and Meena stood together. This victory wasn't just for Sonia; it was for every woman silenced by men like Thakur and Suresh. For every girl who had been told she couldn't fight back. And for every survivor who still carried their scars.

As he walked out of the courthouse, he saw people pouring into the streets. Relief, celebration, and disbelief blended into one. Banners waved, tears were shed. Pelling had found its voice.

Breaking News flashed on PAN India TV screens: *MLA Thakur Arrested – The Empire Falls*

For years, Karan had carried the weight of mistrials, corrupt verdicts, and the ghosts of victims whose justice had been stolen from them. He had feared he wasn't enough.

But today, justice had prevailed.

The case had consumed him, but justice had been delivered at a cost he wasn't sure he could ever repay.

On his way to the station, his phone buzzed. A message from Kiara. For the first time in years, his daughter had reached out. She'd seen what he stood for. She understood now. *'I'm proud of you. Let's meet soon.'* His eyes welled up as he read it.

For Karan, it was closure. Not just for Sonia, but for himself. Anya left for Kolkata to get back to her work.

As he stood waiting for the train at the station, Nisha called out to him, "Karan?" her bruises fading, but her eyes still carrying the weight of everything they had endured. The city had never felt more suffocating.

"Where will you go?" she asked, her voice barely above a whisper.

Karan glanced at the train station in the distance. "Away from all this."

She hesitated. "Take me with you."

He turned to look at her, truly look at her. For years, she had been trapped, just as he had been. Now, the chains were broken.

He nodded.

As the train wound through the mountains, Nisha rested her head against Karan's shoulder, her fingers intertwined with his. The rhythmic clatter of the tracks lulled them into silence, both lost in thought. They didn't speak of the past. They didn't need to. News headlines scrolled across his phone screen. He read a beautiful message from his friend Chief Justice Rao before he put his phone away, for the time being.

Back in Pelling, life moved on.

Leela, Priya, and Meena continued their fight, ensuring that the cracks in the system were filled, that no other man like Thakur would rise again. They had become a force, a movement bigger than themselves. Shakti, in all its power, had prevailed.

Rohan, now alone but free, took a path far away from his father's shadow, working to rebuild a life of his own. He knew redemption wouldn't come easy, but for the first time, he had the chance to try.

And Sonia, her name would never be forgotten. Her parents worked with advocacy groups in her honour, ensuring that her fight continued beyond the courtroom. She was the martyr who had changed the system.

As the train continued its journey, Karan exhaled, the weight of years lifting from his shoulders. The ghosts of the past would always be there, but they no longer defined him.

Justice had been served. And now, he was finally free.

He poured a drink and, taking out his journal, wrote one last line: "Justice is not just about verdicts. It's about courage to do what's right – no matter what."

Verdicts end cases.

They don't end battles

...To Be Continued

Glossary

- ***Aba***: Colloquial expression used in Sikkim and North-Eastern India, similar to "oh" or "well then."
- ***Ante-mortem***: Occurring or existing before death; *ante-mortem* injuries are sustained while the victim was alive.
- ***Bhartiya Nyaya Sanhita***: Indian Penal Code; the criminal code of India that defines offences and prescribes punishments.
- ***Bittiya***: Affectionate term meaning "daughter" in Hindi; used to address young women with respect and warmth.
- ***Dupatta***: A long scarf or shawl worn by women in South Asia, typically draped over the head and shoulders or around the neck; an essential part of traditional Indian attire.
- ***Ghazal***: A poetic form consisting of rhyming couplets and a refrain, with each line sharing the same meter; traditionally expresses themes of love, loss, and longing. Popular in Urdu and Persian poetry, often set to music.
- ***Kukhri***: A curved Nepalese knife with a distinctive inward bend; traditional weapon and utility tool of the Gurkhas. The blade is typically 12-15 inches long with a notch at the base.
- ***Kurta***: A loose collarless shirt or tunic worn in South Asia, typically knee-length for men and varying lengths for women; often paired with *churidar* or *salwar*.

- *Krav Maga*: An Israeli martial art focused on real-world self-defence situations; it emphasises neutralising threats quickly and efficiently. Mentioned as Karan's training background, explaining his ability to handle physical confrontations.
- **Ligature Marks**: Marks left on skin by material (rope, cord, belt) used to strangle or bind the victim; important forensic evidence.
- **Lividity (also *Livor Mortis*)**: Discolouration of skin after death due to settling of blood; helps establish time of death and whether the body was moved.
- **MLA (Member of Legislative Assembly)**: *An elected representative to the state legislative assembly in India; equivalent to a state legislator.*
- *Namaste*: Traditional Hindu/Indian greeting meaning "I bow to you"; performed with palms pressed together in front of the chest. Used for both hello and goodbye, expressing respect.
- *Pallu*: The loose end of a *sari* that drapes over the shoulder; often the most decorative part of the garment with intricate embroidery or patterns.
- **Perjury**: Criminal offence of lying under oath in a judicial proceeding; serious crime that can result in imprisonment.
- **Plaintiff**: Party who brings a case to court; in criminal cases, the state/prosecution conducts the trial, as the crime is against society.
- *Saab / Sahib / Sahab*: Respectful term meaning "sir" or "master" in Hindi/Urdu; used to address men in positions of authority or as a mark of respect. Originated during the British colonial period.

- *Sari*: Traditional Indian garment consisting of a long piece of cloth (5-9 yards) draped around the body, with one end forming a skirt and the other draped over the shoulder; worn with a blouse and petticoat.
- **Sessions Court**: A court in the Indian judicial system presided over by a Sessions Judge; handles serious criminal cases, including those punishable by life imprisonment or the death penalty.

Acknowledgements

I wish to thank and acknowledge the love and affection I have received from all the Honourable Judges, professional sisters and brothers, all my friends, and my support staff.

I wish to thank my beautiful and delightful family, Ritu, Aishwarya, Vivek and Armaan for tolerating my childish playfulness and pranks.

Last but not least, I am thankful to the teams of Nu Voice Press and Hubhawks for their support in making this book come to life. I would also like to thank Nidhi Kaushik, my friend, who kept me motivated throughout this journey.

Other Books by Dr. Kantawala

A haunting legal mystery of guilt and consequence.

"Perfect murder mystery. Must read."

A thriller about mistrust and redemption.

"Gripping and unique storyline."

A romance between a tribal prince and a yoga teacher

"It is so elegant and marvelous."

About the Author

Dr. Sujay Kantawala is a distinguished lawyer and public thinker whose work bridges law, literature, and national discourse. With a legal career spanning more than three decades, he has spearheaded landmark cases across constitutional, environmental, and public interest law, appearing in more than 16 High Courts across the length and breadth of India as well as the Supreme Court.

A passionate advocate for justice and accountability, Dr. Kantawala is known for his clarity of thought, courtroom conviction, and fearlessness in public debate. A familiar voice in debates on various T.V. channels on governance, law, and ethics, he brings to his writing the same intellectual depth and moral scrutiny that define his legal work.

As an author, Dr. Kantawala brings his deep understanding of justice, society, and the human psyche into his writing. His writing reflects a rare blend of intellect and emotion: from legal essays that dissect policy and constitutional ideals, to novels and poetry that explore love, loss, identity, human struggle and the pursuit of meaning.

Connect with Dr. Sujay Kantawala:

- LinkedIn: https://www.linkedin.com/in/sujay-kantawala-63014936/
- Twitter: @sujay_kantawala
- Instagram: @sujaykantawala
- Email: sujaykantawala.author@gmail.com

Follow for updates on legal insights, media commentary, and upcoming books.

